"THIS SHOULD GIVE YOU SOMETHING TO THINK ABOUT while I'm gone," Hawk said.

He closed his hands around her arms and pulled her forward. Angela gasped in protest as he captured a fistful of hair and used it to lever her face upward. Her hands flew up to his chest to push him away, but it was too late because his mouth had already settled on hers.

For a moment she was too stunned to react. It was the last thing she'd expected, a kiss from a man who'd slept beside her two nights running, without even a hint of the passion he was capable of. And there was passion in his kiss, passion and a heat that simmered just beneath the surface of his control. Like a moth to flame, she flirted with the urge to yield to his fire. Her body tingled with a sudden awareness that began in her lips and flared downward, singeing everything in its path until there was no part of her left untouched. . . .

WHAT ARE *LOVESWEPT* ROMANCES?

They are stories of true romance and touching emotion. We believe those two very important ingredients are constants in our highly sensual and very believable stories in the LOVESWEPT *line. Our goal is to give you, the reader, stories of consistently high quality that may sometimes make you laugh, sometimes make you cry, but are always fresh and creative and contain many delightful surprises within their pages.*

Most romance fans read an enormous number of books. Those they truly love, they keep. Others may be traded with friends and soon forgotten. We hope that each LOVESWEPT *romance will be a treasure—a "keeper." We will always try to publish*

LOVE STORIES YOU'LL NEVER FORGET
BY AUTHORS YOU'LL ALWAYS REMEMBER

The Editors

Loveswept ® 767

AMERICAN BACHELORS:

NIGHT OF THE HAWK

VICTORIA LEIGH

BANTAM BOOKS
NEW YORK · TORONTO · LONDON · SYDNEY · AUCKLAND

NIGHT OF THE HAWK
A Bantam Book / December 1995

*If you would be interested in receiving protective vinyl covers for your
Loveswept books, please write to this address for information:*

Loveswept
Bantam Books
P.O. Box 985
Hicksville, NY 11802

ISBN 0-553-44451-4

Published simultaneously in the United States and Canada

*Bantam Books are published by Bantam Books, a division of Bantam Dou-
bleday Dell Publishing Group, Inc. Its trademark, consisting of the words
"Bantam Books" and the portrayal of a rooster, is Registered in U.S.
Patent and Trademark Office and in other countries. Marca Registrada.
Bantam Books, 1540 Broadway, New York, New York 10036.*

PRINTED IN THE UNITED STATES OF AMERICA
OPM   0 9 8 7 6 5 4 3 2

PROLOGUE

"I don't know what it is that you want me to do, Caroline."

"I want you to tell me whether or not I'm Gary's ideal mate." The female voice that reached Fiona through the headset was young and petulant.

Fiona threw an exasperated look across the table to where Austin McEver, deejay and ninety-nine-percent-of-the-time believer, was avoiding her gaze by fiddling with a lever on the control panel. Realizing no help would be forthcoming from that quarter, she glared at the microphone and wished this particular call had been screened more thoroughly. She was supposed to be finding mates for confirmed bachelors, not handing out advice for the love-lorn.

Unrequited love was not, after all, the theme of tonight's program. More to the point, Fiona was a psychic, not a psychologist—which might have been more appropriate with this particular caller. Still, Fiona didn't have the heart to give her the bad news—she'd known right away that Gary and Caroline weren't destined to share their futures—so she approached the issue from another angle.

"Caroline, I'm not certain that it's fair to describe a

twenty-year-old archaeology student with two part-time jobs and a passion for rock climbing as a confirmed bachelor. Have you ever considered that Gary might simply be too busy or, perhaps, too young to commit himself to you?"

Caroline responded so quickly that Fiona knew the young woman hadn't listened to her words of reluctant counsel. "If he loved me, he would spend more time doing things I like."

"You might have a point there, Caroline. I'd think about it if I were you. Thank you so much for calling 'Fiona's Forum.'" Fiona made a cutting motion across her throat, but she needn't have bothered. The deejay was already flicking buttons and leaning toward the microphone.

"This is WRDY radio out of Pine Forest, North Carolina, and you're listening to 'Fiona's Forum' on *Austin in the Evening*. Tonight's subject is men who won't commit to a relationship." Austin took a quick breath and grinned across the table. "Fiona Alexander, world-class psychic and hopeless romantic, believes it's not so much a problem of commitment as it is of finding the right woman . . . and she's here to do just that. Give us a first name, tell us a little about this confirmed bachelor, and Fiona will do her thing. Before you know it, Technicolor fireworks will fill the skies and wedding bells will ring all across the nation—"

Fiona leaned toward her microphone and inserted, "Don't get too carried away, Austin. I only promise to produce the perfect mate. The end result of any relationship is a matter best left to the people involved."

Austin's eyebrows rose inquiringly. "You're saying that not even the perfect mate will be a guarantee of happy-ever-after?"

"A lasting relationship takes more than a mere introduction," Fiona said, resting her chin on her palm. "Much more."

The engineer behind the glass cued another call, and Fiona took it before Austin could draw her any deeper into the subject of love and its disparate denouements. It wasn't that she was insensitive to the end result of her psychic matchmaking. On the contrary, Fiona found it incredibly frustrating to see two people botch up a relationship she'd had a finger in engineering.

Her attention swung to the new caller, who had the voice of a woman to whom menopause was a distant memory.

"My name is Mrs.—"

"First names only, please," Austin cut in.

There was a pause, then she began again. "My name is Sara. It's my neighbor I'm calling about, you see, a very nice young man—although I suppose *young* is a relative term. Frankly anyone under sixty looks young to me."

"How old is this man?" Fiona asked.

"Around forty, I suspect. Of course, I wouldn't dream of asking, because then he'd think I'm nosy. It's just that when I heard you could find the perfect mate, I decided I had to call because some woman out there is missing out on a good thing. I mean, it's not that he's gorgeous or anything prissy like that. Bob—that's his name—is more the rugged sort, real tall with wonderful broad shoulders and the kind of face that only a very strong woman would think was attractive."

Fiona choked back a giggle, and in a separate corner of her mind made note of the fact that the name Bob didn't feel right. It wasn't because the neighbor had made it up to protect his privacy, she sensed. More likely, Bob wasn't his name, and the elderly woman simply didn't know that.

A hawk circled lazily in the stormy skies above, waiting for its prey with the kind of patience that was bred, not learned. . . .

The image was vivid and momentary, gone before she could get a sense of where it had come from. She avoided jumping to the conclusion that it had anything to do with Bob because it could so easily have been "fallout" from any one of the dozen people inside the station as well as other callers waiting on hold.

Returning to the "rugged not prissy" routine, she prompted Sara. "A woman has to be strong to look at Bob?"

"Don't be silly. What I meant was that it would take a very special kind of woman to see beyond the harshness in his features. His eyes too. They're so dark and unreadable, mysterious like I told my friend Edna, with little smile lines shooting out from them. Edna says those lines are from squinting at the sun and that Bob scares her when he smiles —which he doesn't do very often on account of the pain, I suppose."

"What pain?" Fiona thought she heard the words *some psychic* across the telephone line, but dismissed it as static and rubbed the back of her right hand to relieve a strange prickling sensation. It didn't go away, though, and her fingers lingered on the spot.

"He was injured," Sara said, "about six months ago, I suppose. That's when he came to live here, just across the hall from me—after the accident. He said he needed peace and quiet to heal." She gave a sigh that couldn't be interpreted as anything less than compassion. "Such a shame, too, that scar on the back of his hand, the right one. He says it happened years ago, but I can tell it still hurts, even now when his other injuries have mostly healed."

Fiona's gaze was riveted to her right hand, where she'd been massaging the odd sensation. She knew what it was now, the tingling. There was a strong connection between herself and this Bob person, a man she'd never met, yet one whose own psychic powers had a physical impact on her. Despite several years of experience with this kind of phenomenon, she couldn't help the mild panic brought on by the rush of awareness.

She began, "A scar on—"

The elderly caller continued as though Fiona hadn't

spoken. "It was why he took up needlepoint—for the exercise therapy, you know, to get his fingers working again. Bob does such beautiful work too. He made me a new cover for my footstool last month, a roadrunner it was. Such a thoughtful man."

She paused, but not long enough for Fiona to get a word in edgewise. "I'm quite worried about him, you see."

The woman hesitated then, and Fiona prompted her to continue. "Because he's single?" she asked.

"Of course that's why I'm worried. I wouldn't have called you otherwise." Without saying it aloud, Sara managed to convey her disapproval of the previous caller's deviation from the theme. "Bob is a lovely man, and I've never once seen him with a woman—or anyone else for that matter," she added, just in case Fiona and the rest of the North American continent got the wrong impression.

"Does Bob talk to you about this?" Fiona asked.

"If you mean does he bend my ear about how lonely he is, then you've got him all wrong. A body has to work very hard to get any information out of Bob about anything, and then he'll only say as little as he thinks he can get away with." The elderly woman's sniff of disapproval was clear, and it was directed at Fiona, not her neighbor's reluctance to share confidences. "I'd think you would sense that Bob wouldn't talk about himself like that. Are you sure you're a psychic?"

"Yes, I am a psychic," Fiona returned, grinning at Austin. "I don't, however, claim to be omniscient."

"Well, that's all right, then." Sara didn't sound convinced, not to Fiona, not even to Austin, who looked more skeptical than she'd ever seen him.

"Tell me a little more about Bob," Fiona said, absently stroking the back of her hand.

"Well, he admits that he sees women away from his apartment—I got that out of him one day over tea and his favorite gingerbread cookies—but if that's the case, they're no one he cares about, because he'd bring them home then, wouldn't he? I mean, he has a perfectly nice apartment here in San Rafael, a bit light on the personal touch but nothing to be ashamed of. I gave him a plant a few months ago—a simply beautiful African violet that I picked up at the Sausalito flea market. Anyway, I'd hoped he might get the hint and do up the place a bit, but I guess he prefers the Spartan look. Still, he keeps it meticulously clean—now that's something a woman would like in a man, isn't it? He even polished my parquet floor for me last month, a blessing because it's been twenty years since my knees worked that way and the lady who cleans for me always leaves streaks."

Fiona broke in before the woman could tell the world what chemicals Bob recommended for cleaning toilets. "Thank you for sharing all that with us, Sara. Your neighbor sounds like a very, er, unique man. In fact, I'd say you're a little in love with him yourself."

"Everyone from my dentist to the grocery delivery boy has said more or less the same thing, and none of them are psychics. I'm beginning to think I should have asked one of them to help me find Bob a woman."

Fiona almost wished she had, wincing as the tingling in her hand increased to a dull throb. She shook her hand from the wrist in an effort to dislodge the psychic scar, and when that didn't work she made an effort to do something about Bob's love life. If nothing else, breaking the connection with Bob's well-meaning neighbor was certain to ease the discomfort.

She said, "Bob is going to meet his perfect mate sometime in the next few days."

"What is she like?" Abundant skepticism laced Sara's question, but Fiona was in no doubt that the caller was paying very close attention. She had to work hard to focus on the image that was no more than a blur, a casualty, she assumed, of the more dominant phenomenon of the scar. Normally, she could see so clearly. . . .

"Well?" The elderly voice demanded attention, and even Austin was looking at Fiona with noticeable impatience.

"She's about medium height, five five or six, with long thick hair hanging down her back. Red, I think—I'm not sure about that, though. It's hard to tell. She's standing somewhere dark, somewhere without windows." The image sharpened for a brief moment, then disappeared, leaving Fiona with one last impression.

Her breath was a sudden hiss that had the engineer behind the glass panel frowning his disapproval, but Fiona didn't care. All that mattered was that she tell Sara exactly what she'd seen.

"The woman Bob is destined to fall in love with is holding a gun," she said, then closed her eyes to the open-mouthed deejay across the table in an effort to recall the image.

"You see a gun," Sara asked, "but you can't be certain if her hair is red?"

"Sometimes it works like that," Fiona said.

"You're sure it's not one of those fancy corkscrews? I've got a friend who bought one for her nephew when we went shopping last summer, and I made her wait for me outside the bank when I went in to cash my Social Security because I was afraid someone would see it and get us both shot."

"I really think it was a gun."

"A corkscrew would make more sense. Bob sometimes drinks a glass of wine when he sits on the porch in the evening." After a pause she added, "Is this woman aiming the thing at Bob?"

Fiona hesitated, then shook her head in silent defeat. "I hope not."

"I'd hate to think this is her way of telling Bob she's not interested in him."

Fiona couldn't help a tiny smile. "Perhaps Bob respects a woman who has strong opinions."

Approximately one million listeners—a number tallied or inflated by those dreamers in the marketing office—were treated to Austin's near-hysterical cackle before he clapped a hand over his mouth. Fiona tried her best to ignore him.

Sara's dissatisfaction with the results of her call was clear in her voice. "To be honest, Fiona, if a gunslinging babe is your idea of a perfect mate for my sweet neighbor, then I'm glad I didn't ask you to find one for me. At my age, I get all the excitement I need playing canasta with Mr. Tompkins who lives upstairs. And before you ask, yes, he's a confirmed bachelor, too, but I don't need a psychic to predict he'll settle down with me once he gets to the point where he can't climb all those stairs any longer."

Fiona swallowed her own laughter. "I'm sure you're right about that, Sara. Thank you for calling 'Fiona's Forum.' "

"And for tuning in to *Austin in the Evening*," Austin said on cue, then gave the station's call sign and phone number before moving on to plug the sponsor's product.

Tuning out the deejay, Fiona replayed the conversation with Bob's neighbor in her head. It sounded just as absurd the second time around. She was fairly certain that prophesying gun-toting soul mates wasn't exactly what Austin had had in mind when he'd proposed the theme of that night's show. But then, she hadn't imagined she'd stumble across a situation this explosive.

If she didn't take steps, it was likely to blow up right in Bob's face. She wasn't sure it wasn't already too late.

Music had replaced the deejay's voice, and Fiona looked up to meet Austin's questioning gaze. "I assume you have that woman's phone number," she said.

"Of course. We won't put through a call over the air without it."

There were various reasons for that safeguard, none of them important to Fiona except for the fact that they could reach Bob. By calling the woman back, they could get her address. Fiona swallowed hard and tried to give an appearance of calm. "Please arrange for a tape of Bob's part of the program to be sent to him. Express."

"You're afraid Bob's perfect mate is going to do something unromantic with that gun?" Austin asked, his expression a blend of disbelief and curiosity.

She smiled, grateful that his belief in her psychic powers had survived the last few minutes more or less intact. "I'm not sure it's the woman that Bob needs to be concerned about."

"So why send the tape?"

"Because I owe him a warning."

"About the gun?"

Another smile. "If that's how he interprets it, then yes, that too."

The engineer waved to signal a call, and Fiona realized as she leaned toward the microphone that the psychic scar on her hand no longer tingled. The connection between herself and Bob—or whatever his name was—had been broken. It was a shame, she often thought, that her powers allowed only glimpses, not complete stories.

Sometimes, like now, she felt a little cheated.

ONE

The parking place Hawk found across from the dry cleaners was tight, but he managed it with a three-point maneuver that wouldn't have worked if the curb had been a couple of inches higher. His car was a blue hatchback of indeterminate age, a minimal sort of car that suited him because of the anonymity it afforded. It had the added advantage of being cheap—not worth stealing but easy to replace if someone did.

He got out, grabbed his sports bag from the backseat, and locked the car before heading over to the fast-food restaurant on the corner. Inside, he paid for a cup of coffee and sat where he could see the door and the street outside as he drank it. The coffee was hot and black and far inferior to anything he could have brewed in his apartment just two blocks south, but he hadn't wanted anything to eat, and the soft drinks in this place were typically low on carbonation and high on syrup. So here he was, drinking bad coffee and watching his back trail just in case he'd been followed from the small valley airport.

Just because the San Francisco Bay Area was the last place anyone would think to look for him—being, as it was,

virtually on the doorstep of the men hunting for him—
didn't mean he could afford to get sloppy. There were too
many people out there who wanted his head, although after
eight months he figured the number of those actively committed to finding him had diminished. Still, all it would
take was a chance sighting to put the hounds on his trail,
and this time he might not get away.

Even if he was the only one who thought so, he figured
his life was worth a cup or two of lousy coffee.

Ten minutes later Hawk walked out of the restaurant
with the sports bag in his left hand and his brown leather
bomber jacket open in case he needed the gun tucked into
his shoulder holster. Rounding the corner and heading
west, he took a circuitous route to his apartment, noting the
cars and other pedestrians who passed him in the gathering
dusk. He walked steadily, but not so fast as to draw attention to himself, the stiffness in his left shoulder easing now
that he was no longer stuck in the cramped Cessna or behind the wheel of the hatchback.

The bullet wound in that shoulder had been the worst
of his injuries, and it was the only one that still gave him
any trouble. Another month, give or take, and he figured it
wouldn't bother him any more than the back of his right
hand, where a junkie had cut a three-inch gash during a
raid almost six years earlier. Hawk had learned to live with
the occasional twinge or ache, preferring that to the numbness the surgeon had prognosticated after he'd done all he
could to repair the damaged tendons.

Physical therapy and sheer bloody-mindedness had
helped him regain full use of his hand. He was confident
the same would be the case with his shoulder.

Too bad he couldn't say that about the rest of his life.
Knowing he was innocent of betrayal and murder didn't
make the days of hiding any easier to endure. Hawk had
long since given up looking for the magic solution that
would put things back to where they'd been before that

fateful night when his partner had died and he'd started running. His job with the DEA—Drug Enforcement Agency—was finished. Even if he thought they'd give it back to him, the prospect no longer appealed.

The best he could hope for now was vengeance.

By the time he arrived at the Victorian house that had long ago been divided into four separate apartments, Hawk was satisfied his trail was clean. There was a light on in his neighbor's ground-floor window to the right, while his own apartment on the left was dark.

His footsteps were deliberately heavy as he mounted the front wooden steps, his way of letting Mrs. Avery know he was home. Not that he was in the mood for conversation, but he'd rather get it over with now than in an hour or two when she realized he was back and came over to check on him. He planned to be asleep by then.

Besides, he liked his neighbor. Her efforts to be kind without being intrusive had won her a place in his affections right next to his sister Elaine, her two kids, and a cross-eyed dog they'd saved from the pound. Since he couldn't risk contacting Elaine, not even to let her know he was alive and well, Mrs. Avery was the only person in his world with whom he didn't have to be constantly on guard.

There was also the advantage of having someone next door who would notice strangers in his absence. Nothing much escaped Mrs. Avery, and what did wasn't worth bothering about. A weary smile kicked at one corner of his mouth as he remembered the shifty-eyed insurance salesman she'd dispatched with a shove that had sent him tumbling down the steps before Hawk could lay a hand on him. Clearly, both Hawk and the salesman had underestimated the diminutive, bright-eyed widow whose pastel-shaded hair changed hue on a regular monthly schedule.

It had been a soft purple the day she'd outmatched the salesman. Hawk had admired the way she'd casually dusted off her hand, tucked a lavender curl back into place, and invited him inside for tea and cookies, the twinkle in her eyes daring him to make more of the incident than it deserved. He'd drunk her tea without referring once to her bit of exercise, but couldn't help reflecting on former colleagues who would have benefitted from imitating her classy brand of discretion.

All the same, he still paid close attention when someone visited her that he didn't know. Being careful was simply part of who he was.

Mrs. Avery's door opened as he entered the narrow hall running between their apartments. Hawk took one look at her face and knew something was wrong.

"What is it?" he demanded, his gaze hitting the dark corners of the hall as he dropped the sports bag and slid his right hand inside his jacket. He didn't worry about how they'd found him. That would come later, if there was a later. For now, it was a matter of assessing the situation and getting out of it without anyone—Mrs. Avery especially—being hurt.

"It's nothing, Bob. Really." She hesitated, clicking her tongue as she lifted a hand to primp the pink curls framing her face. She sighed, then thrust a thick envelope into his hand. "This came for you, by express. I had to sign for it."

He never got mail, not at this address. No one who knew him had any idea where he was.

His fingers closed around the butt of his Astra revolver as he took the package in his free hand and tossed it toward his door. Then he moved between Mrs. Avery and the street, because if there had been a shooter inside her apartment, she would have been a lot more upset. As it was, he knew he had to kill the lights before he got her back inside. If she would just move so he could reach the switch . . .

It suddenly dawned on him that she hadn't stopped talking, and now that he heard the words, they weren't making any sense.

". . . and I wouldn't have called that radio station, not

for myself, but I was bored and thought it would be a hoot to talk to a real psychic. Although I have to admit that now that I've done it, I'm not at all convinced she's not a fraud. I mean, seriously, Bob, you should hear what she had to say about you."

He blinked twice and decided to leave his gun where it was. After all, he'd been backlit in the hall for over a minute, and if there was a shooter anywhere near, he would have done the job by now. Just to be on the safe side, he reached up and unscrewed the lightbulb in the ceiling.

"Who said what about me?" he asked, setting the hot bulb on the ledge beneath the mailboxes.

"The psychic. Why did you unscrew the bulb?"

"I could hear a crackling noise that meant it was ready to go out," he lied. "I'll replace it now and save someone tripping in the dark. What psychic?"

"The one on the radio. The show's broadcast all over the country, out of the Carolinas or somewhere like that. She claimed to be able to find the perfect mate for any confirmed bachelor. I thought you fit the theme perfectly." Mrs. Avery looked at him curiously. "I didn't hear any crackling."

"My hearing is extraordinarily acute." Making sure Mrs. Avery was standing inside her door but out of range of her windows, he crossed to his own door and inserted the key before bending to pick up the package. "So this is a tape of the call you made?"

"Apparently. Fiona—that's the psychic—had someone call after I was on the program and ask for your address. It came this morning, but you weren't in."

Hawk noticed she didn't ask where he'd been, and he was, as always, grateful for her reticence. He just wished she'd used a little of it before calling the psychic.

No telling what damage she'd done with that single phone call.

"When did you make this call?" he asked.

"Yesterday afternoon. You're not angry with me, are you, Bob? You seem a little nervous."

Hawk softened his expression. The last thing he wanted to do was hurt the one person he'd relied on all these months as a touchstone with reality.

"Don't worry, Mrs. Avery. I was just surprised. I'm sure it will be, er, a hoot to listen to."

She sighed and smiled at him. "Just so you don't take it seriously. Now I suppose I'd better let you go. Mr. Tompkins is going to be down soon and I haven't set up the card table yet."

Hawk waited until she was inside and had shut her door before entering his own apartment. Although he seriously doubted anyone would be waiting—a waste of time when all they had to do was blow him away on his doorstep—he took the usual precautions. As a result, it was another five minutes before he put his gun on the coffee table and stuck the cassette tape into the machine. Moments later he'd sorted out the voices belonging to Fiona, the psychic, and Sara—he hadn't known her first name—and found himself laughing at Sara's "gorgeous not prissy" summation.

He'd just settled back in his chair and was beginning to relax when Sara mentioned the scar on his hand and the needlepoint. Hawk ignored what came after that as he moved quickly through the apartment, gathering up those essentials that weren't already in the sports bag and stuffing them inside.

The program was still running when he detoured on his way out to eject the tape from the machine and shove it into his jacket pocket. Taking care not to make any noise that would alert his neighbor, he let himself out into the dark hall.

He was on the run again, and all because a sweet old lady thought he was lonely. Hawk figured it served him right for letting her past his guard. Still, he hated leaving without saying good-bye. Or thank you for lending him a piece of sanity to hang on to during these past months. He left without saying anything, though, because those who came for him would leave her alone once they realized she knew nothing.

Winding his way through back alleys toward the street where he'd left the car, he realized it was sheer luck that he was still walking. Another five minutes or five hours, and there might have been a story about him splashed across the front page of the *San Rafael Gazette*. . . . RENEGADE DRUG COP DOWNED IN SHOOT-OUT, or some such nonsense.

He had to assume that someone listening to the radio program would hear the bits about the scar and the needle-point and figure out it was him. Even if they weren't one of the people after his head, they would eventually mention it to someone who was, and the hunters would be blowing out his windows faster than Fiona could sense anything was wrong.

He approached his car from behind, then walked past it without so much as a heartbeat's hesitation. All of the windows looked like they'd been done over with a baseball bat. The coincidence in timing worried him, though less so when he noticed two other cars with their windows bashed in. Random violence, he decided, and wished the perp had chosen another night for his rampage. Half a block down, a prowl car was double-parked beneath a streetlight and two cops were in the process of cuffing a man. One of the cops bent over and picked up a bat.

Nothing to do with him . . . maybe. To be on the safe side, Hawk kept walking until he was out of sight of the three men, then hailed a passing cab. It was only a five-minute ride to his backup vehicle, but riding was less exposed than walking when one's back trail was in question.

He sat where he could use the rearview mirror to keep watch on the road behind them and thought about the man with the bat. It wasn't that he didn't believe in coincidences.

It was simply that he didn't like them.

The parking garage where Hawk kept his other car was cut into the ground beneath a thriving business park. He had chosen it because a lot of the people who worked in the adobe-faced buildings overhead left their cars there while traveling. No one paid any attention to a vehicle that didn't move for weeks at a time, so long as the rent was paid every month. It was the third such location he'd used over the past six months, and there was nothing in writing that could tie the rental to him.

The phony papers he'd secured soon after his fall from grace were supposed to protect him from the hunters. So long as the hunters didn't know whether he was in Tampa or Tahiti, he could stay hidden for a very long time.

He really wished Mrs. Avery hadn't made that call.

Hawk kept his hand closed over the butt of his revolver as he walked through the dimly lit garage with its low-hanging steel beams and evenly spaced concrete pillars. As many as a quarter of the parking slots were still filled, but the place was empty except for a man doing something under the hood of a blue four-wheel-drive Jeep Cherokee that just happened to be blocking Hawk's car.

So as not to alert the man, Hawk didn't break his stride as he eased the sports bag onto the floor and slid his gun from its holster to rest against his thigh. He was five yards away when the man looked up and seemed to notice Hawk for the first time.

"Hi there." He sounded flustered, but Hawk ignored the verbal signals and analyzed the scene for flaws.

He was dressed appropriately for a man who actually might work in this complex—pin-striped suit coat draped through the Jeep's open window, shirtsleeves rolled up to his elbows, tie askew, and a preppie haircut that was slightly mussed from a frustrated hand. His expression was part chagrined, part relieved, and if he'd taken his hands out of the engine and held them in plain sight, Hawk might have believed he was nothing more than a man having car trouble.

Hawk stopped where he was, shielding the gun behind his thigh and waiting for the man to continue.

"I don't suppose you know anything about cars, do you?"

"Some."

"Would you mind having a look, then? It just stopped before I'd driven twenty feet." He looked away from Hawk and peered under the hood. "It probably has something to do with the fact that it's been parked for nearly a month, but I haven't a clue and my secretary forgot to renew the auto club. Silly girl, but she's usually so—"

His hands came away from the engine as he suddenly pivoted and aimed a dark-painted automatic at the spot where Hawk had been standing not two seconds earlier. Operating on instinct, Hawk had taken the opportunity of the turned back to move. Before the man could correct his aim, Hawk was beside him and landing a stunning blow to his jaw with his left fist. The automatic—a Beretta, Hawk thought—fell to the cement floor, and Hawk kicked it aside as he whipped the butt of his revolver across the man's face.

The tactic was messy but effective, a broken nose generally being as incapacitating as a half-dozen well-placed punches. There was the added bonus of the opponent remaining conscious for a question-and-answer session. Grabbing the man by the knot of his tie, Hawk was about to drag him into the deep shadows near the wall when the barest hint of sound from behind him made his blood run cold. He glanced over his shoulder. A woman was rising from the ground, her eyes round and accusing, one hand

holding back a thick mane of reddish-brown hair, the othe
holding the Beretta.

He made his move before she used it. With his grip
around the man's tie for leverage and a helping knee to his
butt, Hawk literally flung the man at her, knocking her
over, then followed the two down with his own body. The
automatic flew from her hand and skittered across the oil-
stained floor. He heard the crack of something against the
cement as he landed on top of the pile, but whether it was
the woman's head or the heel of a shoe, he didn't care. All
that mattered was winning this encounter, and if someone
got a little dead in the process, that was okay as long as it
wasn't him.

The male assailant squirmed silently beneath Hawk's
weight—Hawk figured he had six inches and commensurate
pounds on him. He raised up enough to get an angle, then
landed a knife-edged blow to the back of the man's neck.
He went limp, leaving Hawk to decide between trying for
the carotid artery just below the woman's ear—if he could
find the ear; so far, all he could see was a mass of hair
fanning out over the floor—or just letting her be smothered
under the weight of two full-grown men. She wasn't a large
woman, about five and a half feet tall and slender, almost
fragile looking.

Appearances were deceiving. Assassins were never as
fragile as this one looked.

He turned his head and saw the Beretta had skidded out
of reach. Hawk decided if the woman was still armed, it
would have to be a gun or knife taped to her calf beneath
her slim-fitting slacks. Possibly a gun tucked into the hol-
low of her back. Her cream silk blouse hadn't looked as
though it was designed to conceal weapons, and unless she
was armed with something really esoteric like a stiletto dis-
guised as a hair comb, she'd have as much trouble as he
would reaching for anything useful.

It occurred to him then that she wasn't moving or mak

ing any sound whatsoever. While the lack of noise was appropriate for what he supposed was to have been a quiet, no-fuss assassination, it could also mean she was unconscious. Or she was playing possum. He thought he'd better find out which.

Shoving the man's head to the side, he braced one hand against the floor and pushed aside her thick, wavy hair. Blood from the man's broken nose was smeared across her face, and he had to wipe some of it away before he could do what he needed.

With his thumb, he checked beneath her eyelids and was satisfied by the way her eyes rolled back that she was out cold. He worried for a moment that she'd stopped breathing, but after licking his finger and holding it under her nose, he was reassured. The breaths were shallow and weak, but more or less even.

Since he'd already decided which of the two he was taking with him—the man's broken nose would make him memorable if anyone happened to see him, and because of the size and strength factor, the woman would be easier to control—he got off the pile and slid his gun back into its holster. Then he dragged the man off the woman so she could breathe more freely, wiping the blood from his hand on the man's shirt. She responded with a cough and a slight gagging noise, rolled to her side and curled into a tight ball, then subsided back into silence. Just in case she fooled him and came to a couple of hours before he expected, Hawk yanked the silk tie from the man's throat and bound her wrists together.

Feeling particularly paranoid, he tied them behind her back. Then he patted her down for weapons, his hands running over her body with a detachment that didn't allow him to take pleasure in her delicate curves, long supple limbs, and smallish but firmly rounded breasts. He finished his quick examination by digging his fingers into her hair, looking for hair combs that weren't there. When he was done, he left her lying on her side with her face to the cold cement.

In the time it took to haul the man over against the wall and out of sight, pick up the loose gun, and check to see that the Jeep did, in fact, start when he turned the key in the ignition, the woman didn't so much as twitch. He hoped it wasn't because she'd cracked her head against the cement and wouldn't ever regain consciousness. There were things she could tell him that just might save his life.

He decided to take the Jeep because it was a more versatile vehicle than his own and, once he'd made a couple of changes, wouldn't be traceable for a week or more. Opening the rear passenger door, he pulled out a plastic cooler and put it into the back end before returning to the woman. He checked her eyes again, then lifted and carried her over to the Jeep. Trying not to knock her around any more than necessary, he settled her on the floor of the backseat, deciding she'd travel best on her side with her back facing the rear of the vehicle. He pushed her hair from her face so she could breathe, then took out a handkerchief and wiped the blood from her forehead and cheeks. If there was a point when she had to be presentable, it was easier to get the blood off now instead of later, when it had dried and was caked on her skin.

Tossing the soiled linen aside, he checked that the tie was still tight around her wrists and slipped the high-heeled pumps from her feet. There wasn't much else he could do to make her comfortable, what with her hands tied behind her back and her body arched over the driveshaft hump. Hawk had never seen the point in casual cruelty, and he wouldn't hurt her unless he had to. Even so, he wasn't going to untie her, and letting her stretch out on the seat wasn't an option.

He spared another minute to move supplies from his trunk to the back of the Jeep. He covered the woman head to toe with a blanket, put his sports bag on the front passenger seat and dropped the Beretta inside it, then got behind the wheel and headed out. He doubted anyone would be waiting outside with a backup ambush; they'd already sent two people and that was enough manpower to expend on the chance he'd show up there. Still, he slouched low in the seat and kept a watchful eye until he was away from the business park.

Checking his watch, he discovered that only six minutes had passed since he'd entered the garage. If he didn't make any more mistakes, there was a chance he'd be far away before the hunters realized he'd escaped their net.

He'd been stupid to assume he had any leeway once Mrs. Avery and that psychic had broadcast his description all over the nation. On the other hand, his hunters had been foolish to think they could take him so easily.

Steering the Jeep onto the southbound ramp of the Redwood Highway, Hawk wondered why the woman hadn't shot him when she'd had the chance.

TWO

Angela couldn't decide whether to puke or cry.

Since neither option offered much comfort, she settled for sinking her teeth into her bottom lip in an effort to stop them from chattering. The longer she could feign unconsciousness, the more probable it was that she would come up with a plan to get herself out of . . . well, whatever trouble she was in. She wasn't quite clear on that yet.

She knew she was on the floor of a moving vehicle—a truck, she guessed, although she couldn't know for sure with the blanket obscuring her view. It felt like a truck, though, the way it swayed as though it were built higher from the ground than a car. Her hands were tied, there was a throbbing in her head from when she'd slammed it on the cement, and she figured that if her ribs weren't already broken, they soon would be. Potholes, the bane of motorists worldwide, would take care of that.

She had to assume one of the two men from the garage was driving, and she doubted it was the one with the broken nose. It was probably the other man, the big one with the dark eyes and fast moves.

Rolling her face against the thinly carpeted floorboard,

she wondered just how in the hell she'd gotten herself into this situation. Guns, blood, men turning on her as though she were a threat . . . If they'd just taken a minute to look at her, they would have known she wasn't part of their struggle.

Life, *her* life, simply wasn't like this. The worst thing that happened to her in the course of a normal day was having to placate an overanxious speaker while giving him hints on how he could punch up his talk without straying too far from incremental profit margins, federal excise taxes, or whatever thrilling subject material he was the chosen expert on.

If only she hadn't picked up the damned gun.

She squirmed beneath the blanket in an attempt to keep her hip from rubbing so hard against the hump in the floor, and wished she'd gone to the bathroom before she left her office.

The truck hit a bump and blood smeared across the lip she was biting. One more offense to chalk up to the tall stranger who'd turned on her so fast, she hadn't been able to duck. He'd thrown the other man in her face and down they'd all gone in a pile, Angela wondering why she'd bent down to pick up the gun before the breath was knocked from her chest and shooting stars replaced all coherent thought.

Blood and guns. She gagged, remembering the bloodied face of the man with his nose pointing toward his ear. She'd noticed more than she cared to before the other man had shoved him at her and toppled them all into a heap. Even though there were a hundred more discomforts to dwell on, she knew the man's blood was smeared on her face. The thought made her wrinkle her nose in disgust, and she stopped short—just barely—of voicing her revulsion aloud. It occurred to her then that she couldn't feel anything caked on her skin, and she wondered if that was because she'd been unconscious too short a time for the blood to dry or if her subconscious was beginning to shut down all but the most critical senses required for survival.

She *really* wished she hadn't picked up that gun.

Angela realized she was repeating herself, but didn't care. And if her thoughts were beginning to resemble the whining of a beleaguered politician who couldn't get reporters away from questions regarding some creative financing on the part of his campaign manager, she knew that was preferable to letting her mind wander too far into the realm of fear.

There was only so much terror she could handle without losing that last bit of control that kept her from opening her mouth and screaming—a move that would certainly earn her the displeasure of whoever was driving. It seemed prudent to avoid annoying him.

When they next came face-to-face, the dignity afforded by that self-control might be her only asset. With control and a calm demeanor, she might be able to talk her way out of this mess . . . which she wouldn't be in if she'd just gotten into her car and pretended she hadn't seen anything. She could have been on her way to her apartment in Corte Madera or already there and not tied up on the floor of a vehicle hell-bent for somewhere she didn't like thinking about.

If only she'd minded her own business.

Angela forced back a surge of bile—the result, she worried, of car sickness as much as sheer terror—and prayed he'd let her go instead of doing anything worse. The *anything worse* preyed on her mind and ensured her silence as the vehicle pressed deeper into the night, drawing her toward a dark reality she knew she was going to hate.

Hawk drove south across the Golden Gate Bridge, staying with the vehicles that jostled for position as they veered right along the thruways bisecting San Francisco. Following the example of the drivers around him, he ignored the speed limit and cruised just under fifty along the well-lit streets. He made it to the other side of town in record time. Daly City flashed by as traffic picked up the pace, and it wasn't until the sharply curving exit to San Francisco Airport slowed him that he neared posted speed limits.

He followed the signs to the long-term parking lots and parked in a dark corner between a tall van and a wood-paneled station wagon. Switching out the headlights and the overhead lamp, he sat for about five minutes without moving, watching the irregular flow of cars entering the lot. A brown four-door sedan came his way and parked six spaces up in the next row. He waited as the male driver got out and pulled two suitcases from the trunk before heading toward the brightly lit courtesy bus shelter about eighty yards away.

Ten minutes later the bus collected the man along with two others who had parked on the far side of the shelter. No one got off the bus at that shelter, or at the next stop the bus made before leaving the lot. Hawk took a screwdriver from his sports bag, slid out of the Jeep, and closed the door gently behind him. Although he hadn't heard so much as a peep from the rear seat, he opened the back door and lifted the blanket from the woman's face. In the weak light, he looked into her gold-flecked green eyes and saw recognition in them. He also saw fear, and silently credited her with better than adequate acting skills.

Not that he didn't doubt fear was one of the emotions she was experiencing. She wouldn't be human if she wasn't even a little afraid of what he intended to do with her. But fear shouldn't be the only emotion showing, not on the face of a woman who had expected to see him dead not an hour past.

The ability to conceal murderous intent, particularly in her precarious circumstances, was a talent to be handled with cautious respect. Ignoring it would be a fatal mistake.

"There's no one to hear you scream," he said. "If you do, I'll gag you."

"If there's no one to hear, why bother?"

The soft, almost winsome sound of her voice hit a pleasure center deep inside him. Hawk cursed his carelessness in not anticipating a voice to match the undeniably seductive body. He would have to be careful with this one, he told himself. A man was never more exposed than when he was physically attracted to a woman.

"Screaming gets on my nerves. Don't do it." He flicked the blanket aside and checked the knot at her wrists. It held firm, so much so that he realized he'd have to cut her free when it was time. The skin next to the silk tie was red, sore looking, the result of a struggle to free herself. He was indifferent to the self-inflicted pain, and met her gaze again without commenting.

"I don't know who you think I am—"

He cut her off before she could finish the lie. "Talking gets on my nerves too. Don't." He dropped the blanket over her face and shut the door with a soft click.

A quick survey of the parking lot confirmed that no one had come toward the corner while he'd been with the woman. He'd been listening for sounds outside the Jeep, but he'd been listening to the woman, too, and knew better than to depend on a sense that had been partially distracted.

He went over to the sedan and made quick work of removing the license plates, replacing them with a set he'd kept stored in his backup car for just such an occasion. By the time he put the sedan's plates on the appropriated Jeep and tucked the third set—those that had originally been on the Jeep—under a mat in the back of the Jeep, only five minutes had passed since he'd warned the woman not to scream.

The fact that she'd heeded his warning confirmed his opinion that she was a thorough professional. A well-trained assassin would know he meant what he said.

Reassured by her silence, Hawk took another minute to break into the van parked in the next slot and exchange his parking ticket for the one the driver had foolishly left on the dash. He'd already seen through the window that it was dated nearly a week earlier, and he took three twenties out of his wallet to cover the fee. Now, when he drove out, the clerk in the booth wouldn't wonder why he was leaving so soon after arriving.

He got back into the Jeep and had just started the engine when the woman spoke.

"I have to go to the bathroom."

"Not now."

"But I—"

"Shut up." He leaned over the seat and lifted the blanket from her face. "I meant what I said about gagging you."

"That was for screaming," she said, her voice a little harder than before, yet still managing a significant tug at his senses.

"The same goes for talking."

She twisted her head to glare at him. Taking advantage of her attention, Hawk reached into the sports bag and pulled out a silencer. He screwed it onto the end of his gun, gripped the assembled weapon in his right hand with his finger against the trigger, and draped a sweatshirt over it. Then he rested his forearm on the console with the gun aimed somewhere between her breasts and pelvis. The position was awkward, but outside of putting her to sleep, it was the only way he could think of to ensure she didn't do anything stupid on the way through the tollgate. Once he found a quiet place to question her, he didn't want to have to wait for her to wake up.

Fear flared anew in her eyes, and he was satisfied that she understood the threat. "Behave yourself. Don't move. Don't even whisper."

"A bullet won't stop me from needing a bathroom."

He clenched his jaw to keep from laughing. Like her voice, the humor caught him off guard. "We have to pay to get out of here. I'd prefer to do it without any drama. Your choice."

Her nod of acquiescence was barely discernible in the near darkness. "Mind the speed bumps."

"You have a smart mouth."

"Potholes too."

"Be quiet."

Hawk pushed the blanket back over her face with his free hand, then switched on the radio. Under the cover of something that sounded like a combination of African drums and alpenhorns, he tucked the Astra and sweatshirt back into the sports bag. The exercise had been designed to gain her cooperation; he saw no need to chance actually shooting her. Even if she went against the odds and kicked up a ruckus, it made more sense to drive out of it than risk forfeiting whatever information she possessed.

Remembering to stay in first gear—something he'd have done with his right hand otherwise occupied—he drove slowly between the rows of cars toward the exit marked with well-lit booths. Cars from all corners of the lot funneled with cutthroat determination toward the bottleneck. Hawk maneuvered the Jeep into line behind a red Jaguar as a high-pitched yodel caught the rhythm of the stereo-enhanced drums. Nerves already stretched taut were sorely tested, and he would have changed the channel but figured he'd end up with Schubert or Enya—neither of which would do him any good if the woman made noise. Drums and annoying vocals served his purpose if not his pleasure.

She didn't make any noise, though . . . at least, not until he'd paid the clerk, rolled up the window, and switched off the hideous noise. He was heading toward the on-ramp that would put him on Highway 101 south when she cleared her throat. She did it again a few seconds later, and he asked, "What now?"

"Just clearing my throat. Why, is that banned too?"

Even muffled, her voice was dangerously compelling. Before he had a chance to answer, she added, "How long before we stop?"

"As soon as I find a place where we can talk without being disturbed."

"A coffee shop would be nice."

They were clearly not thinking along the same lines. The digital clock on the dash blinked from eleven fifty-nine to midnight, reminding Hawk there were only four good hours of dark left. He knew he had to be out of the area or undercover before dawn.

"They have bathrooms," she went on.

He'd been wondering when that subject would come up again. "Are you always this obsessed by trivialities? I'd think someone in your position would be more concerned with the bigger picture."

"It's my *position* that's keeping my attention focused on the basics."

Hawk smothered a laugh as he cut hard to the left and accelerated onto the freeway, refusing to feel guilty as the unbraced body on the floor ricocheted against the seat. The woman's groan of protest had faded by the time he reached cruising speed, and he allowed himself a few moments' reflection on her curious combination of sassy defiance and wide-eyed fear—both of which were at odds with the image one normally had of a ruthless assassin.

Humor could be an effective weapon if it succeeded in lowering his defenses. Added to the aura of fear she projected and her insidiously appealing voice, Hawk judged she was about as harmless as a piranha on a blood trail.

Easing into the lanes leading to the San Matteo Bridge, he decided it was time to give her something to think about. "We'll be stopping soon. When we do, I'll want you to tell me when and where you were to deliver my body to Constantine." He wanted to know more, a lot more, but that would get the ball rolling. Once she committed that much, the rest would be easy to get out of her.

"Your *body*?" She made it sound as distasteful as something the cat dragged in.

Hawk ignored the insult. "I know Constantine. He wouldn't accept photos."

"Of your *body*?" Once again, her distaste for the word was graphically clear. He could almost hear the follow-up thought. *Who'd want pictures of your body?*

The fact that she didn't say it aloud didn't affect the smile that lifted one corner of his mouth. For a man on the run with one hunter tied up on the floor behind him and God knows how many others on his trail, Hawk was surprised at how at ease he felt. How comfortable. Cheerful, almost. He chalked it up to adrenaline.

"I don't know anyone named Constantine," she added.

He sighed. She was going to be stubborn. "What's your name?"

"Why?"

"What is it?" Even if she gave him a pseudonym, using it would lend a sense of intimacy when the time came.

A small hesitation, then she said, "Angela."

He was certain from the way she said it that Angela was either her real name or that of someone very close to her. He was pleased. "Think about what I asked you, Angela. The faster you give me the answers, the better your chances will be."

"What chances? I don't know what—"

"Shut up and think, Angela. We'll be there soon."

Maneuvering the Jeep into the right-hand lane, Hawk cruised across the last quarter mile of bridge and prepared to take the exit to Freemont. The furnished house he'd rented three months earlier had been paid for in cash and was virtually untraceable back to him. The woman he'd hired to house-sit was an illegal alien who communicated best in Spanish and didn't pry about why he paid her to live there when he could have charged rent. It was enough that she understood he wanted the place available for his use at a moment's notice, and would vacate the premises for as long as he needed to be there. In exchange, she kept the crackheads and dopers from taking up residence in his absence.

She also kept the garage empty, the mechanism for the electric door in working order, and the safety light permanently broken. Fifteen minutes after leaving the bridge, Hawk eased the Jeep across the short, cracked driveway to the garage door, dug the electronic opener from his sports bag, and pointed it at the door. It opened noiselessly, and he killed the headlights before driving inside and clicking the button to close the door.

He leaned over the backseat and spoke to the woman without removing the blanket. "There are some people inside who would as soon kill you as look at you. Keep quiet and they won't even know you're here."

"What's the difference between you and them?"

"Not much."

A short silence, then she said, "I'm tired of you telling me to be quiet."

"So am I." He got out of the Jeep and rang the bell beside the kitchen door before pushing it open. He walked through the spotless kitchen with its Formica-topped table and metal chairs, then went down a short hallway to the living room and waited. Consuela joined him a minute or so later, holding closed the lapels of her terrycloth robe with one hand and rubbing grit from her eyes with the other. Her gray-streaked black hair fell in a single braid down her back.

She stopped at the end of the sofa and looked at him without speaking. Hawk gave the street out front one final check, then pulled the shabby drapes completely closed. When he turned, he bowed his head slightly as a sign of respect for her age and apologized for waking her.

"Es su casa," she replied. It's your house. An abbreviated version of the classic Spanish welcome for guests, in this case more to the point than the courtesy implied.

This was a scene they'd played once before, Hawk's need to ensure that the system worked overcoming his reluctance to chance exposing the hideout. He kept it brief, and in English, because no matter how limited Consuela's English, his Spanish was worse.

"I need to be here tonight."

"I leave in *cinco minutos.*" Five minutes. Even Hawk knew that much.

"Please change the sheets on the bed."

"La cama. Claro qué sí." The bed. Of course. He didn't know whether she imagined he was on his own or not, or if she thought about it at all. That's why he'd chosen her. She was discreet.

Expensive too. He counted out two hundred dollars in twenties and handed them to her. It cost a lot of money to survive on the run, and Hawk had been damn lucky to escape the beach in a truck with cash in it—payment to Constantine from the middlemen. He had no scruples about spending drug money in this case. If nothing else, he was a practical man. Without the money, he wouldn't have had a chance in hell of evading his hunters. With it—as well as the other thing he'd hidden—he had a fighting chance of turning the tables.

Thanks to Mrs. Avery, his timetable for revenge had begun to tick. He only hoped he was ready for it.

Hawk locked the front door behind Consuela and watched until she turned the corner before going back to the garage. He got his sports bag from the front and said, "Not long now," then returned to the house. Putting the bag on the kitchen table, he got out what he needed and sorted through the cupboards for the rest. It took about two minutes to fill the horse-sized gelatin capsule with the white powder and another two for the glue sealing the cap-

THREE

"*What the hell do you think you're doing?*" The words burst out of her mouth with all the frustration and fear and confusion Angela had been trying to keep a handle on since the nightmare had begun.

For hours, it seemed, her imagination had skittered from one ugly scenario to another. Physical abuse, interrogation, humiliation—they'd all figured in what she assumed would be her end if she couldn't convince him she wasn't part of whatever mess she'd stumbled into. But not once, *never*, had she imagined sexual assault was part of the man's plans. Call it naïveté or plain stupidity, he just hadn't seemed the type.

Not, that is, until his fingers started working on her belt and she realized she'd given him more credit than was due.

Angela backed away from those hands so fast, she would have fallen over the toilet if he hadn't reached out to steady her. His reward for hauling her upright was a kick to the shin that she wouldn't have given if she'd remembered she was barefoot. Her scream was a combination of pain and frustration. Like a wounded animal, she lashed out again, ignoring the throbbing pain in her toes as she tried to bring her knee high enough to do some good.

He cut off her knee jab with a slick step sideways, keeping his fingers curled around her arms so that she didn't fall over. It occurred to her that he could just as easily let her fall and avoid having to duck her pathetic blows, and that fueled her growing anger. Throwing the last vestige of caution to the wind, she bent her head and sank her teeth into his forearm.

For her trouble, she got a mouthful of his leather jacket and the satisfaction of knowing she'd annoyed him. He swore at her, short, explicit words that gave her courage, because even anger was preferable to the almost total indifference he'd subjected her to thus far.

Hard fingers bit into her one arm as his other hand fisted in her hair and jerked her head up and away from his arm. She relinquished the bit of leather and clenched her jaw firmly shut as she met his furious gaze.

"What the *hell* do you think you're doing?" he demanded.

"My question exactly." Ignoring the tearing pain in her scalp, she tried to shake her hair free, yet only succeeded in making him tighten his grip. She tried the thing with her knee again, but had to admit defeat when he backed her against the shower door and pinned her legs with a single thigh.

"Will you *stop* that!" he growled. "No one's getting hurt here except you."

"You expect me to just stand there while you rape me?"

"That's not—"

"Oh, shut up!" Surprise flickered in his eyes, then it was gone and she realized his anger had also disappeared. Indifference resurfaced, and she knew she'd lost the battle. It had felt good, though, to throw his own admonition back in his face. Telling him to shut up had done wonders for her self-esteem. Unfortunately, it was also a conversation stopper.

Tiled walls echoed the *whoosh* of frantic breathing, and she wondered, too late, if kicking and biting had been a good idea after all. His body lay hard against her, and it took hardly a moment to realize she was the only one whose breathing was fast and uneven. His was steady and sure, his chest a solid wall that crushed her breasts and quelled her resistance.

Something wet tracked down her cheek and settled in the corner of her mouth. She touched the tip of her tongue to the bead of moisture and tasted salt. Yes, it was a tear all right. Dammit anyway, she hadn't cried since Frank, and only then because he'd taken their cat with him when she'd thrown him out. That had been four years ago, and now a man she'd never met before was making her do it again. She willed the tears to stop, then had to bite her tongue to avoid swearing aloud when another slipped away.

She watched his eyes as he followed the narrow ribbon of water, bracing herself to meet his gaze when it lifted again.

"I didn't bring you here to rape you. I think you know that." His voice was heavy and dark, words without expression that terrorized her because he didn't seem to care one way or the other how she reacted.

Angela gulped back the fear and tried to remember a time when calm was an asset she'd taken for granted. "Sorry, but when a man reaches for my belt, there are only so many conclusions I can jump to."

"I thought you had to go to the bathroom."

She blinked and tried to make her own expression as neutral as his. "I've been able to do that without any help since I was three."

"If you can undo your belt and pants with your hands tied behind your back, then you're more dangerous than I imagined." He retreated a couple of inches, taking care, she noticed, to minimize her selection of targets. The hand buried in her hair eased its grip, and her scalp tingled with its return from numbness.

"You're the one with all the moves around here," she said. "Where on earth did you get the idea I'm dangerous?" The image of that split second when she'd picked up and pointed the gun at him rose unbidden. She flicked it away with a mental whip.

He backed up farther and crossed his arms on his chest. "We're wasting time."

"Then untie me and I'll be as quick as I can."

When he just stood there without speaking, it dawned on her that it had never occurred to him to untie her. She was, in a word, aghast. "You can't possibly—"

"I can."

"But *I* can't—"

"Come here." He pointed to a spot in front of the toilet.

She shook her head, feeling a resurgence of the hated tears. "No."

"This is your last chance." His expression was unreadable, his tone even and unemotional. She believed him, just as she believed everything else he'd said that night. Including the part about rape. That had stopped being a threat the moment he'd said the words.

Her choices were limited and growing more urgent by the minute, with the humiliation factor weighing heavily in favor of stuffing her modesty and getting the thing done.

Angela took the necessary steps to where he'd pointed and fixed her gaze on a fleur-de-lis imprinted on a tile as he helped her through the drill. To be fair, he was efficient and brisk and managed to get through it without making her feel worse than she already did. Almost before she knew it, he was fastening the catch on her slacks and fixing the belt.

She continued staring at the tile, refusing to meet his gaze until he'd led her into the bedroom and pushed her onto the bed. When she scooched back to cower—yes, that's how she felt—against the headboard, he let her go without comment, seeming more intent on digging through his sports bag than on what she was doing. She watched as he pulled out the sweatshirt and the thing that was still inside it, then tried not to look too conspicuously relieved when he unscrewed the silencer from the gun and put it away. The gun went back under his coat, into a holster of some sort, she imagined, then he put his hand into a jacket pocket. When it slid out there was something in his palm. It was white and shaped like a capsule—elephant-sized, if she had to make a guess.

She didn't have a clue what it was.

His gaze flicked up to make sure she was watching as he showed it to her. "You probably know what this is, but to save time, I'll tell you. That way there won't be any misunderstanding."

"I don't know—"

His chastising look cut off her denial, and he held it between his fingers so she could clearly see it. "This is a gelatin capsule. When it's in your stomach, you'll have approximately twenty minutes before the gelatin dissolves. Don't worry about it breaking, because I've glued it shut. Inside the capsule, of course, is enough cocaine to fry your brain and probably kill you—although by then, you won't care."

Her wrists burned where the silk rubbed against her skin and her ribs were sore from bouncing against the driveshaft, but Angela forgot all about them in the wave of sheer terror that washed over her. She stared at the deadly capsule and knew she was dead.

"If you tell me everything I want to know, I'll give you this to make you vomit the capsule back up." He showed her a small plastic bottle of Ipecac syrup that he'd pulled out of his sports bag. "The capsule doesn't have to be in your stomach ten minutes if you cooperate. Of course, you could always tell me what I want to know without going through all this."

"I don't know what you want to know. I'm not who you think—"

"Lies will get you dead, Angela. I know you were part of a team sent to kill me. The tables are turned now, except that I'm giving you a fighting chance."

"I'm not part of a team," she began, desperate to make him listen. "I wasn't part of anything."

"And I don't believe you."

She looked into his eyes, and her protests faded into a soundless whisper as she understood that he wouldn't be convinced she'd been in the wrong place at the wrong time.

Several years earlier she'd faced death and come away with a broken fingernail and a healthy respect for seat belts. In the split second of time when she'd seen the semi bearing down on her and known she had to drive off the road or meet it head-on, she'd imagined her life was over. Bits of said life had flashed before her eyes as her car left the road and flipped over before sliding down the embankment. The images had been vivid and real, happy moments of her past that she would carry with her into whatever lay beyond. When she'd regained consciousness, those images had stayed with her for months, a reminder, perhaps, of how close she'd come.

This was different. Perhaps because she had twenty minutes, not merely a second or two wrenched from the inevitable. Twenty minutes before her brain melded her past and future into a mushy gray lump of nothing.

She tore her gaze from the hideous white death and met his eyes. "I won't swallow that."

He sighed and dug into the bag again, pulling out a small plastic bottle of water. Opening it, he moved toward her, blocking her escape by sitting on her feet, crushing them into the soft mattress without really hurting. "Angela, you know I can make you swallow this just by holding your nose and pushing it inside your mouth until you choke or swallow it."

She shook her head helplessly. If he was going to kill her, he'd have to do it without her help. Tears streaked down her cheeks, and all she could think was what an ass she'd been to cry in the bathroom over something that was no more than an affront to her modesty. If she'd known then how high the stakes would rise, she wouldn't have wasted the emotional effort.

If she'd known and not just suspected that the night would end up like this, she would have yelled her head off every time he told her to shut up. At least then she'd be dead without having twenty minutes to think about it.

If she had it all to do over again, she would never have picked up the gun. She would have stayed in her car and covered her eyes and ears and pretended that if she couldn't see it or hear it, nothing would happen. Just like the tree falling in the forest, its passage ignored for lack of observation.

He put the bottle on the bedside table and caught her chin in hard fingers until she looked at him. "You know there are two other places I can put this where it will do the same job. I had hoped we could do this with a little dignity."

For a moment she didn't understand, then comprehension flooded her thoughts and she was furious that her first reaction was the familiar combination of modesty and humiliation that had plagued her so recently.

"It won't fit." Which was absurd, but it was the first thing that came to her mind. She was shocked when it got a laugh out of him. His reaction stopped the tears, though, and for that she was relieved.

He held the capsule in his fingers and measured it with his eyes before meeting her gaze again. "I think it will." His hand fell from her face and swiped across his own in a quick motion that removed any hint of expression. Before she could think of another objection, he reached for the sports bag and dug around until he found a small tube of Vaseline.

"Is there anything you *don't* carry in that bag?" she asked, eyeing the Vaseline and knowing she would swallow the damned capsule before she let him put it anywhere else.

His gaze was steady and impenetrable. "I don't have any more time to waste. How are we going to do this, Angela?"

With dignity, she said silently, wishing the only real option wasn't one he also preferred. It would have given her pleasure to be contrary, to defy him to the end. She took a deep breath and closed her eyes, trying to dislodge the surreal feeling that was beginning to obscure her thought processes. It didn't work, though, because when she opened her eyes he was still there, offering her a choice of death or death.

She wet her lips and opened her mouth, then tried not to gag as he put the thing on her tongue and told her to swallow. She couldn't, not until he held the water to her lips and kept pouring until she had a choice of drowning or swallowing. It went down her throat, finally, inevitably, helped along by the ciliated pharyngeal muscles she'd learned about in fifth-grade science during an experiment in which Jimmy Caruthers stood on his head and swallowed without the benefit of gravity. She could almost hear the laughter of the kids in class as they'd watched Jimmy unbalance and crash to the linoleum, gravity flexing its brawn on those things it could and did affect.

She felt the brush of cloth across her chin as the man dried the spilled water with a corner of the bedspread, and she wondered if the Jimmy Caruthers flashback was the first of those images she'd see as her life replayed itself. If so, she hoped the content of the snippets improved. Jimmy Caruthers had been an obnoxious boy who'd grown into an equally obnoxious man.

He got off her feet and checked his watch as he sat at

the end of the bed. "Just to get things rolling, Angela, why don't you tell me what name you use with Constantine."

"I've never met anyone named Constantine." The truth, she knew, wouldn't save her, but she couldn't help but think any reply was better than staying mute and letting him win by default.

"Then who did you meet with who represented Constantine?"

She gave it sincere thought, clinging to his questions as a shield against imagining what was going on in her stomach. Constantine? Well, there was Constantinople, but that was a place, not a man, and she doubted he was interested. Constantan was a nickel-and-copper alloy—she knew that thanks to a geology/mining conference she'd put together last year—but she didn't think that would impress him either.

She wondered how it would happen, this massive cocaine overdose that would soon be seeping into her bloodstream. The only drug course she'd taken had emphasized the effects of narcotics on addicts, not how a body would react in the death throes of unintended, unaccustomed ingestion. Would it hurt, with convulsions racking her body and fear seizing her mind? Or would she just go to sleep, the white death of cocaine numbing her in a snowstorm of cold and peace?

"Angela."

She looked up and remembered she hadn't answered him. "I've never heard of Constantine, or met anyone who mentioned such a person."

"What name did you use?"

"The same one I always do. Angela Ferguson." She shifted against the headboard, trying to find a comfortable position for her hands and realizing her fingers were going numb. For a moment she panicked that it was the cocaine, then calmed herself when the new position brought stinging needles of recovery.

She was still in control of herself, and that gave her a certain comfort.

"Are you freelance or part of Constantine's organization?"

"Freelance." He quirked an eyebrow in interest, and she continued. "I've been working for myself six years now. Ask me what I do for a living."

"You're not supposed to be feeding me the questions," he said mildly.

"Yes, well, I guess technically this is your nickel," she replied, studying the harsh, tanned lines of his face and wondering what he'd feel as he disposed of her body. Frustration, perhaps, that she hadn't told him whatever secrets he was convinced she carried? Regret because, in the end, he'd realized she was telling the truth? Distaste when he had to handle a body that was still warm but quickly growing cold?

"Okay, Angela, what do you do for a living?"

He was humoring her, but she saw him glance at his watch and knew he wouldn't do it for long, not with the clock running. It really didn't matter, but talking was less terrifying than thinking.

"I'm a meeting planner," she said. "I put together conferences for different organizations, doing everything from contracting facilities to collecting fees and arranging speaking commitments. It's a busy life. I wouldn't have much time for killing on the side."

"A meeting planner." He regarded her steadily, his gaze dark and unfathomable. "Sounds like a good cover. How many teams did Constantine send after me?"

"How would I know?" Her voice had a petulant ring to it, but Angela was past caring about the niceties. "I've been nose-deep in investment bankers for the last three days. When I so conveniently ran into you, I was unloading my gear from my car. I have an office in the building over that parking lot. Of course, by now someone has probably stolen everything. I know my computer wasn't the best, but when it's free, I suppose that doesn't matter."

"Does Constantine still do the Condor run personally?"

"Condor run? What's that?"

"What he likes to call his biggest drop," he explained, even though she could see he thought he was telling her something she already knew. "Does he still like to go along for the ride?"

"I haven't a clue." She yawned and slouched uncomfortably against the headboard. "Ask me how many investment bankers it takes to screw in a lightbulb, and I'll have an answer. By the way, what's your name? You've told me to shut up so many times, I haven't had a chance to ask."

He hesitated, and she could almost see the mental shrug he gave before answering. "Hawksworth. Most people call me Hawk."

"As opposed to Mr. Hawksworth? I can see why." A wave of hair fell across her eyes, and she tried to move it away with her shoulder, but couldn't. "Don't you have another name?"

"No." He made a show of looking at his watch, then surprised her by leaning forward to brush the hair out of her eyes. "Angela, we've wasted ten minutes. When you were contracted for this job, did anyone mention the name Paul Marchand?"

"The Western Bankers Forum contracted me, and if Paul Marchand was part of the group, I never met him." There had been a Paul Marshall, but Angela doubted he had anything to do with assassinations. With the half bottle of Scotch he put away each day of the conference, she imagined he was too indiscreet to survive long in the killing field.

Not that her qualifications were any better, but this was a case of the mind believing what the eye saw, and she *had* picked up that damned gun.

Her stomach gurgled, and the reminder of what was

down there brought fresh tears to her eyes despite her best efforts to hold them back. It was just that there was so much left undone, little things she would have taken care of if she'd had some warning, not just the twenty minutes he —Hawk, she made herself use his name—gave her. Twenty minutes of answering questions she didn't understand, with her hands tied so she couldn't even scratch her nose. If she'd had cancer or some other disease, she could have at least left her life in order. There were business obligations to cancel, her mother to call—if she could catch up with her. The last Angela had heard, she was somewhere between Singapore and Shanghai, with no firm destination in mind.

There were friends, too, people who wouldn't even miss her for a couple of weeks because everyone knew she'd booked a vacation—alone, mind you—in the Bahamas. She'd been looking forward to it for months, frivolously indulging in business-class tickets and first-class accommodations.

"Angela? We're running out of time."

She focused on him.

"What about my plants, Hawk? I've had the philodendron on the coffee table since high school. I wouldn't want it to go to just anyone." She thought she saw a nerve jerk in his jaw as he clenched it, and chalked it up to frustration. Even in the doom-and-danger world he seemed to inhabit, there must be a point when people talked to save themselves. He must be getting impatient because she hadn't reached her personal breaking point, and even, she thought, a little worried she'd leave it for too late and die anyway.

Angela had had the advantage of knowing all along that her death would be the end result. Even if she'd had the answers, *especially* if she'd had the answers, this man, this Hawk wouldn't have any reason to let her live.

"Is the Condor run still scheduled for next Thursday?" he asked.

"You tell me."

"Are they using the *Sea Charmer*?"

"What is that?"

"Constantine's yacht. *Dammit*, Angela, you've got five minutes before that thing in your stomach begins to dissolve." He thrust his fingers through his hair, the overhead light glancing off the sun-bleached streaks in the otherwise dark brown thickness. "I was there last month, Angela. I watched as Constantine's best off-loaded enough coke to satisfy the habits of most of the West Coast. But I didn't see Constantine. I need to know if he'll be there Thursday."

"*I don't know!*" She surged to her knees and straightened her shoulders in a posture of defiance, which was all she could manage under the circumstances. "I've never heard of Constantine or the *Sea Charmer* or any Condor run. I'm not a killer and I wasn't in that damned garage for any reasons that have anything even remotely to do with you."

"You *are* a killer and you have to know if he'll be at the drop!" Surging up beside her, he curled his fingers around her arms and shook her hard. "I know Constantine. He wouldn't send anyone after me that he didn't trust completely. Constantine surrounds himself with people like you. He wouldn't dream of making the run without his shield. If you're going to be there, so will he."

Angela felt as though her head was going to snap right off her neck, but that didn't worry her near as much as the thing in her stomach.

He stopped shaking her but kept his grip on her arms, his gaze intense. "Tell me, Angela. Tell me now and I'll give you the Ipecac before it's too late."

She took a deep breath and gathered her composure, its familiar presence now a final shroud of dignity. "It was too late the second you made me swallow it. I don't know any-thing, Hawk. Nothing."

The intensity left his expression, and he softened his hold on her. "Then that's that, isn't it?"

So much for an epitaph, she thought, and wondered how much longer she had before the cocaine began to de-stroy her. Sliding backward, she slumped against the head-board, mindless of the ache in her wrists.

Almost as an afterthought, she asked, "So why is it so important? You seem to know where and when. Why do you care if this man Constantine is there or not?"

He looked at her with deeply hooded eyes. "Because if he isn't there, he won't die."

Angela focused all of her concentration on his answer, because she felt, somehow, that knowing *why* she was dying would be miles better than not. "And if he is?"

"Then my death won't be for nothing. I intend on tak-ing him with me." Without dropping his gaze, he picked up the bottle of Ipecac and opened it. Before she knew what he was about, he turned it upside down and poured the con-tents out onto the floor.

She swallowed in surprise, in shock, as the last chance she had of living made a brown mess on the cheap gray carpet.

FOUR

Gold bits sparkled and danced against green as her eyes became a mesmerizing burn of fury and disbelief. Hawk watched without blinking, almost without breathing, as the woman who called herself Angela Ferguson whipped herself into a virtual thunderhead of wrath.

He waited patiently for the explosion, knowing it had to happen just as he'd known she wouldn't break easily. The first fifteen minutes had been a time for fencing, for theatrics. Now the real work could begin. She would know, of course, that the next five were the critical ones. After that, she wouldn't be able to vomit up the disintegrating capsule without at least part of the cocaine entering her system. The old finger-down-the-throat method wasn't as efficient as Ipecac, but she'd know it was still an option. Even if she couldn't get rid of everything in her stomach, she could force up enough to make a life-or-death difference.

Five minutes. He would give her one to get past her anger. He was careful to check the seconds on his watch because every one counted.

"You're killing me so your own death will mean something?" The air fairly vibrated with her rage, but Hawk ignored it.

He looked at his watch and began again. "Will Constantine be at the beach? Is he worried I'll come after him, or does he think I'm going to keep my head down until he forgets about me? Is Marchand using his people in the DEA to help track me?" He didn't ask her again about the date of the run because time was running out and he already had the answer to that one, bought and paid for that same morning from a middle-ranked distributor he'd cultivated during the first stages of his infiltration into Constantine's organization. He'd only asked Angela as a truth check against those things he didn't know.

She straightened an already ramrod posture and took several deep, shaky breaths. "We've gone over this already. I don't—"

His anger got the better of him. Kneeling on the bed with his hands fisted into the mattress on either side of her hips and his face right up against hers, he kept his response clear and precise.

"You are out of time, Angela. The only way that cocaine is coming out of you is in the next three and a half minutes and only then if you vomit real hard. I'll untie you and let you give it a try as soon as you answer every single question."

Her outraged glare slipped into something softer, a look of bewilderment and—he blinked, but it was still there when he looked again—humor. She was laughing at him. "I can't seem to get anything right tonight. Do you have any idea how hard it was *not* to get sick on the drive here?"

He checked his watch again because he didn't want her to see how he reacted to her laughter. "Three minutes, Angela. Tell me about Constantine."

All humor was gone as she composed herself before answering. "For the last time, Hawk. You've got the wrong woman."

"You'll die."

"And so, it seems, will you. Not tonight, perhaps, but I

can see that you know you won't be far behind me." Her voice was low, husky from strain, a siren's song that pulled at his senses at a moment when he couldn't afford to be distracted.

Almost against his will, his hands lifted to thread into the fall of hair at her nape, his fingers tangling in the heavy silk until he cupped her head in his palms. "Tell me, Angela. It doesn't have to end this way."

"This isn't my game plan, Hawk. It's yours, and I didn't even have the advantage of knowing the rules. That's not fair, you know." She yawned, a tiny cat yawn that seemed to puzzle her until she focused on him and remembered. "Is this how it happens, then? I go to sleep and never wake up?"

Her eyelids began to drift closed, and he forced them open with his thumbs. Her pupils were even and dilated until he moved his head, then they shrank against the bright ceiling light. She blinked as he removed his thumbs and shook her head, a tiny moue of disappointment on her lips.

"I thought I had another three minutes. You lied." Her eyes slipped closed again, and she sighed, easing the weight of her head into his hands.

He shook her. "Angela, this won't work. Pretending to sleep won't save you."

She blinked in slow motion, regarding him from behind thick, dark lashes. "Guess you miscalculated, Hawk. The poison is working, and I can't work up enough energy to argue with you anymore." She yawned widely, and when her eyes focused on him again, they were bright with tears. "I only wanted to help, you know. That's why I picked up the gun. I saw everything, and thought that if I could get rid of the gun, he wouldn't have a way to hurt you."

Her head became heavier in his hands, and he realized all that was holding her upright was his touch. Gently, so that he wouldn't hurt her anymore, he shifted her weight into the crook of his arm and settled her head against his shoulder.

He watched her face as she struggled to keep her eyes open . . . and failed. Once, twice, then three times, and her eyelashes rested without moving on her cheeks. A single tear tracked down her face, and he caught it with his finger before it reached her lips.

Lifting his finger to his mouth, he tasted the salt of her silent anguish and knew he'd crossed the line between civilized man and his barbarian antecedents. In his self-righteous quest for revenge, he'd caused incalculable harm to an innocent human being.

Angela was no more an assassin than Mrs. Avery was. She hadn't deserved any of what had happened to her in the past few hours. He should have known no one could act that frightened without being utterly terrified, but her smart mouth had thrown him off. That, and the defenses he'd erected against the seductive pull she exerted on his senses. If his libido hadn't reacted so violently to her allure, he might have looked at her more closely, examined her words, and, perhaps, even listened to what she was saying.

The assassin he'd imagined her to be would know a cocaine overdose was a violent, ugly death. Tremors and convulsions would have been a convincing act, not this gentle slide into unconsciousness.

Cursing himself for being a fool, and an ignorant one at that, he bent his head to her breast and listened to the strong, even beat of her heart. Reassured, he laid her carefully on her side, dug a knife out of his sports bag, and used it on the silk binding her wrists. When he was done and could see the raw welts caused by his enormous error, he swore again.

A series of soft, senseless moans escaped her lips as he dabbed disinfectant on the wounds and bandaged them with gauze he'd found under the bathroom sink. Remembering the way her head had hit the garage floor, he felt her scalp for bumps and was relieved not to find any. When he was done and had packed everything back into the sports bag, he carefully lifted her into his arms.

There was no question that he had to take her with him. He would have preferred explaining to her why it was necessary, but her sleep was deep and sound. The combination of stress, fear, and exhaustion had taken its toll, and he knew she'd sleep until her body told her it was prepared to face the world again.

Taking care with her this time as he maneuvered through the narrow hall, he wished she'd stayed awake long enough to realize she wasn't going to die.

A couple of tablespoons of flour wouldn't kill anyone.

Hawk put her on the backseat of the Jeep, then returned to the house for a pillow and his sports bag. Gathering her long hair in one fist, he tucked the pillow beneath her head, then arranged her hair so that it wouldn't fall over her face or pull on her scalp if she moved. After fastening the center seat belt around her waist, he covered her up to her chin with the blanket. Her knees were bent and the end seat belt jutted against her shoulder, but it was the best he could do. He shut the door and got behind the wheel before the temptation to haul her into his arms and hold her until she awakened got the better of him.

It was all he really wanted to do, for now. Hold her. Stroke her hair and tell her how sorry he was that he'd frightened her so, and how very brave she'd been. He wanted to luxuriate in the feel of her soft, sweet curves as he held her, to imagine a world in which she would come to him willingly, with a smile on her lips and her gold-and-green eyes alive with laughter and need.

He wanted to hold her—now, because there wasn't a chance she'd let him get that close once she awakened and realized the downside to being alive was that neither he nor the nightmare had gone away.

He turned the key in the ignition, then opened the ga-

rage door with the electronic box and backed out. Ten minutes later, they were on the interstate heading north to the
Benicia-Martinez Bridge. Hawk's plan was to head up
through Vallejo on the other side of Benicia and keep going
until he was deep in the hills of Napa Valley, California's
fertile valley of wine and high-ticket tourism. There was a
place he could go there, a place where, for a price, Angela
would be safe.

The kind of people that hunted Hawk would think
nothing of killing her if that was part of their orders. He
had to assume it would be.

From the moment he'd taken her with him from the
parking garage in San Rafael, she'd been marked by Constantine as a lead to Hawk and by the authorities as a suspicious disappearance—if, in fact, they'd been notified. It
didn't really matter. With Marchand in his DEA role moni-
toring and, no doubt, interfering in police activities, there
was nowhere "normal" she could hide. The police might
believe she was an innocent bystander, but Marchand
wouldn't take the chance Hawk had told her something
that would land Marchand right in it.

Paul Marchand, Hawk's supervisor in the DEA, had
made the mistake of succumbing to the lure of drugs and
easy money. Hawk had made the mistake of finding out.
Added to a couple of other complications, he'd been on the
run ever since.

He had to take Angela somewhere beyond the norm,
somewhere she'd be safe until he could organize a way out
for both of them.

He kept the Jeep at a steady five miles over the limit, his
desire to cross the bridge with its manned tollbooths before
Angela woke up tempered by the greater risk of being
pulled over for speeding. His strategy paid off, and soon
they were across the bridge and heading steadily north. He
drove without stopping for an hour, passing through Napa,
then Yountville and Oakville, where the road narrowed to a

single lane in each direction. Calistoga was still fast asleep as he negotiated its quaint streets and kept pressing north. When he finally pulled off onto the gravel road winding into a fold in the tree-covered hills, dawn's pale shadow had just begun the subtle, inexorable process of softening the harsh blackness of the night.

Almost immediately the road forked. Hawk veered right and followed the deeply rutted path for ten minutes before coming to a dry wash. The land ahead was fenced and posted for trespassers and hunters, but he ignored the warnings. Feathering the gas in an effort to minimize the bounce of the truck, he drove through the wash and across the cattle guard at the gate. He then followed the road another mile until it ended at a white painted fence where a paved driveway took over. He stopped and waited with his hands in plain sight on the wheel as two men armed with automatic machine pistols closed in on the truck from either side.

They were dressed in dark jeans, windbreakers, and baseball caps, and looked neither pleased nor alarmed to see him. The man on the far side of the Jeep disappeared from his peripheral vision, and Hawk assumed that particular weapon was now trained on Angela. This would not, he mused, be a good time for her to wake up.

He stared down the barrel of the compact machine pistol and waited until the one on his side indicated he should roll down the window. The man seemed content to let Hawk speak first.

He obliged him. "I want to see Sammy."

"You're not expected."

"I was too busy to call." The grit beneath his eyelids had taken on the texture of coarse-grade sandpaper, and he fought the urge to rub them. Not that he thought Sammy's men were trigger-happy, but he'd rather not take the chance he was wrong.

He held the man's cool, unblinking gaze and said, "Tell him it's Hawk."

"And the woman?"

"She's with me."

Without lowering his weapon, the man backed up several paces and used the mike wrapped around his throat. Hawk listened as the man told someone on the other end about himself and Angela, but he couldn't hear the response that fed into a small ear receiver. Whatever it was caused the man to lower his weapon. His partner must have been plugged into the same channel, because by the time Hawk looked around, he'd shouldered his machine pistol and was striding back toward a small building set just inside the trees.

"Drive on up to the house," the first man said. He kept his weapon handy, and Hawk knew it would stay that way until Sammy told him otherwise.

Hawk nodded curtly and put the truck in gear. By the time he'd parked in front of the sprawling white ranch house that was hidden from the gate by a stand of pine, the man who gave the orders was walking down the flagstone path to meet him. Hawk eased out of the truck and left the front door ajar as he went to meet him.

Sammy—Hawk had never heard him called anything else—was a man of medium height and medium weight who dressed with the kind of flair that would be admired in boardrooms and casinos, and on yachts drifting across the Mediterranean. That morning he wore a cream knit shirt tucked into forest-green chinos that were obviously dry-cleaned, not washed. A black wool jacket—probably cashmere, Hawk guessed—flapped open as he walked, and the dark, curly hair that was trimmed neatly over his ears didn't look as though Sammy had combed it in a hurry. He'd either gotten up early for reasons that had nothing to do with Hawk, or—as Hawk suspected was the case—he'd been alerted the moment Hawk had taken the right fork.

About twenty feet from the Jeep, Hawk stopped and waited for Sammy to come to him. When they were even, Hawk turned so that he could watch the Jeep, a move he knew Sammy wouldn't miss. He'd meant him to notice, because Sammy needed to know Hawk did not intend to be careless with the woman in back.

Sammy didn't offer to shake hands and Hawk wasn't offended by the omission.

"I thought you might show up," Sammy said. "Sooner or later."

"You were too expensive for sooner."

Black eyes flashed in momentary amusement. "From the way I hear Constantine has been abusing your good name, I'd say you could afford just about anything."

Hawk let the comment pass. There was a lot he wanted to learn from Sammy, but he was too tired to pay much attention. Since any conversation with Sammy had a price, he knew enough to wait.

"I need a place for tonight, probably longer."

"The woman too?"

"Yes."

Sammy named a figure that was twice what Hawk had estimated. It worried him—not because of the money, but because he was hotter than he'd thought. Either that, or Sammy already knew who the woman was.

"Anything else I can do for you?" Sammy asked, pushing aside his coat to slide his hands into his pants pockets. He looked down the walk to where the Jeep was parked.

"I'll know more later. We'll talk then."

Sammy nodded his acceptance and pointed to the farthest of three cottages that were separated from the main house by lush green lawns dotted with rhododendron bushes. "It's the same one you used before. Walt will have everything ready by the time you get over there."

"It's been two years since I was here. You have a good memory."

"A computer." Sammy laughed again with his eyes. "I would have remembered without it, though."

Hawk remembered, too, but was considerably less amused than Sammy. The last—and only—time he'd availed himself of Sammy's broad range of services, he'd ended up paying for a jailbreak (a high-placed dealer Hawk had been cultivating), a Mercedes two-door coupe (burned as a diversion), and a substantial bribe for the officer in charge (incentive to look the other way). Added to the cost of Sammy's hospitality for two weeks while he learned everything he needed to know from the dealer, it had been an expensive exercise.

Worth it, though, because he'd gone on to penetrate Constantine's organization—something that had been on the DEA's wish list for a decade.

"I need to get some sleep," Hawk said. "Can you post a man near the cottage in case the woman decides to go for a walk?"

"Naturally."

Hawk knew Sammy would have a man in the area regardless, but it was the only way he could bring up the subject delicately. "I don't want her hurt, not for any reason."

Sammy quirked a single brow. "Will she faint at the sight of a gun?"

"No, but don't leave it where she can pick it up." Turning his back on Sammy's soft laughter, Hawk went down the walk to the truck and checked that Angela was still sleeping before starting the engine. Five minutes later he tucked her barefoot but otherwise fully dressed between the sheets of the king-size bed. He shrugged out of his leather jacket and threw it onto a brightly upholstered chair and pulled off his shoes. His holster and gun went out of sight under his pillow and the sports bag under the bed before he lay down beside her. Covering himself with a quilt he'd found folded at the foot of the bed, he shut his eyes and let the rhythm of her gentle, even breaths lull him to sleep.

Angela was lying on her side when she awakened. Her face was pressed into a soft pillow. One arm was tucked beneath it while her other hand rested on Hawk's chest. He was sleeping on his back, fully dressed and snoring so lightly, she wouldn't have heard if her own breath didn't lie strangled in her throat. The stubble of beard she'd noticed before had darkened, and the lines that fanned out from his eyes were as deep in repose as they were when he was awake. All in all, he looked just as dangerous asleep as he'd been the last time she'd looked at him through eyes misted with tears. Keeping her hand exactly where it was in case he noticed its absence, she counted the beats of his heart and wondered how the hell she was going to get away from him.

Just how her hand had landed there in the first place was a curiosity in itself. She was, out of preference, a solitary sleeper. If there happened to be a man sharing her bed —a rare but not unknown experience—he soon learned she wasn't the cuddly type.

Staring at the man beside her, she decided he had placed her hand on his chest as a means of keeping track of her. She supposed it was better than being tied up, then shivered as the previous night's madness filled her thoughts.

She had always envied those people who had the ability to retain a rosy fuzziness after waking that left them unsure of what day it was, where they were, who they were. A mellow, slow-blinking start to the day was as foreign to Angela as snow in Egypt.

She always came blindingly awake, rushing from deep REM sleep into total awareness with an abruptness that jarred her senses and oftentimes left her winded. Thought patterns that had been with her at the other end of the night came back with clearly detailed precision. Moods weren't softened or forgotten. She always knew who she was, where she was, why she was there, and how she felt about it.

Except today, and the only variable that was out of whack was the *where* one—which left everything else pretty much as it had been when she'd died. Or thought she'd died.

Biting her lip so that the fears inside of her wouldn't escape, she looked across Hawk's massive chest to the peach-colored curtains that were only partially effective against the day's light. This wasn't the dreary little house where she'd tried not to cry and failed. This room had a refined feel to it, a hushed elegance that was ingrained in the soft quilt, smooth sheets, and luxurious drapes. He had brought her here afterward, she realized, feeling markedly uncomfortable as emotions like gratitude and relief roiled through her.

He didn't deserve either.

She'd fallen asleep thinking it was for the last time, yet here she was, alive and surprisingly rested. Anger, real and potent, surged through her, and she would have hit him if she'd thought it would do her any good. She almost did it anyway, going so far as to clench her fist against his steadily beating heart. Blood pounded in her head as thought and reason took the reins and pulled hard, and she realized that if he hadn't awakened when she curled her fingers, she might be able to move her hand and get away with it.

If she was very, *very* careful, she might even escape. It was worth a shot.

Taking care not to shift her body in any other way, she lifted her hand. He didn't stir, and she was congratulating herself when her gaze landed on the gauze around her wrist. Holding that hand in the air above her, she pulled the other out from under the pillow and saw the matching wristband. It didn't make sense that someone so ready to kill her would bandage her wounds, and she thought about that for a second before more immediate questions surfaced.

Just how was she supposed to escape if she didn't know where she was? Lowering her hands to the covers, she began pushing them down and decided it didn't matter where she was. Getting away was a priority, because anywhere was better than her current location. One thing at a time.

It took forever, it seemed, to move the covers enough so that she could roll over without tugging at them, working with hands that trembled despite her resolve not to. When the sheet and blanket were finally down to her thighs, she rolled onto her back, then sat up and prepared to slide from the bed.

A vise of flesh and steel clamped around her arm, yet even in her first rush of panic, she knew he was being very careful not to hurt her. "Don't go outside the cottage," he said. "There are people out there whose job it is to keep you from leaving."

Her hair got in her face as she swung around to look at him, and she had to push it out of her way before she could meet his heavy-lidded gaze. He hadn't moved any more than it took to grab her with his hand, and he dropped that to the covers before she could demand he do so. She almost did a delayed jump through the ceiling, but calmed her speeding heart with deep breaths as she wondered how long he'd been awake.

He spoke before she could think what to say. "No more lies."

She blinked, then did it again because he wasn't making sense. "Excuse me?"

"I said, no more lies. I told three last night. I won't do it again." He rolled onto his side and rose up on one elbow.

"Whether you live or die depends on your doing exactly what I say."

"I imagine the spider said something similar to the fly, and look where that got him."

"I'm not the one you need to be worried about, Angela. I know that's a little hard to believe right at this moment, but things have changed since you went to sleep. I'm on your side now."

"That's not hard to believe," she said, gritting her teeth as waves of remembered terror washed over her. "It's impossible."

"The only way I can make you understand just how much trouble you're in is by telling the truth." He yawned, then shook his head as though it would help him stay awake. "I know it will take a while before you believe me, but it's important that you do, and soon. For your sake as much as mine."

She was disconcerted by what he was saying, and it bothered her that she was paying more attention to that than to her own questions and demands. She tried to get the dialogue back onto a track she could follow. "The only trouble I'm in will be history once I get out of here."

He shook his head again. "It's too late to get out. I know that's my fault, but I can't change what happened. I made a mistake, thought you were someone else."

"Who?"

"An assassin, like the other man in the garage. I assumed you were there to kill me."

"You can't be serious!"

"Very serious," he said. "I know now I was wrong. All we can do is accept that and try to work through the consequences."

"But—"

"No buts, Angel. I'm too worn-out for them right now." He fell back onto the pillow and shut his eyes. "There should be food in the kitchen, and if you're tired of those clothes, you'll probably find a robe somewhere. Take a shower, eat, try not to worry. We'll talk later."

She opened her mouth to protest, then realized she might never have a chance like this again. Hawk was clearly exhausted, much too tired to listen for an opening door. She could be miles away before he noticed she was gone. His reference to "people outside whose job it was to stop her" didn't faze her, because she didn't believe him. He'd lied about the cocaine, just as he'd admitted to lying about other things. True, he had a fearsome-looking gun, but a quick glance told her it wasn't anywhere handy. She'd wait until he was snoring, then she'd sneak away.

"Please don't try to leave the cottage, Angel. What you'll find out there is a lot worse than what's inside."

She thought about reminding him her name was Angela, not Angel, but it didn't seem worth it. Sliding off the bed, she went into the bathroom and looked longingly at the richly appointed shower with its gleaming fixtures, marble floor, and glass siding. It occurred to her that by the time she showered, Hawk would be sound asleep.

The knowledge that she'd have to get back into the same clothes didn't dissuade her so much as the feeling of vulnerability that washed through her. She stared unseeing into the huge mirror over the marble-topped vanity, imagining herself naked and totally defenseless against the man who'd given her her first taste of violence and terror. There was nothing sexual about her fears. That particular brand of assault didn't seem to be in Hawk's repertoire.

Her clothes, wrinkled and soiled though they might be, gave her a sense of control in a world gone mad. Stripping them away would be a form of acquiescence.

Her toes curled into the deep-pile carpet, and it occurred to her that she'd have to find her shoes or escape barefoot. Either way, she intended to be long gone when Hawk next opened his cold, dark eyes. Stretching out a hand to the porcelain tap, she turned on the hot water and scrubbed her face until the white blanching of fear was replaced by a healthy glow. Then she used the toothbrush and comb she found in a drawer, telling herself that basic grooming wasn't the same as taking a shower.

She didn't have to get naked to brush her teeth.

FIVE

Hawk pretended he was asleep when Angela came out of the bathroom and crept past the bed and through the door to the living room/kitchen area beyond. Her bare feet made almost no sound on the thick carpet, and he had to listen hard to track her movements.

A click that must have been the front door opening confirmed his suspicion that she didn't intend to heed his warning. He stayed where he was until a second click announced the door's closing, then swung his feet to the floor and went over to peer through the slit in the drapes.

The Jeep was parked about twenty feet from the cottage, and he watched as she went there first and checked the ignition. The keys were in his pocket, and he was wondering what the chances were she knew how to hotwire a vehicle when she retreated from the Jeep with her high-heeled pumps dangling from one hand.

She paused for a moment as though considering her options, then struck out toward the thick forest bordering the lawns. She walked boldly and without any apparent sense of being watched. He guessed she assumed no one would bother her even if they noticed, an innocence that was refreshing and almost impossible to credit. Hawk couldn't remember a time when he wasn't constantly looking over his shoulder, a day when he could relax without having to rely on someone to watch his back.

Sammy's guard stepped out from behind a cluster of rhododendrons and stood in her path. He was dressed much like the men Hawk had seen earlier, and he was relieved when the man kept his weapon slung over his shoulder. Angela hesitated, then tried to walk around him. Admiration for her sheer guts kicked his mouth into a half smile, and Hawk watched as the guard shook his head and said something to her. Whatever it was stopped her in her tracks. She glanced up at him, listened for a moment longer, then looked back toward the cottage, where two similarly dressed men had come into view. As soon as she saw them, they retreated back to wherever they'd sprung, leaving the first guard to watch as Angela padded back across the lush grass toward the cottage.

Hawk waited until he was sure she'd given up—for the time being, anyway—then got back on the bed and shut his eyes in case she came in and looked at him. It wouldn't serve any purpose for her to know he'd watched her defeat.

The front door clicked softly, and Hawk drifted on the wings of angels into a deep, soul-reviving sleep. If Angela came into the room, he didn't even know it.

The sun that filtered through the bedroom drapes wasn't as strong as it had been when Hawk had last looked. A glance at his watch confirmed it was late afternoon. He'd slept four hours straight, almost eight hours total, and a rumble from the vicinity of his stomach reminded him that it had been a very long time since he'd last eaten.

Aromas of garlic and onion teased his senses and made his mouth water. It didn't take a genius to realize Angela was doing something miraculous out in the kitchen, and as

Hawk got out of bed and shut himself into the bathroom, he wondered if she'd made enough for two.

Three minutes later he went into the living area and saw her seated in a recessed alcove next to the kitchen. The table was set for two. She hadn't waited for him to begin, and ignored him when he pulled out the chair opposite her and sat down. He looked at the plate piled high with pasta, slivers of chicken, spring onions, and asparagus tips, then lifted his gaze to her bent head. She still wore the clothes she'd slept in, although it was apparent she'd found a comb. Her hair was woven into a French braid she'd tied off with a piece of string, and it looked as though she'd changed the bandages on her wrists.

He supposed it was too much to expect her to do everything he'd suggested, and was grateful she wasn't refusing to eat. A sick woman was the last thing he needed right now.

"Thank you," he said, picking up his fork. "My abilities in the kitchen are confined to opening cans and boxes."

She lifted her head to look at him, and he saw that her face was scrubbed clean of cosmetics. Her nose was a little shiny, her lashes dark but not as thick as he remembered, and the color in her cheeks was entirely natural.

He thought she was stunning and only just stopped himself from saying so. Her learning that he was attracted to her wouldn't do anything for her peace of mind. His own equilibrium on that front was delicate enough. Sleeping beside Angela had been a uniquely exotic experience—a combination of frustration over the struggle not to pull her into his arms and fascination for the tenderness he felt toward her. The resulting dreams had been wild and exciting.

"I thought about starving," she said, "but couldn't see the point. I also considered cooking only for myself."

Her voice kicked him in the gut with the same potent energy it had the first time he'd heard it. He remembered the way it had been in his dreams, her silky cries of yearn-ing, of need. He had to take several deep breaths before he could resume eating.

"This is very good," he said. "What made you cook enough for me?"

Doubt and indecision furrowed her brow. "Whether it's enough is yet to be seen. I'm not used to cooking for a man."

He filed the information that there wasn't a man in her life and asked again. "So why bother?"

Her gaze went to his plate, which was already half-empty. "Maybe I put poison in your share. Isn't that what an assassin would do?"

He swirled some pasta onto his fork, stabbed a bit of chicken, and put it into his mouth. After he'd finished chewing, he said, "Sammy would never leave anything so tempting lying around, and I know you didn't bring anything with you. Which brings me back to my original question." He watched a faint blush darken her cheeks and knew he'd embarrassed her. "Why do I rate a spectacular meal like this?"

She bent her head and continued eating, and Hawk realized she didn't know why any more than he did. Either that, or she wasn't going to tell him no matter how many times he asked. So he let it go and concentrated on the food. He was nearly done when she spoke again.

"What happened last night?"

He looked at her carefully. "Quite a lot. Which part are you referring to?"

Her eyebrows veed in delicate confusion. "The last thing I remember was dying. Obviously, that didn't happen."

"You went to sleep." Her eyebrows twitched in exasperation, prompting him to continue. "It wasn't anything I did, if that's what you're bothered about. I assume it was a combination of exhaustion and fear, though I have to admit I was a little surprised."

"I was dead on my feet before I even went down to that garage," she admitted, and her eyes twinkled for a brief moment as her own words must have struck an absurd chord. She chased away the aberration with a determined frown. "Even so, I find it hard to believe I simply fell asleep. I was much too scared to do that."

"Terror takes a lot out of people. In your case, it sounds as though you were already functioning on reserves." He met her gaze without flinching, and was relieved to see more anger than fear in her golden-green eyes. Anger would serve her better, even if it did make her less easy to manage. He added, "Putting you through what I did last night was more than your body could stand. Going to sleep was the only way you could cope."

She looked at him a little longer, then nodded in agreement. "So what did you put in that thing you made me swallow?"

"Flour."

"That's it? Flour?"

Her expression plainly told him she wished he'd been the one to swallow something, and he didn't fool himself into thinking she was imagining anything smaller than a football.

There was a pause as she nibbled on some pasta, then she asked, "Who's Sammy?"

He finished what was on his plate and looked up to find her waiting. "Sammy is the man who owns this place. We're here under his protection."

"Where is here?"

"I can't tell you that."

She pushed her plate aside and rested her fisted hands on the yellow linen place mat. "I thought you said there would be no more lies."

"I did." He stood up, reached for her plate, and carried it with his own to the sink. He rinsed them both before returning to the table for the silverware and glasses. He was putting everything into the dishwasher when he heard her come sit at the bar that jutted out between the kitchen and living room.

He turned his back on the dishes and looked at her. "I said I wouldn't lie to you. I will not, however, tell you things you don't need to know."

"You've made it clear I won't be allowed to leave," she said, neatly avoiding telling him she'd already tried. She glared at him as though it was his fault she'd been turned back by Sammy's men—which it had been, of course, but it wasn't as though he hadn't warned her. She continued. "What harm can it do to tell me where I am? I can't see how that information will do me any good."

"That's not the point. Sammy's compound is a closely guarded secret. He wouldn't like it if I shared its where-abouts with you."

"You mean so I can't find it again?" she asked, and something that resembled hope flared in her eyes.

"Precisely." He turned away and made quick work of the pots she'd used for cooking. When he finished a few minutes later, the counters were clean and Angela had gone to sit in the bay window facing the big house. Curled up on the thick cushion with her back against the wall and arms hugging her drawn-up knees, she stared through the window with an intensity that he knew was designed to block him out. He shifted a heavy, overstuffed chair close to the window and sat down.

"There are some things we need to talk about," he said.

"When are you going to let me go?" she asked, without looking at him.

"Not yet. You'll understand why after we've talked." He propped an elbow on the chair's arm and bounced his fist lightly against his chin as he searched for the best approach. "I think that if I explain everything from the beginning, you'll have a better picture of what's going on."

She turned her head to meet his gaze. "What you did to

me last night was cruel and unforgivable. I thought I was going to die."

"I'm not asking for forgiveness."

She frowned. "Then why bother explaining anything? If you won't let me go, we have nothing to discuss."

"If I let you walk out of here, you're as good as dead."

"I was supposed to die last night, but here I am, wearing an outfit I bought last week that looks like I haven't taken it off since." She plucked at a wrinkled sleeve and sniffed delicately. "Sorry, Hawk, but I don't scare as easily as I did last night."

"I told you, no more lies."

"You've told me a lot of things. Trouble is, I've learned not to take any of them at face value."

Hawk stretched out his long legs, crossing them at the ankles as he contemplated the wilted yet tense picture she made. She was resisting him, fighting because she thought it was the only way to survive. He'd known she wouldn't be easily convinced of the real and continuing danger she'd waltzed into the moment she picked up that gun, but he had hoped she would at least listen.

He tried again. "You won't have to stay here long. But until I can organize a more permanent kind of protection for you, you won't be safe anywhere. This was the best I could do for the short term."

"You're telling me all this"—her hand swept wide in a gesture that encompassed everything in sight—"all this is for my protection? Don't make me laugh."

Hawk smothered a curse at her stubbornness and his own clumsy attempt to right a wrong. Looking beyond Angela to the big house, he saw one of Sammy's men come out a side door and head for the cottage.

"Why didn't you shower?" he asked her.

"Why didn't you shave?"

"Too hungry." He rubbed a hand over the two days' growth on his chin. "This might take a while. Besides, I think I'm going out for a bit. Why don't you go ahead and use the bathroom. I saw a thick robe in there. You won't be cold."

"I'm more comfortable in clothes." Her chin tilted up and she drew her shoulders back, accenting the line of her throat.

"Then I guess I'll have to find you some." He got up and went to the door as Sammy's man crossed the last few yards. He spoke with him briefly, then turned back to Angela. She was still looking out the window, pretending she didn't care what was going on behind her back.

"I have to go over to see Sammy. I'll probably be gone an hour or so." He pointed to a bookcase in the corner. "There's some books and magazines over there."

The look she gave him was carefully guarded. "Aren't you going to tell me what not to do while you're gone?"

He shook his head. "You're a quick study, Angel. I wouldn't insult you by repeating myself."

"Don't call me that. I don't like it." It was clear from the way she said it that she didn't like *him* calling her that.

"Too late, Angel. I do."

He put an end to the discussion by going into the bedroom, where he retrieved his gun from under the pillow. Weighing in on the side of caution—Sammy wouldn't appreciate him arriving at the house armed—he compromised and tucked it into the sports bag. Sammy's sensibilities aside, he had no intention of leaving it around for Angela to pick up. As there were other things in the bag he didn't want her to have either, he took the lot with him.

He grabbed his jacket and took that, too, for much the same reason as he was taking everything else. Even though he doubted Angela would look that closely, the papers sewn into the lining weren't something he wanted to fall into the wrong hands.

When he walked back through the living area, she was still staring out the window, her posture a clear signal that she was ignoring him. He let himself out the door and nodded at the man leaning against the side of the house, the butt of his machine pistol—a micro-Uzi, Hawk noticed—resting on his hip and the bill of his baseball cap pulled low over his eyes.

Hawk walked across the grass to the big house, sorting in his mind the various directions his talk with Sammy might take. Even if Sammy had the information Hawk needed, there was no guarantee he'd sell it. Complex loyalties, bought and paid for, ensured that nothing was certain. It would require a combination of nerve, cash, and timing to get anything from Sammy that wasn't necessarily on the market.

All Hawk knew for certain was that Angela would be in the cottage when he got back. Sammy never went back on services already contracted.

Sammy gave him what he wanted, but it took two hours and more energy than Hawk had to spare. Subtle ground-level lanterns splayed light in his path as he walked back to the cottage in the quickly falling night, his sports bag in one hand and several hangers full of clothes slung over his shoulder. He was tired without being sleepy, yet was fully aware that he wasn't alone out there. He counted two of Sammy's men who purposely showed themselves as he passed by.

Obviously, Angela wasn't the only one being "guarded." Until Sammy passed the word that Hawk had paid for all services, Hawk's movements were as restricted as Angela's. He reached the cottage and was about to open the door when one of the guards came up to him.

"The boss just radioed your clearance. We'd appreciate it, though, if you wouldn't go wandering around without letting us know first—especially in the dark."

Hawk nodded, admiring, as always, Sammy's efficiency.

It hadn't been five minutes since he'd left him checking the stack of hundred-dollar bills under an ultraviolet light.

"The woman still needs to be restricted," he said, knowing it was a repeat of what Sammy must have already told them. Still, he felt better emphasizing the point. He added, "Gently, though. I'll let you know if and when that becomes unnecessary."

The guard nodded and faded away, leaving Hawk to go inside. He stepped through the door, and couldn't help the pang of disappointment at discovering she wasn't still in the living area. Sighing because he'd really wanted to get a few things settled before they slept, he draped the clothes over the back of a chair, put his bag on the floor, and went across to the bedroom.

He pushed the door open quietly, not wanting to disturb her if she was already asleep. She wasn't on the bed, or anywhere else in the room. Crossing to the bathroom, he pushed open the door and switched on the light. Empty.

His heart skipped a beat as anxiety warred with total disbelief, but the moment passed and he was all business— checking closets, under the bed, behind curtains. He went through the whole cottage with an efficiency that showed none of the alarm he was feeling.

He couldn't help thinking, though, that it was dark outside, and there were men with guns who would shoot first and show no regret later. Dammit! Didn't she know how dangerous it was out there?

Obviously not, because she'd somehow slipped out. Hawk didn't waste time going through the cottage twice. Stopping only to extract his own gun from the bag—he didn't plan to shoot anyone, but the idea of being the only man out there without a weapon was unsettling—he opened the door and shouted, "The woman is gone. Find her."

He waited impatiently in the light streaming from the window, knowing better than to move away from the cottage. The delay was frustrating but unavoidable. Running into the night without a plan—not to mention without telling anyone—was the best way to get the same thing Angela was asking for. Killed.

The same guard who had spoken to him earlier rounded the corner of the cottage and joined Hawk in the light. He was calm and, from Hawk's point of view, not the least bit concerned.

He said, "She can't get through the perimeter without us knowing."

"I would have thought she couldn't get out of the cottage either," Hawk growled, "but she's done that."

"We'll all be very interested in learning how too." He paused to listen to something being transmitted into his earphone, then said, "That was the control room. If she's moving about the grounds, they can't locate her." He had the grace to look vaguely uncomfortable. "Sammy isn't pleased."

Neither was Hawk, but he guessed the guard knew that because he didn't say a word about the gun in Hawk's hand.

Angela waited until she could no longer hear the murmur of men's voices, then counted to thirty just to be on the safe side. When the only noise to reach her ears was that of her own breathing amplified inside the small space, she pushed the cabinet door open with the flat of her hand. When it swung back and banged against a nearby chair, her heart leaped into her throat and stayed there until she was certain no one had heard the crack of wood on wood.

It took less skill to crawl out of the small cabinet than it had taken to fold herself inside, but with her limbs nearly numb and her body slick with sweat from the airless, cramped quarters, it was a challenge all the same. In the end, she flopped out onto the living-room carpet in a manner reminiscent of a beached fish and lay on her back until the stabbing pain in her joints subsided to a tolerable level.

The thrill of victory surged through her, and she allowed herself a mental pat on the back before getting on with the serious work of escaping. The next steps weren't as clear as the first, but she didn't allow negative thinking to sway her determination. It was a matter of getting outside and reaching the trees without anyone seeing her. From there, she guessed she'd be playing hide-and-seek as she worked her way to freedom.

It was a game she'd already proven quite adept at.

She didn't try to walk until she thought she could do so without falling over and crashing into something, then had to crawl to the front door anyway when she realized she'd forgotten to close the drapes. Hawk's sports bag was next to the door. She pushed it aside, then changed her mind and zipped it open. There had to be something useful inside, she mused, remembering the seemingly endless succession of items Hawk had extracted from it the night before.

Her hands were shaking as she pulled out a sweatshirt, leather holster, small address book, and a black leather case that she didn't bother opening because it was too small to be of any use. There was a largish blue nylon bag tucked into one corner, and she was reaching for it when she spotted a small, familiar-looking gun.

She hesitated, then put her fingers around the butt end and pulled it out. It was, she guessed, the same automatic she'd picked up off the garage floor. With movements practiced long ago but never forgotten, she pulled out the clip, checked the load, and snapped it back into place. Leaving the safety on because running with a loaded gun was bad enough without it being ready to go off, she tested the weight in her hand and smiled.

Now she had something useful.

Shunning the remaining contents of the bag, Angela crawled around it. Her shoes were where she'd dropped them earlier, but she decided to leave them. Pumps would be worthless in the soft turf, and she already had one hand fully occupied.

Taking a moment to check for noise outside, she rose to her feet and opened the door. After glancing right, left, and center and seeing no one, she ran like hell for a clump of rhododendron bushes nearly thirty yards beyond the lighted path. She dove into the center, triumphant that the only sounds were the snapping of branches and her own excited breathing. No one raised the alarm. No one shouted, "Hey you! Stop or I'll shoot!"

No one was there to suggest—very politely, as had the man that morning—that she return to the cottage. She'd made it halfway to the trees. Another thirty-yard dash, and the rest would be easy.

She crouched shivering on the soft, moist earth, every sense alert as she peered through the thick foliage and scouted the terrain. So long as she didn't lose her nerve, she'd be free before sunrise.

Just to be on the safe side, she decided to wait where she was for a few minutes. Her eyes hadn't quite adjusted to the dark, and she wanted to be damned sure no one was out there when she made her final run. Moments later she was rewarded for her patience when a guard slipped out of the shadows and went inside the cottage. Angela decided he was probably doing another check of the premises, and was a little surprised when he came back out after only a few seconds and disappeared around the back side of the cottage.

Then she forgot all about him as she stared hard into the night and planned her run to the trees.

Hawk didn't notice at first when the guard running beside him fell back. They were in the trees at the north rim of the forest, having already covered nearly half the perimeter without so much as a sign that Angela had come that way. His companion was in constant communication with the other members of the team, and occasionally Hawk spotted their dark shapes moving nearby. Over a dozen men were looking for Angela, with Sammy himself directing the search from the control room.

She didn't stand a chance. Hawk wiped a film of sweat from his forehead and wished she'd taken his advice to stay put. Sammy's men were too well trained to shoot, but there was no telling what would happen if she surprised one of them. She just might get a little hurt before reactions could be controlled.

If she was lucky, all she'd get from tonight's adventure was a scare. Unless she got as far as the perimeter beyond the forest, and then it was anyone's guess what Sammy would do. Hawk tried not to think about it.

A low-pitched whistle pulled him up short, and he looked back to where the guard was signaling him to return. Jogging back, he heard the last bit of what the guard was saying into his mike.

". . . sure she's armed? What is it?" He listened for a moment, then looked at Hawk. "She's got a gun."

Hawk thought of the one he'd left behind and groaned. "There was a Beretta in my bag, but that was inside the cottage."

"So was she." The guard relayed that information, then asked Hawk, "Is it loaded?"

"Yes." He winced at his own stupidity in leaving it behind, but the guard just shrugged it off, then confirmed to the others what Hawk had told him. He added, "Don't anyone approach the woman. If she tries to move out, let her go. We'll cut her off."

"Where is she?" Hawk demanded.

"Near the cottage."

Hawk breathed his first easy breath since he'd discovered Angela missing. With the guard at his heels, he turned and headed back. Now that she'd been found and everyone knew she hadn't gone far enough to find out anything useful regarding their location, the rest was more or less under control. Once he convinced her that shooting was not in her best interests, he would have a heart-to-heart talk with her about the seriousness of the fix she was in. When that was done, he hoped she would be easier to keep track of.

The only loose end was to discover where she'd been hiding. When he found that spot, he'd fill it with cement. He doubted even Sammy would object.

Moonlight shafted down through the trees, lighting their way more effectively than flashlights. Hawk's eyes had long since adjusted to the night, and they kept up a steady pace as they cut back through the forest. The trees thinned eventually, and they halted at the edge of the lawn while still in the forest's protective shadows. Hawk squinted toward the lights of the interior compound as the guard pointed to a clump of rhododendrons.

"She's been inside there since she left the cottage, about three minutes."

"What's keeping her from moving?" Hawk asked.

"Don't know. There are a half-dozen men surrounding the area, but they're keeping out of sight. The only close surveillance is electronic, and they don't have a camera inside the bushes."

Hawk handed his revolver to the guard without paying attention to the man's surprise and began to walk across the lawn, his empty hands in full view. He moved slowly, giving Angela plenty of time to see him and decide what to do about it.

If she was going to shoot, he'd prefer she did it from a distance. It took a decent marksman to hit anything with a handgun, and he didn't think that was one of her talents.

He'd been wrong about her before, though, and the thought didn't give him any comfort as he drew nearer. He was about ten feet away when he heard rustling noises from inside the cluster, followed some distinctly unfeminine muttering.

Angela knew from the moment Hawk stepped out of the trees and started toward her that the jig was up. He walked without hesitation, heading straight for the rhododendrons as though he knew exactly where she was. She didn't know how he knew, and a shiver curled up her spine at the thought that someone had been watching her all along. Her success had been an illusion, her escape nothing more than an exercise in futility.

She mentally kicked herself for wasting time waiting for her eyes to adjust to the dark, then in the next moment admitted that even if she'd reached the trees, they wouldn't have let her go far.

They, not just Hawk. The gun suddenly seemed heavy in her grasp, though she knew it didn't weigh more than a couple of pounds. Staring down at its dull black shape, she supposed she ought to be grateful they hadn't shot her already. If they knew where she was, they certainly knew she was armed. Which might explain why Hawk was the only person in sight. The pistol slipped from her fingers to the ground, and she swore as she sifted through the leaves until she found the cold metal.

"Angela?"

Her heart thudded an extra beat, and she peered through the leaves to see Hawk hunkered down about five feet beyond the branches.

"Angela, are you all right?" His hands were lightly clasped across his knees, and he sounded concerned—for her, not himself. If he was worried about getting his head blown off, he certainly didn't look it. It occurred to her then that he wasn't holding a gun.

"What?" Her knees ached from all the cramped positions that had been imposed on her body over the past twenty-four hours, but she gritted her teeth against the pain and tried to think of a way out.

"It's getting late."

He was worried about the time? She almost laughed. "Your beauty sleep isn't a big concern for me."

"It's also getting chilly out. You don't have a coat."

"Whose fault is that? Mine is in my car back in San Rafael." Shooting him was an option, but she didn't think that would get her far. As he'd told her before, there were men with guns whose job it was to keep her from going anywhere. Just because she couldn't see them didn't mean they weren't there. If she killed Hawk, they might just as easily do the same to her.

Besides, she was certain she couldn't do it—shoot Hawk, the man she'd slept beside and cooked for. It had nothing to do with her reliance on him for survival, the hostage/terrorist syndrome that made certain behavior acceptable under unusual conditions. No, it was Hawk himself, a man who'd clearly taken no pleasure in her embarrassment or her fear. He had slept beside her without making her feel threatened. He'd given his word that she was safe from rape, and she'd believed him.

In a situation that grew more bizarre by the hour, he was a man who seemed to possess both honor and discipline. She admired him for that, and wouldn't have cooked for him otherwise. And if she was being strictly honest, there was something about him that would have drawn her to him under different circumstances, something in his bold, hard strength that touched her and left her shaken and bemused.

It was a combination of things that kept her from using the gun on Hawk, but in the end it came down to her own sense of right and wrong. Escape was essential. Shooting Hawk was not.

She watched as he shrugged out of his leather jacket and put it on the ground beside him.

"What did you do that for?" she asked.

"So we'll be even."

"I'm barefoot."

"You want me to take my shoes off?"

"Not particularly. I was just pointing out another inequity." Even if she wanted to, she couldn't shoot him, she thought. Ten years ago, while vacationing on her parents' ranch, she hadn't been able to shoot the pit bull that had savaged and killed her sister's cat. She'd had the shotgun cocked and aimed, her sights on the dog's bloodied jaws, but she hadn't been able to do it.

Later she'd learned the dog had been responsible for killing a new lamb. Her father's foreman had transported the dog to the vet after the decision had been made to put it down.

She almost wished that same foreman was here to do her dirty work for her again. But only to wound, maybe incapacitate, not kill.

Hawk stood up, turned his back so she could see he wasn't hiding anything, then knelt on the grass. "You'll notice I'm not carrying a gun. It would be a nice gesture if you'd hand yours over. *Very* carefully."

"I ran out of nice gestures when I tried to save your butt last night." She could try taking him hostage and bluff her way back to civilization—however far away that was—but something told her Hawk would risk getting shot rather than let her escape. That something, she realized, was the way he'd walked across the grass knowing she could shoot him anytime.

"I told you earlier that last night was my mistake, Angela. Don't you make an even bigger one."

"I doubt there's a court in the land that would convict me of anything once they heard my side of the story."

"Sammy has his own means of settling things," Hawk said. "The courts you're referring to will remain forever ignorant of anything that happens here."

"You mean if I kill you, Sammy will just get rid of the body and pretend it never happened?" Ludicrous, but not any more outlandish than anything else that had happened in the past twenty-four hours.

"You'd be better off thinking what Sammy would do to you if I'm not here. Two bodies are as easy to dispose of as one." He paused, then added, "Give me the gun, Angela. This isn't a game."

"Don't be so impatient. I'm not exactly defenseless in here, you know." Her toes made dents in the soft ground and she thought that if she'd been wrinkled and soiled before, she was filthy now. While diving into the bushes had seemed prudent at the time, it had left her hands, feet, and clothing coated with grime.

"If I seriously thought you'd shoot," he said, "we wouldn't be having this conversation. I could have let Sammy's men disarm you without so much as showing my face."

"I might have shot one of them."

"I doubt it. Even if you know how to handle that gun, you're not in their league." He paused, then asked, "*Do* you know how to use it?"

"It's a little late to be asking that."

There was a short lull, then he said, "What are you waiting for, Angel? No one out here is going to hurt you— not as long as I'm with you." His voice was low and reassuring, and she realized he could now see her as easily as she saw him.

She flashed the gun for bravado and tried desperately to think of a plan. Unfortunately, nothing came to mind. "You hurt me before."

"That was before I knew better."

"I don't want to be here anymore, Hawk."

"Then come out of there and we'll go inside."

"I didn't mean the bush."

"I know." He stood up and held out his hand toward a break in the branches.

Angela debated, then decided it was no use putting off

the inevitable. In a low crouch that further tormented her knees, she beat her way through the gap and stopped the moment her toes reached the grass on the other side.

His arm was still extended, waiting for the gun, she knew, but there was softness in the gesture that gave it the feeling of a request instead of a demand. Without looking at him, she put the automatic in his palm and turned toward the cottage.

"Thank you."

She glanced over her shoulder and met his gaze. "What for?"

"For not shooting me."

"That's okay. I couldn't shoot the dog either." He didn't ask what dog, and she started walking across the cool grass, knowing he followed. Not because of any sound he made, but because she could sense he was there. He didn't try to touch her, which she was grateful for. The tremors of reaction were a weakness she'd rather keep to herself.

When they got to the cottage door, Hawk reached around her to open it, then waited until she looked up at him before saying, "Did someone else kill the dog when you couldn't?"

"Yes."

"Then you have nothing to worry about." He pushed the door open and followed her inside.

She felt his gaze on her back as she walked across to the bay window and curled up on the seat. Then he went back outside and spoke in low tones to someone in the shadows, leaving Angela to wonder why she didn't feel any satisfaction at knowing Hawk expected to die.

SIX

Angela stared at the sleeveless pink cotton nightgown dangling with alien delicacy from the tips of Hawk's fingers, and frowned. The gown had a deep ruffle around the hem, a satin bow in the center of its slightly scooped bodice, and looked soft and clean.

She didn't want any part of it. "It suits you."

He gathered it into a loose ball and tossed it to her. It landed on the window cushion in a heap. "Don't be stubborn, Angel. I thought you'd appreciate having something clean to put on."

She kicked the gown from the window seat with a deft flick of her toes. It landed on the floor, not far from the cabinet from which she'd begun her great escape. She wondered if Hawk had discovered yet where she'd hidden. "I told you before. I prefer to be dressed."

"That's why pajamas and nightgowns were invented, for people who feel the same way as you."

"It's not the same thing."

"All right, Angel, which is it? Are you afraid I'll attack you if you take off your clothes, or is the gown too sexy for your standards?" He picked it up and shook out the wrinkles. "Sorry, but Sammy didn't have any jammies with feet and a zipper from top to bottom. This was by far the most modest gown available."

Admitting that it was, indeed, modest had nothing to do with it. Since she wasn't prepared to discuss the real issue, she simply said, "If you like it so much, why don't *you* wear it?"

"Because I normally don't wear anything at all." He tossed the gown aside and before she could react, was holding her chin captive, giving her no choice but to meet his heated gaze. "Normally, I sleep nude, particularly if I'm with a woman. In your case, however, I'll settle for taking off my shirt and socks."

His fingers were warm and hard against her skin, the tingling a result of nerves, she thought. Admitting he made her nervous was a lot safer than taking that tingling feeling a step further. She was not prepared to analyze the way he made her feel.

She touched her tongue to her lips, then froze as his gaze narrowed on that part of her. "I won't sleep next to you," she said.

"You'll sleep where you're told." His fingers tightened almost imperceptibly on her face, and he bent his head so close that she could smell the sweet tang of whiskey on his breath. "I explained to you last night that rape wasn't on the agenda."

"You also admitted you'd told lies."

"Three. That wasn't one of them." His hand dropped from her face, but instead of moving away, he pushed her knees toward the window and sat down. It was crowded, *too* crowded, and she tried to shrink back against the wall, but there wasn't a single inch of space available for her retreat. His nearness threatened something vulnerable within her, an indefinable weakness that was as new to her as the terror he'd instilled in her the night before.

He braced one hand against the window frame and the

other beside her head, his body holding her captive even though the only place they touched was at their hips.

He said, "We'll sleep together because that's the only way I'll get any rest. If you try to leave, I'll know it."

"I left this morning, and you slept right through it. You didn't know anything," she said, then nearly bit her tongue off when she realized telling him wouldn't help her escape—a goal she hadn't yet given up on.

"I knew." He took a deep breath and let it out slowly, a technique Angela often used herself when a situation required patience and hers was waning. "You've gone outside twice now. Sammy's men are well trained, but even the best soldiers get jumpy if they're constantly tested."

"Soldiers?"

"An expression, although I'm sure most of them have had some sort of military training. It would be safer for everyone if you didn't try leaving again."

"Afraid I'll get myself killed trying to escape?"

"Yes."

She blanched momentarily, then fought back. "And you want me to believe you brought me here for my protection?"

He did the deep-breathing thing again. "We'll get back to that later. At the moment we're discussing sleeping arrangements—"

"No, you're giving orders, none of which I find appealing." She turned her head to look out into the black night beyond the window and saw her reflection in silhouette with Hawk's. It was disconcerting, the amount of patience he was obviously exercising, when all he really had to do was tie her up and toss her onto the bed as he had the night before.

He didn't have to be reasonable and explain himself, she knew. Nor did he have to argue with her. He didn't even have to be nice to her. With a shiver, she realized how much worse it might have been if he'd let one of Sammy's men fetch her from the rhododendrons and force her back to the cottage. Hawk had accomplished the deed with unruffled tact.

He was being kind, yet it didn't change the fact that she was his prisoner. She glared at his reflection, then turned and did it again face-to-face. "I'm not going to make this easy for you."

"I didn't think you would," he said mildly, "but that doesn't stop me from trying to make it easier for you."

She barely kept herself from flinching when he trailed a single finger down her cheek, then held the fingertip up for her to see. It was brown with dirt from the rhododendron patch. "You need a bath, Angel. I'm not going to force you, but I *do* want a shower and I'm going to take it in precisely one hour."

"And if I don't wish to bathe?" she asked.

Hawk leaned a little closer and sniffed. "Then I guess I'll just have to get used to it. Either way, we're sleeping in that bed *together* tonight and every other night until I say otherwise."

She could no more stop the panic that leaped into her eyes than Hawk could help seeing it.

"I don't know what words will reassure you," he said. "What is it you want me to say?"

"I don't know."

He thought about it for a moment, and knew he couldn't be closeted for days on end with a woman who looked at him through a cloud of mistrust and fear. It was time, he decided, for another level of honesty . . . and he wondered how he knew Angela would respond positively to it.

"Is it because you know I'm attracted to you that makes you not trust what I say?"

Her eyes widened in alarm, and she shook her head vigorously. "But you're not—"

"*Yes*, I am," he interrupted. "You're a beautiful woman,

Angela. A very, *very* desirable one, though now is perhaps not the time to tell you precisely why. Suffice it to say, my physical response to you is strong and absolute."

If possible, her eyes widened even further. "If this is meant to reassure me, I have to tell you it's not working."

He checked the automatic chuckle and continued to hold her nervous gaze. Her small, fine-boned hands were clenched in her lap, and he covered them with one of his—not because he actually thought she'd hit him, but because he felt that by touching her, she might sense the honesty of his words. A fine tremor radiated from her hands to his, a warmth that was strangely satisfying.

He was inordinately pleased when she didn't pull away, proud that she managed to keep her fears and trepidation under control.

"I've never been so hungry for a woman that I've felt the need to force an unwilling one," he said slowly. "And even though I find you incredibly attractive and exciting, even though I want you so much I can hardly think of anything else when I'm with you, *I won't do anything about it.*"

She managed to blush and look stunned at the same time. "That's impossible."

"That I won't do anything?" He shrugged negligently. "Difficult, yes. But not impossible."

"That's not what I meant. You hardly know me."

"I don't have to know you to want you. This is a physical thing we're talking about here, Angel. It doesn't require the emotional depth that a long acquaintance would bring." Hawk *knew* he knew her better than he was admitting, but also knew that saying so wouldn't help his argument. Telling Angela that her bravery, her defiance, and her smart, sexy mouth were part of the package that tantalized his senses would be a tactical error.

When she didn't immediately respond, he said, "You can't have it both ways, Angela. First you're worried that

I'm going to rape you, then you're surprised when I admit to wanting you. Which is it going to be?"

She looked at him crossly. "I'm going to take a shower. Move."

Keeping any sign of victory or satisfaction from his expression, he got up and went over to the chair where more clothes were draped in plastic bags. "I'll hang these in the closet. There should be something here you can wear tomorrow if you decide you want to."

"Sammy keeps a change of clothes for all his surprise guests?"

"I imagine he's discovered that it's sometimes more discreet to have things available than to have to go looking for them."

"You've obviously taken lessons from him."

His brow furrowed. "Excuse me?"

"The sports bag from hell," she returned without missing a beat. "Last night, I was beginning to think it was bottomless."

"And now that you've gone through it, what do you think?"

He looked more than naturally curious, and she wondered what she'd missed. It was worth, she decided, a second look.

"I think," she said, "that I was much better off never even imagining people like you and Sammy existed."

He nodded as though he agreed, but only said, "I thought you'd prefer washing out your own underthings to wearing what Sammy had on hand."

"Couldn't find anything to fit me?" she asked, intending to goad but failing.

His smile was gentle and more dangerous than anything she'd seen yet. "I assume he has whole drawerfuls of the stuff, but given your state of mind, I thought you'd prefer wearing your own bits of lace and satin."

She opened her mouth to ask how he knew so much

about what she wore under her clothes, then blushed hot and red as she remembered his intimate assistance the night before. She had to take several deep breaths before she was able to speak, and when she did, she pretended she hadn't noticed his ungentlemanly reference. "The only thing wrong with my state of mind is the location of my body. I don't want to be here."

"And I can't let you go, so we're at an impasse."

She snagged the pink nightgown in one hand and stood at the bedroom door waiting for him to hang up the clothes, her bare foot tapping soundlessly on the carpet. Hawk no sooner exited the bedroom than she slipped past him and shut the door on his back. Loudly.

The ghost of a smile touched his lips as he went over to the liquor cabinet and poured a finger of Scotch into a heavy cut-glass tumbler. Taking a healthy gulp, Hawk congratulated himself for using Angela's own tactics against her: He'd set out to confuse her—never, of course, veering from the truth—and had succeeded brilliantly.

The fact that she did it to him with less effort than it took to breathe didn't diminish the sweet taste of victory.

Confusion was one of those gnarly sensations that was as unfamiliar to Angela as being out of control. She was pretty sure she didn't like it, but decided it was better than not feeling anything at all—which was precisely what she'd be experiencing if one of Sammy's men got trigger-happy. Guiding the disposable razor up her shin and over her knee, she thought about the man named Hawk and wondered how he'd react to the cold shower she planned for him. By the time she'd soaked in the steaming bath and washed her hair under the shower, she doubted there would be a drop of hot water left in the tank.

He would have no one but himself to blame. He had, after all, insisted she go first.

Angela sighed almost contentedly, then reached forward to add another splash of boiling water to the tub. Condemning Hawk to a cold shower was a small enough act of defiance, but all she could manage at the moment. Except for taking first dibs on the razor, but that was minor. It would still do the necessary job on his face once she'd finished with her legs, but she felt a certain satisfaction knowing it wouldn't be brand-new sharp.

I want you so much I can hardly think of anything else when I'm with you.

Despite the almost achingly hot water, Angela shivered. The heat in his eyes as he'd said those words had shocked her to the core, stirring feelings that had nothing to do with the fear and frustration she'd felt from the moment he'd taken control of her life. She shifted uneasily in the water, determined to ignore the fluttering deep in her belly that in other circumstances would be a valid confirmation of her own sexual response.

In other circumstances, not these. Hawk had threatened her life, and it was outrageous to view him from any perspective other than as his unwilling prisoner. Still, it was impossible to ignore the subdued courtesy with which he'd treated her from the moment he'd realized she wasn't one of the bad guys—whoever *they* were. With the singular exception of his reference to her lingerie, now clean and drying on the heated towel rack, he'd been firm instead of harsh. Considerate, not careless.

Somehow, paying him back with a cold shower didn't seem quite fair, not when he'd made an effort to provide her with basic comforts. It was that dilemma that absorbed her thoughts, confusing a picture that should have been black and white.

Then there was the issue of control. From the moment she'd picked up that gun in the garage, Hawk had taken charge of her life. She wasn't a woman who gave up control easily—never entirely, and certainly never against her will.

With brutal efficiency, he'd stolen away that which she wouldn't dream of giving anyone. And with an ease that took her breath away, he held on to what he'd taken. Her life was in his hands and there was nothing she could do or say to change that.

My physical response to you is strong and absolute.

Another shiver racked her body, a reaction that was as purely sexual as Hawk's response to her. Angela had never been one to lie to herself, but at this particular point in her life she was tempted. It wasn't, she mused, that she didn't already have enough to worry about that a tiny lie shouldn't pass unremarked.

Unfortunately, the lie wasn't tiny. Her body's awareness of Hawk was too strong to ignore, now that he had confronted her with his own attraction.

I've never been so hungry for a woman that I've felt the need to force an unwilling one.

He'd said it with a quiet insistence that made her want to believe his words. She *needed* to believe, if only to keep a sense of sanity in a situation that was already too bizarre for logic and reason. Strangely, she almost took comfort in his frankly sexual disclosure. He desired her, but he wasn't going to do anything about it.

Hawk was in control, of himself as well as the situation.

She believed him, and that *did* surprise her until she recognized that the source of that belief was her own intuition. She'd always prided herself on being a good judge of character.

She was also intensely practical. Last night Hawk had kidnapped and terrorized her. Today he'd kept her prisoner on the grounds that it was for her own protection. He'd made a mistake—believing she was part of an attempt on his life—had admitted the mistake, but the resulting consequences kept him from releasing her.

It made sense, if only because any other explanation failed her. Why else would he do what he'd done last night, then turn around and feign concern for her well-being? It would, she thought, be useful to understand why he'd mistaken her for an assassin. That rather peculiar leap in logic wouldn't occur to most people.

She recalled that Hawk had tried to explain earlier and she hadn't let him. She'd been too consumed by fear—not to mention general annoyance at his usurping her control—to listen. She'd closed her ears, not wanting to hear anything from a man who had, very recently, given every appearance of trying to kill her.

Putting the razor aside, Angela lay back until the waters lapped gently at her breasts, her head cushioned on a towel and her hands resting on the cool porcelain. She was alive and reasonably well, and it was the future she should be concerned with, not the past. It didn't matter that she believed Hawk had made a genuine mistake last night. It wasn't even relevant that he was being kind and considerate in an effort to make up for unwarranted abuses. Her startling attraction to him notwithstanding, she couldn't care less if he was a good guy or bad guy or something in between.

All that was important was that she put as much distance between herself and him as was possible. She didn't belong here any more than people like Hawk and Sammy belonged in her safe, ordinary world. Perhaps, she mused, a new opportunity for escape would present itself in the morning. Failing that, she'd make Hawk's life so uncomfortable he'd let her go in self-defense. With that positive thought, she flicked the drain lever with her big toe and watched as a tiny whirlpool danced between her feet.

Climbing out of the tub on legs made wobbly from extended parboiling, she pulled out the pin that held her hair in a loose knot and shook it free. Her gaze landed on the razor, and she grinned as a naughty idea occurred to her. After a moment's thought as she considered not the *if*, but the *how*, she pulled open a vanity drawer. She knelt on the cool tiles, ducked under the drawer, and ran the fragile blade up and down the wooden spar beneath it. When she was satisfied with the results, she rinsed the razor and put it back where she'd found it.

With a bottle of shampoo in one hand and a facecloth in the other, she stepped into the luxurious shower stall and closed the glass door behind her. On the off chance she'd already used up most of the available hot water, she washed and rinsed her hair in a moderate rush.

She could have taken her time. It took what seemed an eternity before there was, at last, a noticeable reduction in temperature. She got out in a hurry before it cooled too much. It wouldn't do, she thought, for Hawk to test the water and decide to wait. Let him get good and settled before he realized there might be a problem.

She wrapped a towel around her head, then pulled on the pink gown, which covered her knees and everything else more or less adequately. Then she put on one of the thick terry robes hanging on the back of the door, picked up her dirty clothing, and was about to leave when she remembered the lingerie she'd left to dry. The panties, bra, and knee-high stockings were still damp, but she scooped them up all the same and tucked them out of sight.

Sharing a bed with the man was one thing. Leaving her underwear flapping in the breeze—so to speak—was quite another.

She took another few seconds to search through the cabinets and drawers, then added a blow dryer and comb to her pile and left the bathroom to Hawk.

It was nearly midnight when Hawk pulled a short-sleeved Henley knit over his head and tucked it into the clean black jeans Sammy had supplied along with everything else before emerging from the bedroom. He found Angela on the window seat with her knees drawn up to her chest and her fingers curled around a cobalt china mug. Her hair lay thick and soft on her shoulders, the ends curling about halfway down her back, and her face was once again scrubbed clean and bright. The only part of her that wasn't completely covered by the thick white robe was her toes, and only the very tips of those were visible.

She looked cozy and warm, and—with good reason, he reckoned—smug.

He paused just outside the door to give her a good look at the jagged red cut on his jaw where he'd tried to drag the razor through his beard. A shadow of emotion clouded her expression, but it was gone before he could decide whether it was regret or black satisfaction. He didn't really care, except that little tricks like that could achieve surprisingly nasty results. If she'd tried that with anyone less . . . understanding, the backlash might have been more than she could handle.

As it was, he was more annoyed about the hot water—or lack of it—than the razor. Besides, he blamed himself for not checking the blade in the first place. If he'd learned anything, it was that Angela was a brave, bright, and somewhat bullheaded woman.

It was his own fault he'd nearly sliced off his ear.

"Have a nice shower?" she asked.

He was so surprised that she spoke to him without being prompted, he decided to chalk up the cold shower as his own fault too. It wasn't as though he hadn't noticed she'd been in the bathroom well past her allotted time. He should have suspected she was up to something.

He shoved his hands into his back pockets and nodded amiably. "Yes, thank you. Is that coffee you're drinking?"

"Chocolate." Her voice was low and uncertain, and her gaze narrowed on him. "I can't drink coffee at night."

She said it as though she wasn't aware that chocolate was also loaded with caffeine. Hawk just nodded again and went into the kitchen where he found a jar of decaf. After plugging in the electric kettle, he looked in the refrigerator and cabinets for something to eat. He settled on cheese and bread, and asked Angela if she wanted any.

"Maybe later," she said, leaving him to wonder just how long she planned on staying up. Although he'd slept away most of the afternoon, he wanted to get his body clock back on schedule. There was work to do tomorrow and he needed to be fully awake for it. Six uninterrupted hours of sleep would be helpful. He cut off a few slices of cheese and bread, set them on a plate, and put the rest away. Then he poured boiling water into the mug and stirred until the coffee dissolved.

"I hope you don't mind," he said, "but I'd like to be in bed in another hour."

"And if I do mind?" She looked up at him as he carried the plate to the coffee table in front of the sofa and sat down.

He popped a piece of the smoky Edam into his mouth and considered his answer carefully. "The sooner we both get on a regular schedule, the better we'll cope." He paused, expecting rebuttal. He got laughter, full and ripe and sensuous.

He managed not to choke, but it took great effort.

"I don't know about the world you live in, Hawk, but mine isn't organized according to regular anything. I work sixteen-hour days for two or three months running, then go flat out for however long the meeting lasts, usually three or four days. Odd hours are my life."

"You told me last night you were a meeting planner. Also that you were freelance." He finished the food and leaned back into the sofa's deep cushions. "Are you in the middle of a meeting now?"

"Why do you want to know?"

"Because if you're expected to be somewhere, someone will eventually come looking for you. Or asking questions."

She hesitated as though deciding how to answer, and he

interrupted before she'd made up her mind. "Why don't I make this easy for you and tell you what I do know before you answer that?"

She shrugged carelessly, but that casual attitude disappeared before his first sentence was finished. "Your secretary doesn't expect you in the office for two weeks—although I'm not sure why—and your landlord is holding your mail for the same amount of time."

"How did—" she began, but fell silent when he pressed on.

"Your silver Lincoln Towncar has a Macintosh computer in the trunk, assorted fast-food wrappers on the floor, and a box of Godiva chocolates on the passenger seat. In your wallet you have credit cards for every major department store in the United States, a driver's license that's six months from expiring, and a signed donor card that gives everything but your eyes to science." He looked at her curiously. "Why not your eyes?"

Disbelief gave way to embarrassment. "Something to do with a horror film I saw years ago. How do you know all those things about me?"

"Sammy knew. I bought the information."

"But how does he know?"

Hawk shrugged. "It's part of what he does. As you haven't been reported missing to the police, we assume Constantine's people cleaned up the mess in the garage. The man I was fighting with was one of them."

Her eyes went round in remembered horror. "He was bleeding all over the place."

"Just his nose. Painful but not fatal." He stretched his arms high over his head, then dropped them to rest along the back of the sofa. "Anyway, he probably told them about your appearance and from there it was a simple matter of finding your car. You left a door open when you came over to see what the fuss was, right?"

She nodded mutely, and he continued. "Constantine's

people know you're with me. They're looking for both of us now, Angel, and trust me when I say they're leaving no stone unturned."

He expected questions about related details, but she surprised him yet again. "Who is this Constantine you keep mentioning and why does he care if I'm with you or not? I've never done anything to him."

"But he doesn't know that." Hawk leaned forward and rested his forearms on his thighs as he elected to ignore the first part of her question in favor of the second. "Constantine is jumping to the same kind of conclusions I did last night, only he's assuming you're on my side, not his."

"But you attacked me," she persisted. "You threw that man at me and knocked the stuffing out of me."

"He was still stunned from that blow to his nose. Fine distinctions like who was on top and why were beyond him at the moment. I put him to sleep before he had a chance to get his bearings."

Angela looked at him for a long time, sorting through what she already accepted as fact, what Hawk had just told her, and how much of that she believed. So far, she couldn't find a lie in anything he'd said—not that she would know a lie one way or the other, but nothing certifiably untrue had jumped out and bit her yet.

More to the point, what he was saying made sense. It explained everything, up to and including the horrible ordeal he'd put her through with the "cocaine" death threat. It explained it all, but that didn't mean she had to like it.

"Last night, you wanted information from me. What does Constantine want that he thinks I have?" She put the empty mug aside and hugged her legs.

"Me."

"Excuse me?" She felt exasperation bubbling inside, but made an effort to maintain a calm, civilized manner. It was a tactic that served her well in business situations when screaming would only have added to the problem. Unfortunately, the discipline it took was currently making her jaw ache.

Hawk flashed a quick grin, telling her without words he noticed her restraint. When he spoke, though, it was without a single hint of humor. "Constantine has been looking for me for eight months. If he thinks I've got ties to you—which he has to assume since you left the garage with me—he'll try to get at me that way."

"I wasn't exactly a willing passenger."

"Like I said before, he wouldn't know that." There was something that almost resembled compassion in his gaze.

A sinking feeling tugged at her stomach, and she covered her belly with her hand as though that would control it. "Just how badly does Constantine want you?"

"Very." He looked down at his hands for a long moment, then raised his head. The look in his eyes was bleak and resigned, and, she thought, almost unbearably weary. "I took something very important from him."

"What?"

"His son." He didn't blink as he added, "I killed him, and Constantine won't stop hunting me until I'm dead too. Unless I get him first, but that's another story."

"Yes," she agreed softly, "I imagine it is." She held his gaze and finally realized the enormity of what he'd been trying to tell her at intervals all day. She was in a lot of trouble. *Big* trouble, the kind that destroyed lives.

For what she knew wouldn't be the last time, Angela wished she'd never picked up that damned gun.

SEVEN

"What were the other two lies you told me last night?"

A feeling of mild disorientation washed through Hawk as he looked at Angela across the rim of his coffee cup. He'd just admitted to killing a man, and her first response was to change the subject. Somehow, he'd thought she would react more strongly than that. It was hard not to let his surprise show, but he managed.

He said, "Aside from the big lie about the cocaine, you mean?"

"Yes."

"I told you there were people in that house where we first stopped, people who would as soon kill you as look at you." He set the cup on the table. "There was only one person inside and she gets paid to keep her eyes closed and her mouth shut."

"That's two." She caught his gaze and held it. "What's the last one?"

Hawk exhaled a deep breath and wished he'd never told her there were three lies. He could, he knew, simply refuse to answer, but that would only make her suspicious of everything else he needed to tell her.

"You asked," he said, "if I had a name other than Hawksworth."

"You lied about your name?"

"Yes." He kept his expression carefully stern in the hope that she wouldn't press him. He should have known better.

"And here I thought we were talking about important stuff," she said. "So what is it?"

"Not something you need to know."

"You're not going to tell me?"

"No."

A look of pure mischief lit up her eyes. "If I put my mind to it, I could make you tell me. I saw a canister of flour in the kitchen while I was cooking."

Hawk just stared at her, keeping his mouth shut and expression blank in lieu of knowing how to react. It hadn't been twenty-four hours since he'd threatened her with death via cocaine/flour, and she was joking about it? Clearly Angela was possessed of a wicked sense of humor.

"What's wrong, Hawk?" she asked, smiling. "Is it against the rules to make a joke?"

Her smile filled him with a kind of pleasure he hadn't known since long before the nightmare had begun, and it gave him hope. At least he thought the vaguely familiar emotion was hope. There had been so damned little of it in the last few months that he wasn't sure.

"Sorry, Angel," he said with an answering smile. "You took me by surprise. I'll do better next time." Getting up from the sofa, he gathered his dishes and took them into the kitchen.

"Hawk?"

He turned and met her gaze. All humor was gone from her expression, erased so well that it was hard to believe she'd been near laughter just moments before. "Yes?"

"Are you going to tell me about the man you killed?"

"I'm going to have to sometime," he said, "but it's getting late. Like I said before, I need some sleep. There are things I have to do tomorrow."

"We're staying here another day?"

"Yes. It would be helpful," he added, "if I knew where you were supposed to be going for the two weeks your secretary said you'd be out of the office."

"Why?"

"Because I don't want anyone running to the police when you don't show up as planned." He knew she wouldn't tell him, but even a lie would give him a little information.

"Ask Sammy," she snapped. "He seems to know everything else." She got up and brought her cup over to the sink, being careful, he noticed, not to chance brushing against him. She was, he acknowledged with a sigh of regret, a very smart woman.

She paused and looked up at him. "You really should do something about that scratch."

"Taken care of. I had some Bacitracin in my bag."

"Of course you did," she said with a harrumph of annoyance. "I should have known a man who carries Vaseline and Ipecac wouldn't travel without antibiotic cream. I'm surprised you didn't have your own razor."

"I do," he said, without rising to the bait. "By the time I realized I should have used it and not the one Sammy provided, I was out of the mood."

Hawk could have sworn that almost got a smile, but she ducked her head before he could tell for sure, and turned away. He let her go into the bedroom first, giving her a shot at the bathroom and waiting until he heard her climb between the sheets before following. When he did, she'd already turned out the lights. He moved easily in the dark, positioning the sports bag where he could find it and his gun where she couldn't. Then he pulled off his shirt and socks, lifted the blanket, and eased his tired body down on top of the sheets.

It wasn't the way he preferred sleeping with a beautiful woman, but the only one he could think of in order to keep a chaste distance between them. Reaching for her in his sleep wasn't beyond his imagination, and he doubted she would appreciate the natural physical reaction that holding her tucked tight against his hips would provoke.

He turned his head on the pillow and was surprised to see the whites of her eyes as she looked at him in the dark. "What is it, Angel? Can't sleep?"

She closed her eyes without answering, leaving him with his own thoughts for company as he waited for her to fall asleep. It was a full hour before he was certain her rhythmic breaths were consistent with those of a woman sleeping, and he used the time to try to come up with a backup plan in case the next day's excursion proved unproductive. By the time he followed her into sleep, he still didn't have one.

Hours later, when Angela turned to Hawk in her sleep and laid her hand trustingly on his chest as she'd done the night before, he covered it with his own and knew that while his priorities hadn't changed, the motivations behind them had.

He still had to stop Constantine. Now, though, he would do it not just to avenge the dead, but to protect a woman who was very much alive.

Hawk didn't think he'd awakened Angela when he slid out of bed at six and went to shower and shave, but she was up and drinking coffee in the window seat when he came out of the bedroom fully dressed. She didn't respond when he said good morning, so he went across to the kitchen, where he found a pot of coffee on the stove. After taking off the funnel to dump the filter and wet grounds into the wastebasket, he poured himself a cup and went across the room to top off hers.

She held out her cup without meeting his gaze, then waited until he'd put the pot back on the stove and returned to sit on the sofa before looking at him. Her hair was still mussed from sleep, a thick, luxurious tangle that spun the morning light into red gold.

"You said last night you have things to do today," she said. Her voice was low and rusty, a sensual rub on his senses that made him yearn for a world in which he could wake up to that voice every morning. She cleared her throat and added, "Does that mean you're going somewhere?"

"Yes."

"Where?"

"I can't tell you." He took a cautious sip of the richly aromatic coffee, then another when it didn't scald his tongue. She made good coffee, he thought, but decided against telling her. She appeared to have something on her mind that precluded nonessential conversation.

"How long will you be gone?"

"A few hours, maybe all day." He knew why she wanted to know and that worried him. "Nothing's changed since yesterday, Angela. You still can't leave here. While I'm out, someone will be by to check on you every hour. Hiding won't get you anything except hot and cramped."

"I'll go mad sitting here all day with nothing to do."

"There are books and magazines," he reminded her. "Sorry about the lack of TV and radio, but they would give you too much information about where we are."

"There's a jigsaw puzzle in the cupboard," she said. "It's a picture of the Bridge of Sighs in Venice. Is it safe to assume that's not a clue?"

Hawk felt his mouth twitch with a threatened smile. He mastered it. "We're not in Italy."

"I didn't think so."

"While I'm away I don't want you visiting Sammy or talking with any of his men. You can't convince them to let you go because I've paid them to keep you here. Nothing you have to offer will change that."

"I wasn't about to put my body on the line, if that's what you're worried about." She ducked her head and pulled the terrycloth robe down to cover her toes. When she looked up at him again, there was a glint of frustration in her eyes. "Why don't you want me to talk to them?"

"Because Sammy doesn't trust you."

"Me? What have I done to him, or is this another of those assumptions like the one your friend Constantine made?"

"Constantine is no friend of mine."

"Whatever." She waved her fingers in the air between them. "Tell me what I've done to Sammy."

Hawk finished his coffee and got some more before answering. "It's who you are, not anything you've done. Most of the people who avail themselves of Sammy's services don't have the kind of regard for law and order that you do. It would never occur to them to tell the authorities about his setup here."

"And he thinks I would?" she said, her tone ringing the "how dare he?" bell so clearly, the words were superfluous.

"He knows you will." The quick blush in her cheeks confirmed his assumption. He decided it was time to tell her exactly what that meant to her position. "I've told you Sammy won't let you escape because I'm paying him not to let that happen. What I haven't told you is that if Sammy thinks you'll compromise him in any way, he won't let me take you out of here when it's time. Once he's made that decision, no amount of money will convince him otherwise."

"And just what does he plan to do with me in that case? Hide me here until I die a natural death?"

She was trying to attribute normal behavior to an abnormal situation, he realized. He couldn't let her do that. It wasn't safe for either of them.

"Use your imagination, Angela," he said, keeping his voice even because there wasn't any need to confuse things with emotion. She needed to understand the content without being sidetracked by how he felt about things.

He'd brought her to Sammy's because there hadn't been any closer options. The risks were acceptable. As long as she did what he told her, Sammy would let them both leave without feeling the need to silence Angela forever.

If, in her bid for freedom the previous night, she'd managed to get through the barrier of trees that surrounded Sammy's compound and seen what lay beyond, no amount of discussion would have saved her. Even at night, the landscape in and around the Napa Valley was distinct. Fields of grapes in their tidy rows would narrow the search to this and the Sonoma wine country. Angela might not have known where she was, but a trained investigator would have figured out where to begin looking. Hawk knew he should have had this discussion with her last night, but he'd elected to soothe her fears, not compound them.

Now, though, her hands shook visibly as she put her mug aside and took several deep breaths. "But I don't even know where we are. How can I tell anyone anything?"

"That won't stop you from trying. I know that. So does Sammy." He put his own mug on the table and touched his steepled fingers to his unshaven chin. "Stay in the cottage, Angel. When they come to check on you, it would be best if you didn't appear to be studying their faces for later reference. Don't meet their eyes if you can avoid it, and don't ask any questions."

"I suppose you don't want me to look out the windows, either," she said, with a touch of her old fight.

"If I didn't, you wouldn't be sitting there now, but, frankly, outside of locking you in the bathroom, I don't see how I could enforce such a directive. I'd rather not have to do that."

"I can't believe that locking me in the bathroom would offend your sensibilities."

"It wouldn't. I just don't see the necessity. You can't see anything useful from here. The house and grounds could be anywhere, and Sammy is keeping out of sight. The only activity you'll see is guards in the distance and the one who comes to the door." He paused, then added, "If you need anything, tell the guard when he comes."

"I don't want to stay here." There was a plea in her expression that he forced himself to ignore.

"I can't take you with me." He didn't tell her what to do if he didn't come back because he'd already covered that with Sammy. He knew Sammy would protect Angela until it was no longer feasible. Police pressures, as well as those Constantine might exert, could alter circumstances beyond Sammy's immediate control.

There were no guarantees, but Hawk hadn't had any choices either. The one man he had decided to trust with the problem of Angela was in Denver, and Hawk didn't want to send her to him without insurance—which was why he had to take the chance today and go back to San Rafael. Without the material he'd left hidden in Mrs. Avery's living room, the job of protecting Angela would be a lifelong one.

He got up and took his mug into the kitchen, then went into the bedroom for his things. When he came back, the leather shoulder holster was hidden beneath his jacket and he carried his and Angela's dirty clothes in one hand and the sports bag in the other.

He went over to the bay window and stood beside her until she looked up at him. "I'll give these to someone to clean," he said, showing her the fistful of clothing. "You know where to find the things I got from Sammy. Please get dressed as soon as I leave."

"Why?"

"Because you'll have to open the door to the guard in an hour and I think you'll feel better about it if you're wearing something else." He didn't mention that he'd feel better too. The last thing he wanted to think about was what would happen if the guard came and Angela didn't answer the door because she was in the shower.

Her eyes were fathomless pools of green and gold as she looked up at him. "Just one thing before you go, Hawk."

"What?"

"Did you kill Constantine's son deliberately, or was it an accident?"

"I killed Nico because he deserved to die." Before horror and revulsion overwhelmed her, he added, "I did it not two minutes after I'd watched Nico point a gun at my partner and blow his head off."

She blanched at the brutal description, but recovered quickly, her brow wrinkling in confusion. "What do you mean, your partner?"

"Jack and I were DEA agents assigned to infiltrate Constantine's organization. That night, I was hiding on the beach in order to get evidence on film. Jack was supposed to meet me afterward and get the video to our boss. Something went wrong. Now he's dead and I'm on the run."

"Constantine's organization," she said after a long hesitation. "He's in drugs?"

"Yes. He isn't the biggest trafficker on the coast, but he tops the vicious scale. I'll give you an example, if you like. A while back he caught up with one of his low-level couriers who was trying to go straight." Hawk took a deep breath, then gave it to her without holding anything back. "Constantine used a knife on the kid until there wasn't anywhere he wasn't bleeding, then had him staked in the middle of a public beach. When a young girl stumbled across him the next morning, he was still alive and begging for someone to kill him. He died before the ambulance came."

He saw the horrified expression on Angela's face and knew that if nothing else, she'd do her best to keep her distance from Constantine. "That was three years ago. Last

I heard, the girl is still in therapy. The nightmares of what she saw won't go away."

He turned and had the front door pushed open when she called his name. He paused without looking back. "What now?"

"Why are you on the run if you're a cop?"

"Agent," he corrected her. He threw his bag and the clothes into a pile just outside the door, then turned and faced her because he couldn't stand leaving without knowing how she was reacting to it all. Surprise sizzled his nerves when Angela got up and came to stand just a few feet away, but he put her nearness down to her need to watch his face more than a desire to be close.

He stood with his back propping the door open and looked down into her fresh, shining face. "I'm running because everyone thinks *I* did it, that *I* killed Jack. There was another man there, who laughed when Constantine told his son to kill Jack. His name is Paul Marchand, and he'll make damned sure I don't live to tell anyone what happened that night. If he doesn't get me, Constantine will."

"Who is Paul Marchand?"

"My boss at the DEA." Hawk cut across her shocked gasp and added, "That's why I can't let you go to the cops. Marchand will know everything Constantine knows about you, and he'll use you to get to me. It would be naive to imagine otherwise."

"You're saying all cops are dirty?" Plainly, she didn't buy that at all.

"No, but when Marchand tags you as Constantine's lover and says he intends to use you to get to Constantine, they'll turn you over to him without listening to a word you say. And believe me, Angel, he's senior enough to pull it off."

"He'd say that about me?"

"Or something like it. The point is you won't be safe until Marchand has been exposed, and I can't do that yet."

Before she could ask any more questions, he said, "That should give you something to think about while I'm gone. So will this."

He reached out and closed his hands around her arms, then pulled her forward until the hem of her robe flapped around his calves. She gasped again, in protest this time, as he captured a fistful of hair and used it to lever her face upward. Her hands flew to his chest to push him away, but it was too late. His mouth had already settled on hers.

For a moment Angela was too stunned to react. It was the last thing she'd expected, a kiss from a man who'd slept beside her two nights running without even a hint at the passion he was capable of. And there was passion in his kiss, even though he did nothing more than rest his lips on hers. Passion, and a heat that simmered just beneath the surface of his control. Like a moth drawn to flame, she flirted with the urge to yield to his fire. Her body tingled with a sudden awareness that began in her lips and flared downward, singeing everything in its path until there was no part of her left untouched.

Her response was a fiery compulsion that would have overwhelmed her entirely had she not suddenly looked up and found him staring at her. He held her gaze without blinking, watching almost impassively until he was sure he had her complete attention.

Then his eyes darkened, and he kissed her in earnest.

It was wrong. Angela knew that, yet the flame of her response burned so hot and bright that it took an enormous effort of will to ignore it. Hawk must have felt the beginnings of her resistance, but it made no difference. His freshly shaven face felt smooth and cool against her own, but her focus was on his lips as they slanted hard and firm across her mouth and stole her breath. He kissed her and watched her as he did it, and there was something about it all that told her this was more than it appeared to be, but she couldn't think straight enough to figure out what.

Her only touchstone with reality was knowing Hawk was in control, of himself as well as her, but even that reassurance didn't stop her budding rage. *He was kissing her—kissing her and holding her and making her want things she wasn't supposed to want from a man she was supposed to fear. It wasn't right!*

Angela felt a scream building deep inside, but there was nowhere for it to go, so thoroughly did his mouth possess hers. Her arms were imprisoned between their bodies, but still she squirmed and struggled. Her attempts to free herself only compelled him to tighten his steely embrace as he backed her against the doorjamb and stilled her thrashing legs with a heavy thigh.

When she was breathless and her vision was dotted with multicolored spots, he took his mouth away and rested his forehead against hers. It took a moment before she realized he was talking softly, almost so low she couldn't hear, even though his mouth was only a few inches from her ears.

"You'll ruin the effect if you scream, Angel," he said, then dropped another kiss on her lips, which felt swollen and hot. "I saw in your eyes that you knew I wasn't just kissing you for the hell of it."

"You—" she began, but he kissed her again, harder this time, though with the same underlying gentleness she'd sensed before.

It was over almost before it had begun, and he took advantage of her momentary speechlessness to say, "Whisper, don't yell."

She ground her teeth and glared at him, but she did whisper. "Get your hands off me."

"In time, when I've explained."

"*You're* the one who promised this wouldn't happen," she said furiously, thinking if he weren't so big and she wasn't squashed against the doorframe, she'd give him a good kick. Unfortunately, at the moment she could barely move her little finger.

"My promise," he said, "was with respect to something much more involved than a simple kiss. It stands. And that's all this was. A kiss. When Sammy gets the report of what just happened, he will assume that my interest in your safety is personal. That will be a strong factor in any decisions he needs to make about you." She started to argue, but Hawk added, "Sammy now understands he'll have more than an unhappy customer to deal with if anything happens to you."

Angela scowled at him even though what he'd said made a certain amount of sense. That wasn't the point, though. "You could have just told him."

"Actions speak louder than words."

"I wasn't exactly a willing partner," she pointed out, stealing a glance toward the lawn without seeing the audience she assumed was there.

"No one was close enough to see that." He looked at her for a while longer, then untangled his fist from her hair and eased his body off hers.

The sudden coolness of the morning air surprised her, and she gripped the doorframe at her back with hands that trembled. "You might have just asked instead of grabbing me like that."

"Somehow, Angel, I didn't think you would agree." A smile curved one corner of his mouth, then faded as his gaze centered on her lips. "Your response was exquisite. I didn't expect that."

"I didn't—"

"You did. Before you remembered you shouldn't, there was a moment when you responded to my kiss and took pleasure from it." He stroked a finger across her flushed cheek. "You may not think you're ready to trust me yet, but your instincts are trying to tell you otherwise."

"You're reading too much into it," she said evenly. "You took me by surprise, that's all."

"If that's the case, Angel, why have I awakened two nights running to find your hand covering my heart?"

Not waiting for her answer, he picked up the things he'd dropped by the door, then walked down the path to a blue sedan that someone had left in place of the Jeep. After tossing everything inside, he got behind the wheel and drove the hundred yards to Sammy's, where one of the guards waited at the edge of the drive.

Angela watched as Hawk handed their clothing out through the open window before continuing down the asphalt drive to be swallowed up by the thick screen of trees. Retreating slowly into the cottage, she remembered what he'd said about giving her something to think about.

She also remembered his warning to get dressed. Judging the latter as more critical, she went into the bedroom and got to it. The thinking she put aside for later when she had food on the inside, clothes on the outside, and the strength that would come from both.

EIGHT

Angela was tidying up the mess her mushroom, cheese, and green-pepper omelette had generated when the sound of men shouting reached her ears over the hiss of water in the sink. She shut off the tap and grabbed a dish towel on her way to the kitchen window to see what was going on.

For a moment all she saw was one of the guards running toward the big house while a pair of others sprinted into the forest. When she looked more carefully, she noticed a man standing on the steps leading to the big house's wrap-around veranda. Although the distance was too great for her to be able to tell much, she could see he had black curly hair and was dressed in a light brown jacket and slacks. He appeared to be of medium height, was slender, and had a medium-dark complexion that she guessed could be anything from Mediterranean to American Indian—although the curly hair pretty much left out the Indian faction. She squinted in an attempt to get a better picture as the guard ran up to the man and stopped.

The contrast between the guard's dark clothing and the other man's quite different attire made her realize who she must be looking at. The man had to be Sammy, and she'd just done the one thing Hawk had cautioned her against: She'd seen too much.

Her hand flew to her mouth to stifle the gasp she knew he couldn't hear, and she backed away from the window. She didn't move fast enough, though, because she could still see out when the guard turned and began running toward the cottage. There was a chance, she thought frantically, that everything would be okay if she just pretended she hadn't looked outside. Flinging the dish towel onto the counter, she ran for the bookshelves and grabbed the first book she touched. Then she jumped into a chair with its back to the bay window, flipped the book open to a point just shy of the middle, and tried to still her racing heart. The charade wouldn't work if the guard noticed she was breathing too heavily for someone who was supposed to be reading.

Glancing up, she caught her reflection in the floor-to-ceiling mirror centered between the bookshelves and bedroom door. The flustered, frightened woman she felt like wasn't the person who looked back at her. Dressed in soft, snug jeans and a full-sleeved V-neck white cotton sweater with her hair woven neatly into a French braid and her face clean of makeup, she looked amazingly composed and calm. Tucking one trembling hand under her thigh and holding the book with the other, she waited for the knock on the door and wondered for the first time what had happened to make Sammy come out of hiding.

A panic worse than the first one made her drop the book to the floor as she realized the shouting and Sammy's behavior must have something to do with Hawk. She scrambled to her feet and, heedless of the appalling risks, ran to the door and pulled it open, spooking the guard. He was only slightly taller than she, but his muscular build made him seem gigantic as he stood there blocking the light.

Disregarding yet another of Hawk's instructions, An-

gela stared into the shadowy area beneath his baseball cap
and met his gaze. "What's going on?"

"The boss wants to see you up at the house," he said,
ignoring her question. "Now, please."

"Why? Has something happened to Hawk?" He'd
hardly been gone thirty minutes. How much trouble could
he get into in such a short time? she wondered, then remembered it had taken less than a minute to pick up that
gun in the garage.

"Sammy wants you to come *now*."

"Then tell me what's happened!" It terrified her, the
thought that she might never see Hawk again, but she
chalked her reaction up to the fear Hawk had instilled in
her regarding Sammy. She wanted to be left here alone
even less than she wanted to get away from Hawk. There
was a sinking feeling in the vicinity of her stomach as she
contemplated this new twist in the overall mess she was in.
It wasn't, she realized, anything good.

The guard just shook his head and grabbed her arm,
then noticed she was barefoot. "Get your shoes."

She shook off his hand, and the fact that he let her do it
was a strange reassurance. Although she realized he'd probably done so to let her get her shoes, it gave her a sense of
power to know she'd done it. Stepping behind the door, she
found her pumps and slid her feet into them. When she
came back around the door, she was three inches taller and
determined not to let anyone see how horribly frightened
she was.

This time the guard didn't grab her, just stood aside and
waited for her to come on her own. She went, preceding
him up the path to the big house at a pace that was obviously too slow, because they'd only gone a few steps when
he asked her to speed it up. Angela was so busy imagining
what was wrong that she bit back the retort that he should
try running in high heels, and did her best.

The man she'd seen from the window came outside to

meet them. This was not a good sign, she knew, but when she got up the nerve to meet his gaze, his expression was only mildly annoyed. That puzzled her.

"Please accept my apologies for interrupting your morning, Miss Ferguson," he said with an accent that was so slight, Angela couldn't place it.

An apology wasn't quite what she'd expected, but she took it in stride. "That's okay. I wasn't doing anything important."

A smile flickered across his expression. "A small problem has arisen regarding your visit."

"Problem?" The guard behind her said something she didn't catch, but when she turned to see what he wanted, she saw he wasn't speaking to her at all. As she watched he said something else, and she realized he must be communicating through the thing wrapped around his throat.

She turned back to the man she'd guessed was Sammy. "What kind of problem?"

"To put it simply, the bounty Constantine put on you was too much for one of my employees to resist."

"A bounty on me?" The sinking feeling in her stomach got worse as everything Hawk had told her firmed up into a singularly ugly scenario—a scenario she could no longer afford to doubt. Constantine was after Hawk and would stop at nothing to get him.

"You and Hawk both," Sammy said, "although I've been given to understand he'll settle for either one of you." He paused to clear his throat, and Angela realized he was uncomfortable to the point of being embarrassed. "We were fortunate to discover the man's lapse in judgment, but the damage was already done."

She glanced around the compound and couldn't see anything to worry about. The only guard was the one standing a few feet away, and except for the fact that he appeared to be in constant communication with one or more people, he looked calm and unbothered. Just because he'd taken his gun from the sling across his back and now balanced it on one forearm with the butt firmly in his hand didn't necessarily mean he was getting ready for trouble. If things were really serious, she mused, his finger would be on the trigger and not outside the guard like it was.

She looked back at Sammy and said, "Would you mind getting to the point? I mean, I'd like to know now if you're going to hand me over or just shoot me and be done with it. It's not that I'm lobbying for either, mind you, but I've never liked not knowing what to expect."

"The point, Miss Ferguson, is that this compound will soon be under siege by Constantine's men. I have decided it would be prudent that you not remain here, as I can no longer guarantee your safety."

"So you're handing me over." She clenched her jaw to keep her teeth from chattering. "Hawk will probably demand a refund."

"He will, of course, have one, but when I spoke to Hawk to apprise him of the situation, he seemed to think he would be getting his money's worth."

"You spoke to Hawk?"

"Mmm. He's got a phone in the car." He studied her carefully, then seemed to reach a decision. "I told him I had arranged to have you taken from the compound and to a place where he could resume responsibility for your safety. If he had agreed, you would already be gone from here."

She blinked a couple of times because the information coming in wasn't making any sense. "Are you saying there's another option that's less gruesome than the ones you mentioned?"

"Miss Ferguson—"

"Call me Angela, Sammy. Hawk does and he's only known me two days."

He bowed his head slightly. "Angela, then. It was not my intention to mislead you. Hawk paid me for a service which I am honor-bound to provide. Part of that service is to keep Constantine and certain law-enforcement agencies from getting their hands on you. While my men are perfectly capable of defending the compound, the attention that such a pitched battle would draw is counterproductive. The authorities would feel the necessity to intrude, and I would have failed to fulfill my part of the agreement."

"Don't you think that Hawk's distrust of the cops verges on paranoia?" she said. "I mean, it just doesn't seem possible that this Marchand person could waltz through the system and get to me or Hawk without raising a little suspicious dust in the process."

"Hawk mentioned you were naive," Sammy said. "He did not tell me you were stupid. If Hawk says Marchand will do it, he should know. He worked for the man long enough to understand the kind of power he can and will use as leverage to survive. What Marchand did to Hawk's partner was just a sample."

Angela let the insult go without comment because there was something more important in what Sammy had just said. "Hawk told me about Marchand and Nico and the rest. Did it happen like he said?"

Sammy's gaze narrowed on her face. "You let a man kiss you like Hawk did this morning, and you are not sure whether you believe in him? From appearances, I assumed there was at least a degree of trust between you." He held up a peremptory hand to stave off any response, which was good because she didn't have one. "Back to the subject at hand, Miss—Angela. Hawk is at present returning to the compound for you. He insisted."

"But that doesn't make any sense," she protested. "I thought you said this place was going to be under siege."

"I believe it already is." He looked at the guard, who nodded in confirmation. "However, they will be waiting for Hawk or yourself to make your break out of here. They will not expect someone to try getting in. If Hawk succeeds—"

"What do you mean *if*?"

"Exactly that. If he can break through—which, by the way, he has a good chance of doing with my men covering him from inside the perimeter—then he should be here very soon." He looked at his watch just as the sound of gunfire erupted in the distance.

Angela's heart was already thudding double time as she spun to stare at the trees. There was nothing to see, and when the gunfire ceased a moment later, there was nothing to prove anything had happened. She turned back to the men, but her mouth was too dry for her to ask any of the horrible questions racing through her mind.

Hawk was out there somewhere, coming back for her and risking his life in the process. It wasn't even necessary, not if Sammy was to be believed. Even though she didn't know how, Sammy appeared confident of his ability to get her out of the compound in one piece.

If Hawk wasn't already dead, she was going to make him wish he was. *What could he be thinking about?*

The guard touched the receiver in his ear, listened hard, then flashed his employer a quick smile. "It worked. Hawk smashed through the gate and was halfway up the hill before they realized he wasn't just a drive-by."

Sammy nodded. "Not opening the gate for him was brilliant, Frank. Good thinking. Remind me to add the damage to his bill."

"He made it?" she asked, but she didn't really need an answer. Sammy's casual reference to what Hawk owed him was more convincing that any reassurance.

"He should be here any second now." Sammy turned to the guard and said, "I think we should get them on their way in case anyone heard the ruckus."

The guard said something into his mike, but Angela didn't hear what, because the growl of a racing engine made her swing around. She was just in time to see the blue sedan Hawk had driven away in come flying through the trees and up the drive. He screeched to a stop and was out the door and jogging toward them before Angela had a chance to catch her breath.

He looked straight past her to Sammy. "Sorry about the gate."

"Wait till you get the bill," Angela murmured, annoyed at herself because Hawk hadn't looked at her and she didn't like how that made her feel.

Hawk turned and stared at her. "I thought I told you to stay inside."

"Not my fault." She crossed her arms over her chest and stared right back.

"I am afraid I took the liberty of asking Miss Ferguson to join us outside," Sammy said. "In case you did not survive the trip back, I thought it best to handle things personally."

"I figured he was going to shoot me and didn't want to mess up the cottage," Angela said, and was surprised at the gray pallor in Hawk's face. "Obviously, you were wrong in thinking Sammy doesn't trust me."

Hawk's snort of disbelief was accompanied by a similar sound from the guard. Sammy just smiled at her very gently and said, "It is a moot point now that Hawk has returned. However, if he had not made it, I am afraid you might not have found the situation so amusing."

Angela was about to demand to know what he meant by that—*she* wasn't laughing at anything!—when a loud thrumming filled the air and she looked up to see a small black-painted helicopter swoop across the trees to hover over a wide expanse of lawn. Spellbound, she watched as it settled on the ground, then glanced to the side where Hawk had been standing. He wasn't there anymore, and it was a frightening few seconds before she spotted him near the car with the everpresent sports bag in one hand.

He came back and shouted at her over the din. "That's our ride. Take off your shoes."

On principle, she argued. "Why?"

Hawk looked at Sammy as though to say, "See what I have to put up with," then told her to do it or get left behind. Even though she doubted Hawk would have come back only to desert her over a minor issue, she decided not to take the chance that she might be wrong. When she straightened with shoes in hand, it was in time to see Sammy pull a dark scarf from his pocket and hand it to Hawk.

Sammy turned to her. "If he had explained that he did not want you to fall or break an ankle between here and the helicopter, you would probably have responded better. Unfortunately, there is not always time to explain things and a situation might arise when your life will depend on doing exactly as Hawk says, even though you do not understand why. I would suggest you remember that." He shifted his gaze to Hawk. "There will be a car and maps waiting when you land. If there is anything more you need, ask someone else. I have a feeling things will be a little difficult around here for a few days."

Hawk nodded curtly, then grabbed Angela by the hand and headed across the lawn to the waiting helicopter. The guard went with them and climbed into the front seat beside the pilot, leaving Hawk to half lift, half push Angela into the back, then slide in beside her. He'd hardly closed the door when the ground fell out from under them as the pilot guided the machine into the air. The racket was deafening, but after the first second she hardly noticed, because Hawk was leaning over her with the scarf in his hands and a determined look on his face.

He put it over her eyes and held it there despite her best efforts to pull away. She was too startled by the suddenness of his action even to begin to sort out why he was doing it, so she reacted without thinking, struggled because it was her first impulse.

When she felt the heat of his breath against the side of her face, she realized he was talking to her. It took every ounce of willpower she possessed to concentrate on what he was saying.

". . . your own protection, Angel. If the guard thinks you've seen something, he'll tell the pilot to land back at the compound. *Stop* fighting me," he said, and his urgency finally sank in.

She stopped tearing at the cloth and dropped her hands to her lap, stunned that she'd so misjudged Sammy. He'd seemed such a reasonable, polite man, but if what Hawk was saying was true, he was as much of a threat as Constantine and Marchand.

Hawk kept talking to her as he tied a knot in the scarf over her braid. "That's it, Angel. Just relax and we'll get out of here in one piece. I'm going to put your seat belt on now." She had to move her hands as he brought the thing over her lap and buckled it. She felt him sit back and fiddle with his own belt, then he was talking into her ear again. "I'm going to put headphones over your ears to cut down on the noise, but they aren't plugged in so you won't hear anyone talking."

She reached out and caught a fistful of his jacket to keep him from moving away. She waited until she felt something brush her lips and decided it was probably his ear. "I've never been in a helicopter before, but I have to warn you I get carsick real easy."

"Don't worry about it," he said, and she knew he was smiling because it sounded that way. "We won't be in the air long."

A moment later the 'copter did something that made her stomach turn over, and she was about to repeat her warning to Hawk when he put something into her hands and showed her by touch how to open it. Then he covered her ears with the thickly cushioned earphones, thus reducing the racket by a factor of ten or better.

Clutching the airsick bag in one hand and her stomach with the other, Angela sat still as a statue beside the man who had risked everything to come back for her. Why had he done it?

NINE

It was the little things that Angela was learning to be grateful for in this violent, terrifying world Hawk had introduced her to. Common, everyday triumphs such as not getting stuck in rush-hour traffic, having an umbrella handy when the heavens opened up, or arriving home to find—for a change—that her firewood delivery *hadn't* been dumped in the neighbor's parking slot, were replaced by even more basic victories. Not getting sick in the helicopter was a major coup.

Hawk obviously agreed. He slid behind the wheel of the black pickup, then looked over to where she sat rigidly in the passenger seat and said, "I know it wasn't easy for you in the helicopter, but outside of knocking you out, there was no other way. I'm not sure *I* could have made that trip blindfolded without being sick."

"If you mention the word *sick* again," she said between shallow breaths, "I'll disappoint you all over the floor."

"Sorry." There was a definite upward curve at the corner of his mouth as he started the engine and drove across tarmac to the road beyond.

The helicopter had dropped them at what appeared to

be a deserted airfield that was surrounded by fields of crops she didn't recognize. That didn't worry her because she'd never been any good at identifying various foods or grains by the way they grew. Unfortunately, whatever clues regarding their location she might have gleaned from the neat rows of green that flashed past the truck's window remained untapped.

She decided that if she wanted to know where she was, she would just have to watch for signs. In the meantime they were on a narrow asphalt road that could pass for a farm road in California or a major highway in Mexico. No clues there. The fact that they were in the only vehicle in sight wasn't a help either.

"The maps are probably in the glove compartment," Hawk said. "Can you get them out and see if you can figure out how far we are from a town of some sort?"

So much for having to do things the hard way, she thought. If Hawk would let her see maps, *where* she was was no longer a state secret. "I can't."

"Why not?"

"Besides the fact that I never, ever read anything in a moving car," she said calmly, "it wouldn't do me any good to look at a map when I don't have any idea where we are. I'm lacking a point of reference."

"I figure we're about seventy miles northwest of Sacramento," he said after shooting her a look that was a silent touché.

The realization that they were close to familiar territory was so comforting, she forgot all about the butterflies in her stomach. She was reaching for the glove compartment when Hawk said, "Can you drive one of these?" He indicated the stick shift protruding from the floor.

"Yes."

He pulled the truck to a stop at the side of the road, put it into neutral, and got out with the engine still humming. Then he came around to the passenger door and opened it.

"You drive," he said. "I'll do the maps."

"Really?"

"Really." He reached up, closed his hands around her waist, and lifted her out in one lithe movement. Her feet had no sooner touched the ground than he let her go and swung up into the seat she'd vacated. "I'd help you in the other side, but I don't want you running off without me."

"I could have just climbed over the gears," she said, declining to reply to his assumption that she would have taken the chance of escaping. It wasn't that the impulse wasn't there, only that she wasn't positive she would have acted on it.

Things that had just been frightening before were more so now that she was beginning to comprehend the full extent of the threat. The explosive sound of gunfire back at Sammy's had been very persuasive in that regard, and Angela was too smart to imagine she could survive on her own in a world so alien.

"I thought you'd appreciate the fresh air," Hawk said. He opened the glove box and began sorting through the maps while Angela went around to the driver's side and got in.

The truck was a basic no-frills model that evoked pangs of nostalgia for her Towncar. There was no automatic button to move the seat forward, a crank where there should have been a button to work the windows, and the outside mirror had to be adjusted by hand. Even with all those deterrents, she had the pickup in gear and moving down the road long before Hawk looked up from the map.

"Which way do I go?" she asked brightly. The sense of freedom that came from being behind the wheel was intoxicating to the point of making her want to laugh. She didn't, though, because the somber look Hawk gave her didn't encourage such frivolity.

"Straight is fine," he said, "as it's the only option."

"For now maybe, but when we get to a decision point—"

"When you get to one, I'll tell you." He folded the maps and put them on the floor. "You can drive so long as you behave."

"What's that supposed to mean?" A cloud darkened her personal horizon with that reminder of the situation she hadn't yet escaped.

"It means that if you're still set on getting away from me and try to do something to attract attention, then I'll have to drive while you sit with your hands tied to the seat."

She could tell he meant it because he spoke in the same emotionless tone he'd used every other time he'd given her an order he expected her to obey.

"I'm sick to death of being threatened."

"I thought the word *sick* was banned."

"That was before I got behind the wheel. I'm pretty invincible so long as I'm driving." She forced back a smile that threatened and frowned instead. "Answer me something, Hawk."

"If I can."

"Why did you come back to Sammy's for me? He said he'd made arrangements for us to hook up outside the compound." Even though the truck was only moving a decorous fifty miles per hour, the road wasn't so reliable that she felt she could take her eyes off it for longer than a second. Luckily, that was all it took to reassure herself that Hawk wasn't wearing his "it's not something you need to know" expression. She continued. "There was no need, Hawk, for you to risk your life. Why did you?"

"Sammy had been betrayed once already. I wasn't willing to take the chance it would happen again."

She chewed his answer over for a few minutes. Yes, it was logical for Hawk to imagine lightning might strike twice, but even so, that didn't explain the risk he'd taken.

Just because Constantine was convinced he could get to Hawk by using her, it didn't necessarily follow that Hawk would respond.

"That's not good enough," she said finally. "If you'd been caught or killed, it would have accomplished nothing. This whole vendetta you have with Constantine would have ended right there."

The truck hit a pothole, and Hawk waited until she'd wrestled it back into the middle of the road before replying. "I took you to Sammy's for your own protection. I came back for you for the same reason."

"Because you feel responsible for me."

"Because I *am* responsible for you. I thought you understood that."

"I'm beginning to," she murmured, touching the brakes when she saw a stop sign ahead. "Trouble is, if I buy into that part, then there isn't anything left of what you told me that I can afford to doubt."

"That bothers you?"

She downshifted to a halt and folded her arms across the wheel. "It terrifies me, Hawk. I don't think I was this scared the night you made me swallow cocaine."

"I don't know, Angel. You looked pretty scared to me. What makes this seem worse?"

"Because back then I was naive enough to believe there had to be a way out, that no matter what, this nightmare *would* end and everything would go back to the way it was." She ran her tongue over her dry lips and turned to look at him. The expression on his face was what she was coming to recognize as "classic Hawk"—unreadable, impervious, cold. A shiver curled through her as she responded to a chill in the air between them.

She went on. "I don't think I believe that anymore. In fact, I'm pretty sure we're going to die, both of us. Everything before that is just tap dancing."

His expression didn't change. A car whooshed by on the

road in front of them, but Hawk kept looking at her, through her, until she couldn't stand it any longer and had to turn away. Another car went by in the other direction, and she was wondering what kind of plans the person driving it had for the next day, the next year, when Hawk finally spoke.

"Turn left, Angel," he said. "It's about ten miles to the main highway."

Out of the corner of her eye, she saw him pick up a map and unfold it on his lap. Following his lead, she dropped the subject and steered the truck onto the crossroad. She couldn't think of any reason not to. Hawk might share her assessment, but he wasn't the type to give up without a fight. Talking about it was obviously something he wasn't prepared to do at this point, and she knew she needed to overcome that reticence if she was going to be any good to him. It would probably help, she mused, if he knew exactly where she stood, and she decided to make it clear for him when they stopped for something to eat.

Despite her dire prediction of their imminent demise, she couldn't help but think there must be something they could do to survive. Both of them—because it was important to her that Hawk lived through this as well.

He hadn't needed to come back to Sammy's for her, but he had and she owed him for that.

Then there was the matter of the kiss. Sammy had been right when he'd said a woman didn't let a man kiss her like Hawk had without there being something between them— a spark, a recognition, a feeling. True, he'd taken her by surprise, but her defenses hadn't kicked into play until she'd remembered she wasn't supposed to like the feel of his body against hers or the warm, firm play of his lips on her mouth.

Hawk had felt her response, and no amount of lying to herself would erase it. And while she was still reluctant to admit just how attracted she was to him, she was beginning to recognize that feeling as belonging to the world she'd left and not the one she now inhabited with Hawk. The outrageous and unfamiliar circumstances she found herself in allowed, perhaps even nurtured, a different perspective on what she normally regarded as acceptable or even rational.

She *was* attracted to Hawk; she made herself admit it. But she'd been attracted to other men in her life and never had she experienced the "jumping out of a plane without a 'chute" sensation she felt just by being close to him. It wasn't the most comfortable of feelings, and one she would have marked up to the situation as a whole if it weren't for the fact that it only happened when he was near or when she was thinking about him.

Curling her fingers around the wheel, Angela wondered just how much tap dancing Hawk had in mind.

Hawk stared at the map until he'd memorized everything on it, then put it down and looked out the window at the flat fields zooming past. Angela's reading of their situation essentially matched his own, but he'd found that even though he knew it would give her comfort, he couldn't lie to her. He'd promised her that much.

On the other hand, she was working from the hypothesis that a confrontation with Constantine and/or Marchand was inevitable. Two other options were open to them that she didn't know about, but he kept quiet about both of them. Until he figured out which he was going to use, she was better off not knowing. Besides, he wasn't at all certain either would work.

In the meantime he wanted to put as much distance as possible between them and Sammy's compound. Glancing aside, he saw how Angela's fingers gripped the wheel and wondered what she was thinking about.

"The interstate is just ahead," he said. "Do you want me to drive?"

"No."

"Sure? You look a bit tense."

"I always look tense when I'm tense," she said. "Until I met you, it wasn't something that happened often enough to worry about."

He angled his body so that he could look at her without having to turn his head. "We're heading north for a while. If you're hungry, we can stop for something."

"I had breakfast," she said, then was quiet as she negotiated the on-ramp and accelerated to blend with the traffic heading north. The speedometer was a steady sixty-five and she'd rolled her window most of the way back up when she glanced at him again. "Are you hungry, or was that just small talk?"

"I've got lots of things we can talk about without resorting to food or the weather, but no, I'm not hungry. I got something to eat before Sammy called." He adjusted the vents on the dash to let more fresh air into the cab. "You never did tell me where you were going for the two weeks your secretary didn't expect you in the office."

"I didn't tell you because it seemed contrary to my best interests to do so." She shrugged, and he thought he noticed a slight relaxing in the way she held the steering wheel. That surprised him. It was precisely the opposite reaction he expected to his question. "I had reservations for a vacation in St. Lucia," she continued. "I'd just finished a big conference and was hauling the last load of materials from the hotel to my office when I ran into you. My plan had been to go home and pack, catch a few hours' sleep, and get up early enough to miss rush-hour traffic to the airport."

"A vacation, huh?"

"Mmm. Two whole weeks of solitude and sun and nary a telephone in sight—not in *my* sight anyway. They probably have them, but are savvy enough to keep them hidden. The result is an environment where decision making is confined to when, where, and how much to eat and what to wear while doing it. I've been going there every year since I discovered it."

Hawk was fascinated by the look of near bliss on her face. "Tell me more."

She smiled without taking her gaze from the road ahead. "The hotel is one of those ridiculously posh places where the rich go to be pampered and the famous go to get away from being famous. I visited it a few years ago with the idea of using it for a small conference, but couldn't bear to spoil it with business. It's the only place I've ever gone where I've been able to get away from it all."

"You have to go all the way to St. Lucia for that?"

She shot him a chiding look. "Everyone has their refuge. I spend my life trotting three steps ahead of everyone else so that when crises arise, I'm ready for them. The only fancy footwork I have to do in St. Lucia involves hot sand on long white beaches."

"Now you're making me feel guilty," he grumbled, not liking the feeling.

"You should. I haven't had a real vacation in a year." She glowered at him, but there was a smile in her eyes as she did it. "No one will know I'm missing except for the hotel, and they won't do anything about it unless someone asks—which, of course, no one will because I've never told a soul where I go."

He studied her carefully. "Why are you telling me all this now?"

"Because it's something you need to know. Otherwise, you wouldn't have asked."

"That explains why *I* want to know. Your reasons for telling me aren't as clear."

She shrugged. "I've had to choose between believing everything you've told me about drug lords and dead partners and corrupt bosses, or deciding it's all a lie—in which case I'm forced to find another explanation for your behavior. I can't. As preposterous as your story sounds, it hangs together." She shrugged again. "Of course, I'm relying pretty heavily on instinct here. Without my instincts telling me to trust you, nothing you said would matter because I'd be too busy plotting how to get away to hear a single word."

A minute or so passed as Hawk let the refreshing logic of her words sink in. He wasn't sure what he'd expected when he'd told her about Constantine and Marchand, but her forthright acceptance of the status quo left him a little stunned. It puzzled him, too, because she was so calm about it all, but he guessed he should have anticipated that. With the minor—but quite understandable—exception of the night he'd forced her to swallow what she believed was cocaine, she'd kept the hysterics at bay and had held on to her dignity with a quiet courage he admired.

The better he got to know her, the more he liked what he saw. She was brave and gorgeous, and her sexy voice had a way of wrapping itself around his senses until his pleasure centers pulsed hot and hard. If only— Hawk cut the thought off before it got started. There wasn't any use in wishing for what he couldn't have.

She glanced at him. "I can't decide if you're quiet because you think I said all that as a ruse to get you to trust me so I can make a break for it, or if you're calculating how long we can keep this truck before Sammy decides your money ran out and tells someone about it." A strand of burnished red escaped her braid, and she lifted a hand to tuck it behind her ear.

The smile that curved his mouth felt good. "Sammy wouldn't do that. It isn't good business."

"So we keep the truck?"

"No. We'll lose it in Redding. I'll feel better once we've

cut all ties with Sammy. No telling how many of his men rose to Constantine's bait."

"That's about a hundred miles away. Are you sure we're okay until then?"

"As sure as I can be. Sammy's reputation suffered a blow today. He won't stay in business long if it gets out he messed up twice in one day."

She looked at him again as though weighing his conviction, then Hawk felt a subtle increase in the truck's speed. When he looked at the speedometer, the needle was on the high side of seventy.

"Getting pulled over for speeding isn't what I had in mind when I said not to draw attention to us," he said.

"In case you hadn't noticed, we were the only vehicle on the road paying any attention at all to the speed limit," she answered, and the reprimand in her voice was clear. "Now we look just like everyone else."

"The 'keeping up with all the other speeders' defense rarely works. Trust me, Angel. I know a lot of cops."

"Don't worry about it, Hawk," she said with a quick smile. "I'll be too busy explaining why I'm driving a truck I don't own without a license—not to mention in the presence of a man carrying a concealed weapon. The subject of speeding probably won't even come up."

They dumped the truck at the Redding airport, caught a taxi into town, then went into a family restaurant where Hawk picked up a copy of the nickel ads before leading Angela toward a booth tucked into a corner next to the kitchen door. They'd clearly missed whatever lunchtime rush there was, and only one other table was occupied.

A waitress watched indifferently from a counter stool until they were settled and had checked the menu, then she stubbed out her cigarette and walked across the room. Her apron was stained with something that Angela guessed was anything from grease to cherry pie, her eyelids drooped with tiredness, and the tag pinned beneath her slumped shoulders said her name was Mabel.

"Long shift, Mabel?" Angela asked after she'd given her order for a hamburger and fries.

"Just came on." Mabel licked her pencil and looked down at Hawk, who was still studying the menu. "If you're real hungry, Cook does a nice chicken-fried steak. My Walter says it's the best thing on the menu."

Hawk glanced up and offered a nod of thanks for the hint. "That would be good. We'll have coffee too."

"It comes with the steak," Mabel said, "but not with the burger."

"Bring her some anyway," Hawk said, hiding a smile.

"You get dessert with the steak."

"I saw some lemon pie in the case when we came in. Can you save me some of that, please?"

"Me too?" Angela asked, her mouth watering in anticipation.

"It's extra for you."

"That's okay," Hawk said. He waited until Mabel had shuffled away into the kitchen, then flattened the nickel ads on the table and took out a pen.

Angela watched as he circled a couple of ads before asking what he was looking for.

"A car," he said, without looking up. "Or a truck. It doesn't matter."

"I saw a couple of used-car dealerships on the way here. Wouldn't that be easier?"

He glanced up at her, the look in his eyes mildly chiding. "It wouldn't take Constantine any time at all to trace us through one of those places. Even if we pay cash, the salesman will still be able to describe us." He tapped an index finger on the paper. "He'll never be able to find us this way."

"We still have to register the car," she pointed out.

"We won't have it long enough to worry about that. As far as the seller is concerned, that's our problem." He looked back down at the paper and circled another ad as Mabel arrived with two mugs and a carafe of coffee. She slopped some into each mug, then went back to the stool at the end and lit up another cigarette.

Hawk folded the paper open to the page where he'd circled two different ads and stood up. "There's a phone out by the front door. Stay here and keep an eye on my stuff," he said, nodding toward the sports bag.

"Aren't you afraid I'll duck out through the kitchen?" she asked, her expression determinedly bland as she looked up at him.

His gaze was dark and thoughtful. "You told me in the truck you trusted me. I'm returning the compliment."

"I won't run, you know," she said softly, and was surprised when he reached out to stroke a finger down her cheek. Her skin warmed where he'd touched it, and she couldn't stop herself from covering the ribbon of sensation with her hand.

"I know you won't, Angel," he said in a voice that was deep and strangely gentle. "Even if you wanted to, I think you know I'd just bring you back."

"Because you feel responsible for me?"

He smiled enigmatically, but only said, "There's that too," then turned and walked away.

Angela watched him go, then looked away because his loose-hipped walk did something to her pulse rate, and *that* was already thrumming on high in response to the things he'd left unsaid. Staring at the collection of fifties-era condiment containers at the end of the table, she thought about the way Hawk's potent masculinity affected her . . . and wondered what she was going to do about it.

When Mabel arrived with their food, Angela was disgusted with herself because not only hadn't she come to any conclusions, she'd missed a golden opportunity to go through Hawk's bag.

Just because they were on the same side didn't mean she couldn't be curious.

TEN

It was late afternoon before they finally left Redding, but Hawk seemed in no crushing hurry and Angela was too delighted to be out among people who'd never heard of Constantine or Marchand to wonder why.

The truck he'd found was a dark green Chevy Blazer with fifty-five thousand miles on the odometer and pockmarks scattered across the hood and roof from a freak hailstorm. Even though the owner swore the engine was in top shape, Hawk spent half an hour looking under the hood and followed that with a short test-drive, leaving Angela on the seller's front porch and his sports bag beside her. Just as Angela was set to zip open the bag, the seller's wife came out onto the porch with coffee.

When they returned, the very happy owner went inside for the necessary paperwork and Hawk sat down on the other side of the sports bag and unzipped a side pocket. Reaching inside, he pulled out a fistful of cash and proceeded to peel a dozen or so notes—all fifties—from it. Those he stuffed back into the bag, then began counting what was left as the gasp Angela had been holding finally escaped.

"Hush, Angel," he murmured, without looking up from what he was doing.

"Don't hush me, Hawk," she returned fiercely, albeit in a whisper. "What are you doing with all that cash?"

"How'd you expect me to pay for the truck? With a credit card?"

Her gaze narrowed on the money as she quickly calculated to the nearest thousand how much he was holding. "You're spending a lot on the truck. Don't you think we should get something cheaper and save the cash for other things?"

"This is only a small part of what I've got available. Don't worry, Angel. There's enough left over for anything we need." He finished counting and zipped the bag closed as the owner returned through the screen door.

Contrary to Angela's fears, the owner not only didn't question why Hawk was paying in cash, he seemed to expect it. He gave Hawk the necessary documents, wished him luck with the Chevy, then watched them drive away with an expression on his face that rivaled a canary-fed cat for smugness.

"Didn't your mother teach you to bargain before spending your hard-earned money?" she asked Hawk.

"The two or three hundred dollars I might have got wasn't worth the time," he said with a shrug. "Besides, it's not my money. I stole it from Constantine."

"You *what*?"

"The night I killed Nico. Things were a little confusing —which was good because I wasn't supposed to be there in the first place, and for a few critical minutes nobody realized I was the one who'd fired the shot. I managed to climb into one of their vehicles and make a run for it before Marchand spotted me and they caught on. Luckily, they were slow and I got away. The money was in the truck I appropriated."

"How much money, Hawk?"

He grinned, something she'd never seen him do before. "A lot. What do you say we go spend some more of it?"

She pressed her fingers to her temples and moaned. "Is there anything you *didn't* do to make sure you went to the top of Constantine's hit list and stayed there?"

"Yeah. I didn't put him out of business, but I'm working on that."

They stopped at a shopping mall and spent some of Constantine's money on a change of clothes for each of them, flat comfortable shoes for Angela, and a sackful of high-calorie, low-nutrition snacks that they mutually agreed would keep them going until dinner. Hawk threw in a couple of healthy-looking energy bars, too, but Angela got the feeling he did this because he knew he should and not because he actually intended to eat them. So long as he didn't make her eat them either, it was okay with her.

They headed west on Highway 299 toward the coast, Angela driving again. She asked Hawk what he had in mind in the way of a plan, or were they, as she put it rather succinctly, "going to wander aimlessly until Constantine died a natural death and Marchand retired?"

"If I thought we could keep our heads down and hide for the rest of our lives," he said, "I'd say let's do it. Unfortunately, Constantine won't stop looking until he's found us."

"Not to mention the fact that someone will, eventually, miss me." She geared down to follow a heavy semi up a long, steady incline. "So what's the plan?"

"There's a man in Colorado named Blackthorne who I can trust to look after you. The only problem is getting you to him."

"You're sending me away?" She hadn't considered that, and the tense, hunted feeling that had receded since morning suddenly returned.

"Of course I'm sending you away. I would have done it sooner, but Sammy's place was closer and I wanted to get something from my apartment in San Rafael to send with you." He squeezed the bridge of his nose between his thumb and forefinger. "That's where I was headed this morning when all hell broke loose."

"So that's where we're going now? San Rafael?" So far, Angela didn't think much of the plan. San Rafael was exactly where they *shouldn't* be headed—not to mention the fact that if that was his plan, they'd traveled a hundred and fifty miles in the wrong direction that afternoon.

"No," he said reasonably. "We're going to Portland, Oregon, where you should be able to get on a plane east without any trouble."

She shot him an exasperated look. "You need a lesson in map reading, Hawk. If we'd stayed on the interstate, we would have been in Portland in six or eight hours. This way will take twice as long."

"The scenic route will be safer," he said. "Besides, I called Blackthorne's office at lunch, and he's out of town until tomorrow night. If we don't dawdle too much, this should time out perfectly."

"Who is this guy Blackthorne?"

"Someone I worked with a few years back. He's not a cop, but that's all for the better in this case. He'll know what to do with you."

"If he's so good, why aren't you coming too?"

"I've got other things to do."

Angela opened her mouth to ask another question—she had a couple dozen, minimum—but he interrupted before she could get started.

"I'm going to grab a nap, Angel. Try to keep your curiosity corralled for another few hours." He didn't wait to see if she agreed, just levered the seat into a semireclining position and lay back.

By the time Angela could take her eyes off the traffic to

look at him, his eyes were closed. She couldn't resist one
last question, though, maybe two. "What about San Rafael?
Are you going back there?"

"Right after I put you on that plane," he said, without
opening his eyes.

"It sounds to me like a particularly stupid thing to do,"
she muttered. "You're just asking for trouble."

"Stupid was picking up that gun the other night," Hawk
said matter-of-factly. "*I'm* taking a calculated risk."

"It's that important?"

"It is."

"Then why did you leave it—whatever *it* is—behind in
the first place?" She knew she sounded more than a little
peeved. "You carry everything else in that bag of yours. I
can't see where one more thing would matter."

He opened his eyes and rolled his head on the seat to
look at her. "You're not going to let me get any sleep, are
you?"

"I just can't see why you take risks when you don't have
to—and that includes coming back for me this morning."
She hung on tighter to the wheel and shifted in the seat
until she found a more comfortable position. "You should
have checked for lumbar support before you bought this.
I've been driving twenty minutes and already my back
aches."

"Pull over, Angel."

She looked at him in surprise. "I wasn't really com-
plaining. . . . Well, maybe I was, but I didn't mean to. I
can still drive, Hawk, so long as I remember to keep my
back straight. You go ahead and sleep. I'll be fine."

"Pull over anyway," he said quietly. "Please."

She did a mental shrug and did as he asked, or perhaps
commanded. With Hawk, the distinction was moot. Courtesy tags like *please* and *thank you* were a device he used to
soften his orders, but they were still orders. Traffic was
sparse in the falling twilight, and she was able to find a spot

just off the road in the deep shadows of towering ever-
greens. Braking to a stop and shutting off the engine, she
looked aside to find Hawk watching her from the reclining
seat.

"What?" she asked after a long, silent minute.

"You still don't get it, do you?"

"Get what?"

"This." He reached out one hand and cupped the side
of her face before she realized what he was about. When he
began stroking her cheek with his thumb, any protests—
whether valid or not—died unsaid. The confusion that had
plagued her regarding her own responses to Hawk lost im-
portance beneath the gentleness of his caress, and she
leaned into his hand because it seemed the most natural
thing to do.

"I've spent eight months planning how I was going to
hit back at Constantine," he said evenly, "but suddenly you
waltz into the picture with your smart mouth and gold-
dusted eyes, and I discover I'm not quite so willing to die
for the pleasure of putting Constantine in his grave."

"You're not going after him anymore?" she asked, and
her heart missed a beat as things she had taken for granted
began to change.

"I don't know what I'm going to do. Right now,
though, I just want to kiss you." His gaze focused on her
mouth, where his thumb was testing the suppleness of her
bottom lip. He exerted an almost imperceptible pressure
there, and was rewarded when her lips parted slightly.

"That's all?" she asked on a whisper of sound. "You
want to kiss me?"

"For starters, Angel. Like I did before, but better. This
morning, I didn't give you a choice. I snuck up on your
blind side and kissed you before you knew what I was
about." Hawk smiled crookedly, then sat up and flipped the
lever to right the seat without taking his hand from her
face. "I want to do it again, Angel. There's something

about the way you responded to me that's been tormenting me all day."

"Tormenting?"

"Mmm. Those few seconds before you remembered you shouldn't be kissing me at all weren't enough to tell."

"Tell what?"

"Whether you're going to melt in my arms . . . or burn. Either one is fine, Angel, but not knowing which it's going to be is driving me right out of my mind."

In the fading light, gold pricks of light in her eyes shone out at him from twin emerald skies. The pink tip of her tongue slid between her lips, slicing a wet path across the pad of his thumb. He sucked in a deep, sharp breath and let it out with a rough groan. Then, because he couldn't not do it, he closed his hands around her waist and lifted her clean across the center console. He settled her in his lap with her shoulders in the crook of his arm and her legs draped across the console.

She didn't feign outrage or struggle or even look too surprised. In fact, there was a little smile on her mouth that told him she'd expected as much. Hawk even suspected that she wondered what had taken him so long. Blood pooled in his groin as her slight weight rested in his lap, and he knew just by looking into her eyes that she was fully aware of his hard arousal pressing against her hip.

She did surprise him, though, when she lifted a hand to his face and stroked the area on either side of the "shaving accident" scratch. "I shouldn't have hurt you."

"You didn't. It was my own fault for not giving you more credit."

"But it was just yesterday," she murmured. "It seems so long ago."

"What are you thinking?" he asked when her expression turned thoughtful.

"You're not the only one whose plan has changed over the last two days," she said after a short hesitation. "Before

I met you, the most urgent goal in my life was to get away for some quality solitude. Now the idea of being alone, without you, makes me feel empty inside. When I first realized how you make me feel, I was uneasy and a little ashamed, because it didn't seem right that I should be attracted to you. The situation was too bizarre, too intense."

"And now?"

"Now I realize I was trying to judge my reactions by normal standards, and they simply don't apply. There hasn't been anything normal or ordinary about this situation from the beginning." A look that was part shy, part daring flickered across her face as she lifted her hands and wrapped them around his neck. "The intensity probably accelerated the course of events, but it didn't create them. I might not have a lot of experience in recognizing my body's responses, but I can't believe I'd feel what I feel now if I really wasn't attracted to you, regardless of the circumstances."

She wrinkled her nose and looked earnestly at him. "Does that make sense?"

"Some." He cocked his head. "Are you trying to justify why you feel good sitting on my lap?"

"No," she said, and her smile looked a little embarrassed. "I'm trying to tell you that if you came back to Sammy's because the idea of sex with me was too good to miss, then you're in for a major disappointment. My experience in that field is limited to a couple of unmemorable affairs when I was just starting out on my own, followed by one live-in boyfriend named Frank who confined his sexual repertoire to a single uninteresting position and wasn't open to suggestions."

Hawk wasn't sure how they'd come to be talking about her sexual experience, but he didn't really mind. Discovering she'd had just one lover of any consequence, and an inept one to boot, kept him from being too annoyed by the subject of other men.

Showing her that there was more to lovemaking, however, would have to wait at least until he'd finished the job in San Rafael. Until then, talking was all they could do about it—unless he counted kissing, but she was stalling for some reason and the last thing he wanted to do was rush her.

When they kissed, all he wanted to see in her eyes was desire, not reluctance.

"I'm surprised you stayed with him," he said.

"He stayed with me. By the time I realized that sex wasn't Frank's only dull facet, it took more time than I could spare to convince him to move out. I probably wouldn't even have noticed when he finally did leave, except that he took the cat he'd bought me for my birthday."

She let out a long sigh that warmed his chest through his shirt. "I wouldn't have told you all this, but you've hinted you came back for me for reasons other than a sense of responsibility, and it wouldn't be honest to lead you on. I'm not good at what I think you want from me."

Hawk kept a straight face, although how he did it was a mystery. It was so endearing, the way she matter-of-factly laid open her imagined shortcomings. The only appropriate response, he decided, was to reply with corresponding frankness.

"Sex with you will be good," he said simply, "although in your case, I'd rather refer to it as making love."

"I just told you I wasn't—"

He touched a finger to her lips, and her words were lost. "You'll have to trust me on this one, Angel. If you were more experienced, you'd know that by the way we respond to each other."

"We'll be good, you think?"

"Very good."

Her partially lowered lashes hid her expression, but her body signaled in other ways that she took pleasure from his assurance. First, there was the barely perceptible quickening in the pulse at her throat, and her breaths came out shallow and fast. Then her nipples hardened to thrust against her knitted sweater, and a moan escaped her lips as he slid his hand from her waist to the firm curve of her hip.

Her fingers tightened at his nape, and she lifted her face until their mouths almost touched. "I seem to remember you telling me you weren't going to do anything about, um, how you felt," she murmured.

"That was before I realized I didn't have a choice," he said thickly. "When I kissed you this morning, when your lips trembled under mine, I knew everything had changed."

"You changed?"

"No, Angel," he said as he lowered his head another millimeter. "You did. You discovered you wanted me too."

"Your confidence overwhelms me."

He froze and narrowed his gaze on hers, and it wasn't until he saw that her eyes were dancing and her mouth curved with laughter that he realized she was teasing. He wasn't used to that. "What are you doing on my lap if that isn't the case?"

"You put me here."

"So I did." He felt the beginnings of his own smile. "I did not, however, put your hands around my neck. You did that on your own."

She nodded in agreement. "That was back when I thought you were going to kiss me. If I'd known you were going to talk me to death, I wouldn't have bothered."

It wasn't a fair assessment of the situation, Angela realized, because she'd been the one doing the talking. But it had seemed so important to say those things, and despite the rather rambling way they'd come out, she felt better because her conclusions were sound.

She was attracted to Hawk in a way that transcended logic. As she looked into his eyes and saw the desire that was as unmistakable as it was fierce, she realized that all the talking in the world couldn't explain the sense of rightness she felt in his arms.

It was just there, right and strong.

She didn't have a chance to take another breath before his mouth was on hers and he was doing exactly what they both wanted, kissing her. And she was kissing him, opening her mouth for the thrust of his tongue because she knew instinctively that he wanted her like that, fast and hot and without barriers.

It was the kind of kiss she'd learned the mechanics of back in high school and never enjoyed much. With Hawk, everything changed, up to and including her perception of pleasure. It began in her lips as they moved against his, a tingling awareness of pressure and friction that was exciting in itself but only part of the whole. His tongue evoked even stronger sensations, stroking across hers, curling around and doing it again, teasing her into following his lead until she took him up on it and ran the tip of her tongue across his smooth, even teeth, and then deeper.

Someone groaned. She thought it was Hawk, but it might have been her, because the heat of their kiss was beginning to affect her all over, in her breasts—especially the crests where they brushed against his chest—and in the place between her legs that was just inches from where his hand gripped her hip.

Hawk thrust his tongue into her mouth, slowly withdrew, then did it again. And again, until a rhythm was established. Angela responded by moving her hips, riding under the gentle guidance of his hand until she brushed against his erection in the same rhythm. He slipped his hand under her sweater, debated a moment when he encountered her silk camisole, then went under that, too, pushing it up and away until his hand was curved around her breast and her hard velvety nipple was between his fingers.

He hadn't meant to take it this far, the kiss he'd been

waiting for so long, all day . . . an aeon, what was the difference? But her response was so intense, so alive, he couldn't resist touching, enjoying her heat. Her breast was full and heavy in his hand, and he thought about what she must be feeling between her legs, the moisture that had to be gathering there. He wondered what she'd do if he unzipped her jeans and slid his fingers inside her panties.

She moaned, or maybe he did. It didn't matter, because the pleasure was exquisite and he wanted more of it. He moved his hand across her hip to her belly, then down, pushing into the vee between her legs, parting them so he could cup her there and feel her heat. The sound came again, and Hawk realized she was trying to say something and couldn't do that very well with his tongue in her mouth.

He lifted his head an inch, then squeezed her nipple, wanting to hear how much she liked it. A cry of pleasure was his reward, and he hugged her tighter against his groin, stilling the rhythm that was driving him wild, but keeping his hand between her legs. He stroked her there, rubbing his fingers hard against the soft jeans, and stole a kiss when another cry escaped her lips. She unlocked her hands from his neck and grabbed his wrist through her sweater as though to pull him away. He almost took his hand from her breast right then until he realized she was holding him closer, harder against her heated flesh.

"We can't," she finally said, and he agreed, but couldn't resist teasing her nipple some more.

"Don't worry, Angel. We're not going any further with this, not now," he said roughly, his voice stuck somewhere beneath the lump in his throat. "Just let me hold you a little longer, touch you."

He covered her mouth again, and this time matched the rhythm of his tongue to that of his hand between her legs. She writhed against him with such sweet, uninhibited passion that it was increasingly difficult not to say the hell with his scruples and take her right there in the truck.

He didn't, though. He couldn't. Instead, he continued giving her pleasure in the only way he dared. Besides being awkward, anything more was out of the question, his own fulfillment included. It wasn't possible to make love to her the way he wanted to, with her naked in his arms as he thrust himself inside her again and again. . . . Impossible, because after he put her on that plane for Denver, there was a good chance he'd never see her again.

Precautions weren't one hundred percent guaranteed, and he was damned if he'd let her fly out of his life if there was even one chance that she carried his child. His future.

He couldn't do that to either of them, not when it was almost certain he didn't have a future.

Her soft moan nearly broke his resolve, and it took a mighty effort to shift her a safe distance down his thighs so he could continue his caresses without the enticing weight of her body against his erection. He devoured her mouth in another long, wet kiss, then spread her legs a bit more to allow his hand freer access.

"Don't, Angel," he said when she tried to recover the gap between their bodies. "Just lie back and let me—"

"Let you what, Hawk?" she demanded, pushing his hands away and wriggling as close to upright as she could manage. "Let you show me how far gone I am that I don't even care how selfish I'm being?"

"Don't be ridiculous. This seat's too small for anything else."

"In which case, we should get back on the road." She smoothed her sweater down, leaving her nipples clearly outlined in the process.

Hawk couldn't help reaching out to pluck at one of the beaded nubs, and was rewarded by the sharp hiss of air between her teeth. He rolled the nipple between his fingers and luxuriated in the look of pure passion on her face.

"That's right, Angel. It feels good, doesn't it? Just lie back against my arm and—"

"And nothing!" She swatted his hand away and glared at him, her eyes shooting golden sparks as the color rose high in her cheeks. "Look here, Hawksworth, I've been there, done it, got the T-shirt, and I'm telling you now, I've had *enough*!"

"What are you babbling about?" he asked. "Enough of what?"

"The way you always have to be in control," she said heatedly. "It's always 'do this,' 'don't do that,' 'hush,' 'shut up,' or something just as obnoxious. I can't decide whether I feel more like a toddler or a dog." With that, she used his stomach and shoulders for leverage and began to clamber back over to the driver's seat.

Hawk tried to help, but she elbowed his hands aside and he ducked back out of her way because a black eye or worse wasn't what he had in mind when he'd started kissing her. He waited until she was settled behind the wheel and deigned to look at him before speaking.

"I'm sorry, Angel," he said quietly. "I wasn't trying to control you. I wanted to give you pleasure."

"I know that, Hawk. It's just that I didn't want . . ." Her gaze softened. She nibbled on her bottom lip for a moment, then finally said, "I didn't want it to be like that."

"With me in control?"

"You have to admit you've got a habit of taking charge of every little thing." She looked down to where her hands were clasped tightly in her lap.

Hawk reached out to lift her chin with the tip of his index finger. "You're overreacting, Angela. At no point since I pulled you onto my lap were you without control. You could have stopped me at any time."

"I tried—"

"Not really." He shook his head slowly and dropped his hand from her face. "Until you realized I was going to make love to you with my hands and not the rest of me, you weren't objecting to anything. If you feel otherwise, then I'm obviously doing something very wrong."

"You're not."

"Then what's all this about, hmm?"

"It's about two days of having my world turned upside down." She thrust her fingers into her hair, and some of it came free from the braid and fell in long strands across her eyes. She looked at him through the dark red ribbons of hair. "It's also a bit of reaction to what just happened. I can't remember ever feeling anything even close to that before. It scared me."

"I would never hurt you."

"I know that," she said, and heaved a huge sigh. "Maybe we should just get back on the road, what do you think?"

"I think it's time for dinner. There should be something close by."

"Okay." Angela turned straight in the seat, but before she could start the engine, Hawk stopped her with a gentle touch on her hand. She glanced at him. "What?"

"I was right on both counts."

"Right about what?" she asked, and even in the fading light could see the heat of desire rekindle in his eyes.

"You did both, Angel," he said huskily. "You melted, then you burned so hot I nearly lost my head. And do you know something else?"

"What?"

"It scared me too."

ELEVEN

It was pitch-dark when they hit the coast and turned north. Hawk had been at the wheel for an hour, and Angela had surprised them both by confining the conversation to occasional comments on the scenery they couldn't appreciate but recalled from previous trips. Discussion of Constantine, et al, was more than she could handle, because whatever Hawk was planning, it was bound to be something that would take him out of her life forever.

That frightened her, sifting past the general fear and nervousness she'd experienced over the past few days and leaving her shell-shocked as she realized how important Hawk had become to her. Her worry about the subject grew until she blocked it from her thoughts and concentrated on the sixties-era music she had found on the radio.

She was beginning to think Hawk planned to drive all night when he pulled into the parking lot of an aging motel whose neon vacancy sign could only be understood if you knew what it was supposed to say and filled in the blanks. Angela waited in the truck while Hawk went inside, then she helped him carry their meager possessions into a ground-floor room at the end of the L-shaped building.

There were two double beds in the room that was otherwise furnished with the standard childproof, theftproof, nondistinctive bits and pieces that were reassuring to some travelers but an anathema to Angela. She liked seeing a flavor of the outside environment in the places she stayed. She kept her mouth shut, though, because she was tired, and not to put too much emphasis on a difficult topic, it seemed petty to spend any time thinking about the room's decorative motifs when this might be the last night she slept with Hawk.

Slept with him. The euphemistic qualities of that phrase had never seemed quite so absurd. She'd slept with Hawk, but she'd never done it in the sense of, well, *doing* it. She jerked her gaze from the wall where she'd been comparing the merits of blank space with the hideous peony oil painting hanging between the beds, and found Hawk watching her from the bathroom door.

"What's wrong?" he asked, wiping a wet rag over his eyes.

"My vocabulary is shrinking to that of a teenager, and I'm thinking seriously about cutting that painting from its frame and burning it, but otherwise there's nothing to be concerned about." She tossed the shopping bag she'd been carrying on the floor and flopped down on a hard-cushioned chair. "How about you?"

He studied her for a long moment, then shook his head. "You sound like you need some sleep."

"I'm too tired to sleep," she grumbled, but didn't resist when he came across the room and pulled her from the chair.

They stood toe to toe, but there was something in the way Hawk kept his body from brushing hers that told her he had no intention of sleeping with her or doing *it* or anything else. She blinked back her disappointment, then looked up at him. "What happened, Hawk? Change your mind?"

"No, Angel. Never that." He cupped her face in his hand and kissed her briefly, then went to sit in the chair by the window that was covered in dull, rust-colored drapes. He continued without looking at her. "We can't make love because I don't have anything with me to protect you."

Make love. Oh yeah, that was how some adults said it. Angela loved hearing the words from Hawk. They made her smile.

"Check your bag, Hawk. You're bound to find what you need in there."

He glanced at her, and there was an answering smile in his eyes. "I don't have to check. I know what I don't have."

"That isn't the real reason, is it?" she asked after a moment.

"No, it isn't."

"Tell me." She sat on the edge of the bed nearest him and waited. When he finally replied, he gave her the kind of explanation she hated, because she agreed with him and didn't want to.

"You want to make love tonight because you think you'll never see me again after tomorrow," he said evenly. "I'm not going to let it happen for that same reason."

"We don't have to think this out, you know," she said, and knew the frustration in her body was clear in her voice. "We can approach this from the mindless, live-for-today attitude that was so popular in the eighties."

"No, we can't."

"You're doing that control thing again," she argued.

"I'm making sense and you know it." He started rubbing his right hand where a scar cut across it as though it was bothering him.

"Your hand hurt?" she asked, and only just stopped short of reaching out to touch where he rubbed.

"Some. Go get ready for bed, Angel," he said wearily. "It's getting late."

It was on the tip of her tongue to point out that he was

telling her what to do again, but she couldn't bring herself to say it, not when he looked so tired and she didn't mean it anyway. She went into the bathroom and got out of her clothes, pulling on the knee-length T-shirt she'd bought that afternoon and taking time to wash her undies. She left them dripping on the towel rack when she went back out, and if she gave any thought to that or the way she was dressed versus how things had been at Sammy's, it was a very small thought.

There was a light on over by the window where Hawk slouched in the chair, his feet propped up on the chair opposite. He had something in his hand that looked like a roll of material, and when she got closer she realized he held a threaded needle in his other hand.

"What are you doing?"

"Sewing," he said, without looking up.

Angela rubbed her eyes and got closer for a better look. "That's not sewing," she said in amazement. "It's fancywork."

"Fancywork?" he repeated. "I haven't heard it called that since my grandmother died. Nowadays we call this particular kind of sewing needlepoint." He put another stitch into the canvas, and she watched fascinated as he drew the yarn back out.

"Why are you doing it?" She leaned closer still.

"Because it's good therapy." He adjusted his grip on the rolled canvas and set in another stitch. "You're in my light."

She walked around to the other side and squatted down beside his chair. "Therapy for what? Your hand?"

"That too," he said agreeably, then surprised her by telling her how he'd gotten the wound. "My grandmother was still living then, and she brought a canvas and yarn with her when she came to visit me after the surgeon did his best to repair the damage. She suggested I give it a try as therapy."

"You learned to sew because your grandmother suggested it?" Angela couldn't picture Hawk going along with the notion so meekly.

"She bullied me into it," he admitted with a grin. "By the time I realized it was doing me some good, I was hooked. I do it now even if my hand isn't bothering me."

It was a side to Hawk she never would have believed if she hadn't seen it for herself. "Why are you doing it now?"

He turned his head to meet her gaze. "It's something to do with my hands, Angel. If I said please, would you go to bed and quit tempting my better judgment? I really don't have much willpower left, and that nightshirt is almost sexier than if you wore nothing at all."

"I'll do it, Hawk," she said, her fingers curling around the arm of his chair, "but not because you said please."

"Then why?"

She leaned forward and kissed him lightly on the mouth, then retreated before her traitorous control deserted her. "I'm going to bed because I'm a lot like you."

"How so?"

"I've never been so hungry for a man that I've felt the need to force an unwilling one."

The following morning, Hawk got up and dressed quietly, not showering or shaving because he didn't want to awaken Angela. He could clean up later, but for now she looked too peaceful to disturb, too carefree. Besides, he wasn't in a hurry to move, so he sat by the window and worked on the needlepoint canvas until the parking lot outside became busy with people getting on their way. He shook her awake and left her to the shower he'd turned on moments before, then joined the sleepy travelers outside. Even though there wasn't a chance that they had been followed, particularly once they'd dumped Sammy's truck, habit made him take precautions. Moving around amid other people was one of them.

Doors to several of the motel's rooms stood open as families trailed back and forth to their vehicles, loading the things they'd brought in the night before. Hawk walked past them and on to the coffee shop attached to the motel, where he waited at the counter nearly fifteen minutes to buy two large coffees, blueberry muffins, and a day-old newspaper out of Portland. The papers were late that morning, the waitress informed him when he asked, and he gathered from her tone that it was the rule rather than the exception.

He had to wait again to pay, because the man behind the desk needed to change the tape in the cash register and he wasn't very good at it. Hawk considered walking out without his change from a twenty, but leaving that much would call unwelcome attention, so he waited and tried not to growl in his impatience because that would be remembered too.

There was still a lot of loading activity as he walked across the parking lot with the breakfast bag in his left hand and the paper tucked under his arm. He knew something was wrong before he was halfway across the lot. The door of the room he'd shared with Angela stood wide-open and there was something on the hood of the truck that hadn't been there when he'd left. Blood was pounding so loudly in his ears that he didn't hear the sound of the bag and paper hitting the ground as he began running toward the room, reaching for his Astra without breaking stride.

His peripheral vision identified the thing on the truck as a cellular phone. It rang as he got to the door, but Hawk ignored it and, with his gun pointed ahead, ducked through the doorway, wary and alert. The room was empty and he'd expected that, but he checked the bathroom just in case. She wasn't there, but he saw she'd left her nightshirt folded on the bed with the clothes she'd worn the day before. The tidy pile told Hawk she'd probably been dressed when they came for her.

They—as in Constantine's people—had taken Angela because it was cleaner than trying to take Hawk in front of witnesses. He wouldn't have gone quietly, whereas Angela could be easily coerced into doing so. It was also apparent that Constantine wanted him alive. Otherwise, they would have handled things much differently, and it would have been his blood staining the parking lot and not just a little coffee.

He saw his sports bag in the corner where he'd left it and wondered why they hadn't taken that too. There was still quite a lot of money inside. Otherwise, nothing in the room indicated a struggle, and he was relieved she'd been smart enough to realize that a fight was useless. It would have made no difference to the end result, except that she would have been hurt in some way by men who were indifferent to suffering.

Angela had learned the hard way how to survive, and it was all his fault. The fact that he'd let down his guard long enough for Constantine's men to get to her was something he'd deal with when he had time for recriminations.

He took a couple of deep breaths to steady himself and put his gun away. Then he went back out to the truck and picked up the phone that hadn't stopped ringing. A voice he didn't recognize gave him all the information they wanted him to have, and Hawk listened carefully to the instructions without writing anything down. They were simple, really, not much more than a time and a place and the usual guidance about no cops, no deal.

He disconnected and ignored the furtively curious looks from a family packing up their car three doors down. He went back into the room, shut the door, and tossed the phone into the wastebasket. It was probably bugged and he didn't have time to take it apart and find out. He gathered Angela's things and stuffed them into a shopping bag, then put his sports bag on the bed and began to empty it. He found what he was looking for stuck into a bottom corner of one of the side compartments.

Satisfied that he at least knew *how* they'd been tracked, Hawk crushed the tiny transmitter under his foot, then refilled the bag. He was certain the guard at Sammy's who'd sold out to Constantine was responsible. Angela had told him about the man who'd slipped into the cottage two nights earlier, when she'd been hiding in the rhododendron bushes. But he couldn't waste time with regrets now. He had his own program to think about.

The exchange of one auburn-haired female hostage for one renegade DEA agent was slated for midnight. He had less than sixteen hours to figure out how to ensure Constantine didn't renege on the deal and kill Angela too.

Micah Blackthorne still hadn't returned to his base in Denver, but Hawk used a variation of the "matter of life or death" argument and convinced the man in charge to get a message to his boss. Blackthorne called him back five minutes later at the pay phone in a family restaurant a few miles south of the motel. Hawk wasn't bothered that Constantine's men were probably watching, because arranging for the return of the money he'd taken was part of the deal. He couldn't very well do that without using the phone. So long as they weren't listening, he didn't care. Even so, he kept his back to the dining room because he needed to get at the paper in the lining of his jacket and he preferred to do that unobserved.

His only real concern was that Blackthorne wouldn't believe he hadn't killed his partner. He needn't have worried.

Blackthorne identified himself first, then said, "I've been hoping you'd remember you still had friends out here. What took you so long?"

"Everything was under control until a couple of days ago," Hawk said. "Besides, I didn't want to involve anyone in what I thought needed to be done."

"Thought, as in past tense?"

"Yes. It was my intention to take out the man on top," he said, and knew Blackthorne would understand he was talking about Constantine. "With myself as the only witness and my good name a touch soiled, it seemed like the only way to get justice done."

"Who really killed your partner?" Blackthorne asked. "The man you're after?"

"His son. I returned the favor that same night. The complicating factor was my ex-boss. He was at the scene."

There was a silence as Blackthorne assimilated the information. "He's walking on both sides of the fence, then. That's interesting. No wonder you went to ground." He hesitated, then asked, "So what's changed that made you call me?"

Hawk told him about Angela, a concise report that left out some of the details but gave Blackthorne all the information he needed. Blackthorne listened without interrupting, then asked what he could do to help.

Hawk told him what he wanted and how much he could pay. Blackthorne agreed, and Hawk began to pull at the threads in his jacket so he could give Blackthorne the bank-account codes he'd need to get at the money Hawk had stashed. Blackthorne, though, said they'd settle up later, when it was over.

Which meant, Hawk realized as he put down the phone, that Blackthorne was a hell of a lot more confident than Hawk about the outcome. It gave him something to hang on to as he sat at a nearby table and waited for Blackthorne to call again.

"The *Sea Charmer* is moored about an hour south of your position," Blackthorne said when he called back over an hour later. "It's a small marina, but with enough movement in and around other boats for reasonable cover. If the diver goes in after dusk, he shouldn't have too much difficulty placing the explosives without being noticed."

They were working on the assumption that Angela would be aboard the *Sea Charmer* at midnight. It made sense, given the deserted beach where Hawk was to present himself and his assumption that Constantine not only wanted to kill him personally, but that he'd do it on his boat. Constantine wouldn't risk coming ashore, not when he was in a position to force Hawk to come to him.

Hawk didn't ask how Blackthorne had gotten the information in such a short time. Blackthorne was a man with connections, a lot like Sammy but with a sense of justice in place of Sammy's strictly mercenary attributes.

"Have you got anyone in mind who can get here in time?" Hawk asked, checking his watch. Dusk was about nine hours away.

"There's a man up in Portland who can get there in plenty of time," Blackthorne said. "He gave me a list of equipment, and I've got someone else working that end. Another man should be at the marina anytime now. He'll keep an eye on the *Sea Charmer*, but I doubt he'll see anything. They won't risk bringing her aboard until the last minute, and then they'll probably pick her up en route to the beach."

Hawk agreed and added, "I'd forgotten how efficient you could be."

"It's a good plan," Blackthorne said in return. "The only part I don't like is the end. You haven't left yourself a way out."

"There isn't one."

"Why don't you let me work on that? I can get some men into the area—"

"I can't take that chance," Hawk cut in. "He'll kill Angela if he smells a trap."

Blackthorne hesitated, then said, "Trust me. You know I'll do it right."

Hawk thought about it. "Yes. Thank you."

"Have you given any thought to a backup plan in case they don't use the *Sea Charmer*?"

"I know that beach," Hawk said without emotion. "There's no way in hell any kind of backup can get close enough to do any good. If that's how it plays out, the only thing left will be to make sure Constantine doesn't get away with it. I'd appreciate anything you can do."

"You can depend on it."

They set up another call for later that day to confirm details, then Hawk left the restaurant and got into the truck. He drove to the closest town with a bank and went inside, taking his sports bag with him. He opened an account, chatted with the manager about nothing in particular, then left and drove north until he found another bank.

It was a charade that he repeated a half-dozen times over the next few hours. Anyone following him would assume he was gathering a large amount of cash. He figured this particular demand was Constantine's way of keeping him busy until it was dark enough for the *Sea Charmer* to leave its mooring unnoticed.

It was the longest day of his life. It was one of the most disciplined as well, because it took all the control he could summon to do the things that needed to be done and not dwell on what Angela might be suffering at Constantine's hands. Thinking about her terror would cloud his professional judgment, and that wouldn't do her any good when it came to the crunch.

When night finally arrived, it found Hawk sitting alone in a diner about ten miles from the beach where he had a midnight date. He would know then whether he'd guessed right about the *Sea Charmer*. He would also know if Angela trusted him enough to do exactly what he told her.

Her life depended on it.

TWELVE

It had been dark an hour or more when the two men guarding Angela got the word to move her. Sitting alone in a tiny bedroom with nothing to do except count the cracks in the walls, she heard the telephone ring in the adjacent room and wasn't surprised when one of the guards came for her a couple of minutes later.

It was the older of the two, the same one who had asked her earlier if she wanted food. He hadn't seemed to care when she'd answered him with silence and a scowl. He hadn't brought her any food either. Nor had he come into the room except occasionally to check that she was still there—although where he expected her to go was a mystery. There wasn't even a window to scramble through, and the attached bathroom was somewhere she was inclined to spend as little time as possible exploring, although there were signs that the local mice population didn't share her squeamishness.

The guard told her in short, clear sentences what was expected of her and what would happen if she disregarded his orders. He delivered his threats in the same kind of flat, disinterested tone Hawk had used in the beginning. The only difference was that, unlike Hawk, this man wasn't lying.

She knew that, just as she'd known they would have shot Hawk dead at the motel if she'd tried to warn him. They hadn't needed to point out that she would be as dead as Hawk if she did anything stupid. There were certain things she was learning to take for granted, and that was one of them.

Another was the knowledge that Hawk would be doing something to salvage what he could from this mess. That was all that had kept her from degenerating into a quivering mass of nerves and tears. Hawk would do something— exactly what, she couldn't even begin to guess.

As she walked between the two men to the waiting car, she held her head up high and her shoulders squared—a model of bravery, a performance Hawk would have been proud of.

Inside the car, she slid across the backseat as the guard got in beside her, gritting her teeth to keep them from chattering. Angela was terrified, but she'd be damned if she let anyone know it.

Hawk got to the beach about ten minutes before midnight and left the pockmarked Chevy on ground that was more dirt than sand, a couple hundred yards from the water. Getting out, he shucked his jacket despite the coolness of the night and locked it inside with everything he'd dumped from his sports bag. His gun was already hidden under the rear seat, and the automatic pistol Angela was so fond of picking up was behind the spare tire. Neither weapon was so well hidden that a determined search wouldn't uncover it, but this tactic was better than leaving them in plain sight and *much* better than coming to the beach without them at all.

Not that Hawk expected to get a chance to use either. If

things went as he figured, he'd be on the *Sea Charmer* before long, and everything that was going to happen would take place onboard. He grabbed a small flashlight, then locked the Chevy and pocketed the keys.

The moon was but a tiny crescent of silver that night, easily outshone by a billion stars in the cloudless sky. Wearing only a T-shirt, jeans, and trainers, and carrying the sports bag, Hawk walked across the deep sand toward the ebbing tide. He didn't use the flashlight, but kept his gaze fixed on the water. At first, he didn't see anything, then thought he detected a dark blob riding the calm sea. He was still staring when it turned broadside and light from an uncovered porthole danced across the waves.

The *Sea Charmer* was at anchor about a mile offshore. He flashed his light twice, then for the first time in sixteen long hours, he drew a deep, easy breath. There was hope now that it would all work out. The only thing left to discover was whether Angela was onboard. The sound of a small engine from the direction of the boat told him he didn't have long to wait.

Several minutes later a rubber dinghy stopped just shy of the beach where Hawk waited with his legs spread wide and his hands loose at his sides. There were two men, but only one came onto the beach. The other stayed in the dinghy and pointed at what looked like a big Steyr machine pistol in his direction while his partner frisked Hawk. The keys and flashlight were left on the sand along with his watch, and the guard took his wallet. Hawk had expected that. Constantine wouldn't want to make it too easy for the authorities to identify his body—if and when it washed up onshore.

The guard unzipped the sports bag and dug through the stacks of bills inside. When he found the videotape, he nearly threw it out on the sand, but Hawk was quick to tell him it was something Constantine would be interested in.

The guard shrugged, put it back inside, and zipped the bag closed.

Hawk's tennis shoes were also forfeit. He kicked them off and got into the dinghy without arguing, although he considered the precaution unnecessary. If it was a tracking device they were concerned about, it would have made more sense to drop the shoes into the salt water and short-circuit the thing. If, on the other hand, they simply wanted to make sure he was completely defenseless—kicking someone, even in tennis shoes, could do major damage—they should have known better. There were a lot of people in Hawk's profession who were deadly in bare feet.

Unfortunately, Hawk wasn't one of them. It didn't matter, though, because bare feet suited him just fine. If he was lucky enough to enter the water while he was still alive, it would make swimming a whole lot easier.

In the ten minutes it took to reach the *Sea Charmer*, Hawk kept his nerves steady by rehearsing what he needed to say to Angela when he saw her. Everything depended on her understanding what he told her.

If she was there.

The *Sea Charmer* was a seagoing cruiser about thirty feet long and built for speed. Hawk had once heard that Constantine bought it cheap from the estate of a man who'd learned the hard way that Constantine didn't tolerate accountants who skimmed off the top.

The dinghy bumped up against the stern of the *Sea Charmer*, and Hawk noticed someone had turned out the light he'd seen from afar. Constantine was obviously not taking any chances of the cruiser being identified.

Because he'd been training his night vision from the moment he'd stepped from the Chevy, he didn't have any trouble counting noses when he climbed up and over the side of the cruiser. As far as he could tell, there were only five people besides himself. Two were his guards from the dinghy, now positioned behind him, and another man

Hawk didn't recognize stood on the flying bridge holding a clumsy-looking machine pistol. Unless there were more in the cabin below, the only other two people on the cruiser were Constantine and the woman standing next to him with her hands tied behind her back and pinpricks of fire in her eyes.

Hawk assessed her with a quick, dispassionate look, then glanced away before he saw anything in her expression that would obscure his thinking with emotion. She was alive and, as far as he could tell, unharmed. It was enough for him to know she'd come through the ordeal without major physical damage; the emotional part he couldn't do anything about. He would have to rely on Blackthorne to see to whatever professional help she might need.

Hawk couldn't afford to think about how he wished he'd be around to do it himself, so he swung his gaze to the tall, thin man beside her and waited, smiling, for the first salvo.

Angela hadn't needed Constantine to tell her to keep her mouth shut as Hawk was escorted onboard. Even if she'd known how to apologize for opening the door to Constantine's men in the first place, she wasn't about to do it in front of an audience. Sorrys and the like could come later.

In the two hours since she'd been brought to the boat, she hadn't said a single word—unless two snarls and a moan counted as speaking. The snarls had been directed at Constantine, a slimy, greasy man with the voice of a snake and a tall, scrawny stature reminiscent of Ichabod Crane—oversized Adam's apple included. Her only other vocal expression, that one moan, had escaped despite her best attempts to keep her seasick symptoms to herself. Luckily, Constantine had gone up on deck and the guard with her had just snickered something about how whining wouldn't get her anywhere.

Angela didn't know what they'd do if she threw up all

over the galley, but couldn't imagine it would be worse than getting herself locked in the tiny bathroom. That's what Constantine told her he'd do not long after they'd left the harbor and she'd started to turn green. That threat had served to keep her thoughts more focused on avoiding making a mess than on what would happen when Hawk arrived.

She believed without a single doubt that he would stop at nothing to get her away from Constantine. That wasn't what worried her. Hawk's agenda concerning Constantine hadn't gone away, and she knew that if he could use this situation to further his goal, he'd do it.

Hawk had always meant to die with Constantine. She couldn't even bear thinking about it.

She watched him climb lithely over the railing and straighten to face in her general direction. She concentrated on keeping her expression confined to less personal emotions like terror and anger. The things she felt for Hawk were too private to chance letting anyone else see, too strong for anyone to miss if she wasn't careful.

When he came to stand in the center of the deck with his legs spread for balance and his head held straight and proud, she thought Constantine must be crazy if he imagined he could get the best of Hawk. For the first time since morning, she began to hope.

She kept that concealed too—a fairly simple task as Hawk spent less than a second looking at her before switching his gaze to Constantine. When Hawk smiled, though, her control over her expression began to waver.

Smiling was not on the list of things she'd imagined he would do upon arriving. She frowned in disapproval.

"I wasn't sure you'd come," Constantine said abruptly, his snake's voice almost succeeding in making Angela cringe. "The report I got from the compound was somewhat confusing. I couldn't decide if she was your prisoner or your lover."

"Both," Hawk said, and didn't so much as spare her a single glance when Angela gasped. "But I expect you already know that. When I couldn't break your little assassin, it seemed a good idea to play along. I assumed she would eventually lead me to you."

"No, Hawk, you—" she began, but that was all she got out before Constantine's backhanded slap sent her reeling. She landed in the corner of a bench seat, and couldn't help crying out when her body came down hard on her tied wrists.

Tears of pain filled her eyes as she looked up at Hawk. "But—"

"Shut up." Hawk didn't even glance in her direction when he said it, and she was suddenly reduced to that same level of fear as the night he'd made her swallow cocaine. This time, though, she was determined to master the tears. Shifting in the seat until she was somewhat upright, she gritted her teeth and stared at the men facing off on the deck . . . and wondered what the hell Hawk was up to.

"She's nothing to do with me," Constantine said, "but if that's what you think, why did you come for her?"

"I didn't. I came for myself." Hawk hooked his thumbs in his belt loops and looked as though he didn't know three powerful guns were aimed straight at him. "I have something I thought you might be interested in buying. The woman was my ticket to you."

"Ticket!" Angela couldn't help protesting, but she kept it to one word and stayed in her seat when Constantine raised his arm as though to swat her down.

Hawk looked at her fiercely. "Keep your mouth shut, honey," he said with an emphasis on *honey* that made it sound like dog doodoo.

"But, Hawk, you know I'm not—"

"That's it!" Without so much as a glance in Constantine's direction, Hawk pulled his T-shirt over his head and strode over to her. Bending down, he gripped her jaw with one hand and forced her mouth open. When he began to stuff the wadded-up shirt into her mouth, she screamed. A muffled squeak was all she could manage, though, and by the time he'd wrapped the end of the shirt around her neck to secure the gag, even a squeak was beyond her. She had to settle for glaring up at him in mute appeal for an explanation. He must have seen it, because he softened his grip on her jaw. Even so, he continued, for a moment, to force her to look at him . . . and to see the plea in his eyes.

She didn't understand, of course, not any of it. But he wasn't asking her for that, she realized. Hawk was asking her to trust him, and that was something she could do without any kind of explanation. She blinked once and nodded almost imperceptibly against his hand. It was all she dared, because one of the guards had come over and was watching them both.

Hawk turned his back to her and confronted Constantine again. "Now where were we . . . ? Oh yes, the reason I wanted to see you."

"Putting aside the issue of the woman for the moment, Hawk, I would have thought I was the last person in the world you'd be interested in seeing." Constantine went over to the ladder leading to the upper deck and leaned against it. "Last time we met, you killed my son. What makes you think I'd be willing to forget that?"

"Because you're a businessman," Hawk said without any seeming hurry. "I never thought you were the type to let personal issues interfere with business."

"The death of my son was more than a personal issue," Constantine said, but Angela thought he said it without conviction. It was hard to be sure, though, because the T-shirt in her mouth was affecting her hearing. "However, before I kill you, you might as well tell me what you're selling."

"A videotape." Hawk dug the fingers of one hand into his shoulder as though to ease a strained muscle. In the soft light of the stars, Angela thought she could see a scar there, but she couldn't be sure.

"That night on the beach, I'd dug into a sand dune," Hawk continued. "I taped everything."

Constantine's eyes narrowed to black slits. "That explains why you seemed to pop up from nowhere. However, I'm not sure I believe the part about the video. If my memory serves me correctly, the only thing I saw in your hand was a gun." He shook his head slowly. "I didn't notice a camcorder, Hawk."

"The dune collapsed when I crawled out. I left it behind." He rubbed his shoulder again. "One of your guys caught me in the shoulder as I drove away. By the time I felt like going back, it took a couple of days to find the damned thing."

"But you did." Constantine didn't look as sure of himself as he had just moments earlier, but she didn't think that meant much to the overall picture. He was still a man with a very big grudge. Then he changed the subject back to one she was even less comfortable with. "About the woman."

"What about her?" Hawk didn't even spare her a glance, but she sent him and everyone else mean glares anyway. If he wanted her to play along, her eyes were all she could use for acting.

"Before we get into any more details about that video, I'd like to be convinced she isn't anything to you."

A corner of Hawk's mouth lifted in a careless smile. "I keep telling you, Constantine. She's not my problem."

"Then I guess you won't mind if I ask Jerry to shoot her," Constantine said, nodding toward the guard closest to her. Angela didn't have to pretend to be afraid, and she sent a frantic look at Hawk that went ignored.

"I suppose that's one way to get the job done." Hawk shrugged negligently and looked down at the deck. "So long as you don't mind the mess, you can do whatever you want. It's your boat."

"You have a better idea?"

Angela didn't wait to hear it. Seeing that the guards' attention was focused on Hawk, she shoved herself from the bench and bolted for the side. Just what she was planning to do in the water with her hands tied and her mouth full of T-shirt, she didn't know. All she cared about was avoiding having her brains splattered across the deck.

She didn't make it, and not because any of the guards was quick enough to stop her. Hawk beat them to it, catching her easily with a long arm around her waist. He hauled her tight against his side and squeezed so tight she thought her ribs would give under the pressure. What with the makeshift gag and Hawk's arm forcing the air from her lungs, all thought of struggle was forgotten as the need to breathe overcame her. She was on the point of passing out when the pressure of his arm eased and he caught her jaw in a grip that was almost gentle.

"That was a waste of effort, honey," he said, putting the same vaguely disgusted emphasis on the endearment. "Unless you can swim with your hands tied behind your back, there's nowhere to go but down."

It occurred to her then that he'd always called her Angel, not honey. It was a small point, but it made her wonder if it was a way of telling her something. She didn't know, but tried to pay closer attention.

Hawk looked away to where Constantine still lounged against the ladder. "I was going to suggest a slightly cleaner way of disposing of her, but she almost beat me to it."

"You want to throw her overboard?" Constantine shook his head. "Not good enough, Hawk. We're too close to shore. She might be a strong swimmer."

"With her hands tied? I doubt it."

Constantine took a minute to consider the proposition, but Angela ignored him and focused on the message Hawk was trying to send her. It wasn't much, just the slight, rhythmic caress of his hand where it splayed flat against her side as he held her to him. The fingers against her jaw were moving, too, pressing gently and rhythmically and with a subtlety that escaped the notice of Constantine's sharp gaze.

Hawk was telling her someting, and she couldn't figure it out except to realize that he was still on her side. Not that she'd doubted it. Well, maybe for a minute there she'd suffered a bit of panic, but listening to Hawk as he consulted with Constantine about the dubious merits of a messy deck had thrown her for a loop. She still hadn't figured out his game plan when it suddenly moved into another stage.

His fingers at her jaw and side tightened simultaneoulsy, then he swore and acted as though he was having trouble holding her. "Stop fighting, honey," he said gruffly, and hefted her right off her feet. "Dammit, I said *stop* it."

It took a couple of midair shakes for Angela to realize she was supposed to be fighting him. She obliged by kicking him in the shin, and got a surprised grunt for that effort. She was making a serious try at getting enough leverage for a knee kick to the groin when he tightened his grip and squeezed the air from her again.

Her moment of defiance, she guessed, was over. It didn't take any acting to let her head fall forward as she tried to recover two lungsful of air through her nose.

"Let's get this over with," she heard Hawk say, and was about to kick him again when he squeezed her closer—this time without depriving her of her air supply.

"Agreed," Constantine said, "but with one modification. I want her feet tied too."

"Not worried what someone's going to think when the body washes up onshore, are you?" Hawk asked, but the rhythmic caress at her waist began again, and she concentrated on that and not the morbid discussion going on over her head.

"It's nothing to do with me," Constantine said. "As far

as anyone at the marina is concerned, the *Sea Charmer* never left her slip."

Angela finally had enough air in her lungs and was breathing deeply when she heard someone come toward her. She stiffened, then kicked out when a hand grabbed her ankle. It didn't do her any good, though, because her kick missed and the guard managed—with Hawk's generous help—to tie her ankles together.

She began to shake then, because if Hawk was counting on her ability to swim in this condition, he'd seriously overestimated her water skills. The caress at her waist became firmer without losing the rhythm, but even that promise of hope couldn't stop the tears that spilled from her eyes.

If Hawk noticed she was crying, he ignored it as he pulled the T-shirt away and tossed it aside. Her tongue was big in her mouth, dry and impossible to get words around —though she tried. Oh yes, she tried, but when Hawk swung her high in his arms and carried her to the side, there didn't seem to be anything left to say.

"Now take a big breath, honey," he said with a cruel smile that she prayed was for the guard's benefit. "It won't save you, but at least you'll have time to say your goodbyes."

Angela heard him, but it was all too much for her. A big breath? Who was he kidding? What was another minute or so when she was going to drown anyway? She stared into his eyes and read such fierce determination in them that she did as he'd told her and filled her lungs with the sweet manna of life.

One minute and thirty-four seconds—that had been her personal record for holding her breath, achieved in grade school, but it was like riding a bike, right? Could she do it again, only this time for bigger stakes than a can of soda and a pat on the back from her brother's sidekick? She wasn't sure. . . .

Hawk's arms suddenly shifted her weight and let go. In

the split second before hitting the water, Angela met his gaze and silently swore that if she drowned, she'd never do what he said ever again. For now, though, she had no choice but to do this one last thing precisely according to Hawk's direction. And if that meant holding her breath until her lungs burst, then by God, that's what she'd do.

One minute thirty-four seconds and counting.

She slammed full length against the sea, and before she could gather her wits about her and decide exactly what Hawk expected her to do besides keep her mouth shut, the cold water closed over her body and began to suck her into its depths. The shock of cold and dark nearly made her lose what precious air she had left. It wasn't as easy as she remembered, holding her breath, because it was getting darker and colder and she was getting more scared with every passing second.

She'd forgotten to count, she realized, and started from one because her lungs had no doubt expanded since she was ten.

Two, three, four . . .

There were other things in the water with her too. At least, she assumed there were; it was really too dark to tell. A scene that was a cross between *Jaws* and *Moby Dick* flashed across her mind, and she thought it was a good thing her hands and feet were tied. Making thrashing movements would attract the more dreadful denizens of the deep. The chance alliteration almost made her laugh, but she couldn't do that and hold her breath, not unless she wanted to disappoint Hawk.

Ten, eleven, twelve . . .

Angela knew she was sinking because her ears hurt and she had to assume it was from the pressure. She wondered if she should swallow to relieve the pressure or if that would waste the air she held in her mouth. She swallowed anyway.

Twenty-three, twenty-four, twenty-five . . .

She couldn't hold the air in her lungs, not all of it, so

she let a little out through her mouth and had to remind herself not to try to replace it. If felt better, for a second.

Forty-one, forty-two, forty-three . . .

It was amazing how long it took to count to ninety-four, and she wondered if she was going too slow or too fast. It didn't matter, she realized. No one was going to give her a soda or even a medal for getting it right. Hawk would care, though. . . .

Eighty—no, that was supposed to be seventy, wasn't it? She let a little more air escape, then realized she must be hallucinating because she could see something coming toward her—a light, a fish that glowed, a confused firefly. Suddenly a mask appeared with a face attached behind it. A diving mask, she realized, and she remembered with startling clarity her first summer of swimming lessons. Her mother had been the one to take her, and she'd had this thing about not letting her wear goggles, something silly about Angela not needing them, that she was perfectly fine in the water without them. Angela had begged and pleaded and pointed out that her best friend had a pair, but her mother had stood firm. Her best friend, Cindy. That was her name, wasn't it? What was she doing here?

But the face behind the mask belonged to a man, so it couldn't be Cindy. That confused Angela and she let some more air out while she thought about it. She didn't spend long at it because she'd just realized the man had an arm around her shoulders and was holding something against her mouth. She wasn't sure what to do . . . like that first time when Hawk kissed her and she'd wanted to open her mouth to him, but hadn't, hadn't even admitted thinking it, because he was the enemy. Then, not now, and besides, Hawk had a plan and she was supposed to be counting. . . .

The man pushed the thing harder, and she thought about telling him it hurt when it dawned on her that *hallucinations didn't hurt*! She started struggling then because she didn't want to drown and there was someone here who could help her if she could only explain. His arm remained firm across her shoulders, and he took the thing from her mouth and pointed to his own and she *finally* got the idea. Lord she was slow! He didn't seem to hold it against her, though, because he tried again, putting the thing back to her mouth, and this time she opened enough to take it inside.

As Angela struggled to learn the do's and don'ts of breathing through the mouthpiece, she thought about Hawk's plan and how she'd rate it on a scale of ten. Putting aside the fact that she might have died from heart failure, and not counting the pneumonia she'd undoubtedly be stricken with by morning, there were still several flaws in his plan that bothered her—not least of which was Hawk's arrogant faith that she'd even be capable of learning something new under what anyone would regard as trying conditions. What if the man hadn't found her? After all, it was a big ocean. Then she looked over his shoulder and noticed not one, but two other men also decked out in scuba gear.

She was breathing more easily now. The first man nodded his approval and gestured for her to keep it up while another cut her free, and then they were all swimming away, Angela in the center and held firmly against the side of the one who had found her. As she allowed herself to be guided from the scene of her brush with death, she awarded Hawk's plan a six and hoped he had a better one for himself.

She'd never forgive him if he didn't.

THIRTEEN

So far, so good.

The splash marking Angela's entrance into the water had barely subsided when Hawk turned away. He had, he calculated, about ten, maybe fifteen minutes to get into position. After that, it was anyone's guess what would happen. Blackthorne hadn't been specific, and Hawk hadn't pressed him except to emphasize that nothing would interfere with Angela's rescue.

Now that the worst was over and Angela was, he assumed, in the hands of Blackthorne's very capable associates, he found himself almost hoping that something *would* happen to keep him alive long enough to see her again. The frantic, disbelieving look in her eyes as he'd dropped her into the sea wasn't something he wanted to take to his grave.

He had known within thirty seconds of boarding the *Sea Charmer* that there was only one weapon he was likely to get his hands on, but it was so obvious that he was almost certain it was a trap. A speargun was *de rigueur* for a seagoing cruiser, and this one was double-barreled and appeared to be loaded and ready. On a normal boat, that would have been considered a serious breach of safety standards. On the *Sea Charmer*, it was probably normal operating procedure. Unless it was a trap, and that was something Hawk would soon find out. For the time being, he concentrated on keeping his gaze from wandering too often to the wall under the flying deck on which the thing was mounted.

He looked over to where Constantine was talking into a cellular phone and wasn't surprised to realize the person on the other end was Paul Marchand. It made sense that Constantine would call his man inside the DEA to discuss Hawk's presence and the video. What didn't make sense was why Hawk hadn't used the video to extricate himself from the murder charge. He had come onto the *Sea Charmer* knowing that was his plan's biggest weakness, but there hadn't been another way around it. It had been all he could come up with that would stall Constantine long enough for him to get Angela off the boat.

Constantine clicked the phone shut and smiled thinly. "Marchand said that he doesn't believe there's a video. I'm inclined to agree with him."

"No?" A quick glance told Hawk the guards were still alert, but their positions had changed since he'd tossed Angela overboard. One man was standing close to Constantine, while the other was leaning against the stern rail. Hawk pretty much had the port side to himself, except for the lookout on the flying deck, and that man's visibility was limited to the back part of the deck unless he hung upside down over the rail.

"No," Constantine said. "If you had one, you would have used it before now."

"Then I guess you don't want to look at the copy, and I emphasize *copy*, that I brought along with me." He traced a line on the deck with his toe and tried to sound nonchalant. Bringing even a "copy" had been a risk, because he didn't know if luxury accessories aboard the *Sea Charmer* extended to a VCR. As the copy was nothing more than a blank tape, it was a substantial risk indeed. "The original is being kept in a safe place. Unless, of course, I don't go back for it, in which case it will be sent along to the proper authorities."

"You don't trust me?" Constantine's question produced a snicker from the guard standing nearest, and Hawk smiled as well.

"There is the matter of a personal grudge you might bear me." Hawk shifted his body a foot or so to the left as though to compensate for the slight roll of the boat, a position that left him closer to the speargun. "If I hadn't run out of money, I might not have come at all. But there you have it."

Constantine pointed at the sports bag. "What's in there if not my money?"

"Paper, mostly." Hawk took advantage of a larger swell to inch closer to the gun. "Like I said before, I'm broke."

Constantine snapped his fingers in the direction of the sports bag, and the guard he'd called Jerry handed it to him without taking his aim from Hawk. Unzipping it, Constantine pulled out a banded stack that was about half an inch thick with a ten-dollar note on either end and tore it open. The nicely cut pieces of newspaper Hawk had gotten from one of Blackthorne's people, slipped into his bag at one of the banks he'd visited, were no contest for the slight ocean breeze, which sucked them into the air and scattered them across the deck and surrounding waves.

In a frustrated frenzy, Constantine ripped three more bundles apart with the same results. Hawk was reluctantly admiring the guards' persistent vigilance—they hadn't taken their eyes off him—when two things happened at once. Constantine grabbed Jerry's Steyr and swung the heavy machine pistol around to point it at Hawk; and the skies suddenly exploded with light and color. Blackthorne's surprise, Hawk assumed, and was filled with confidence.

The flares wouldn't have been released if Angela wasn't safe and sound.

Hawk didn't wait to see if the guards were *that* good. Springing aside, he dove for the speargun and had it in hand and aimed straight at Constantine before the drug lord recovered from the surprise of the flares. The guards were slow, too, but it didn't matter because they'd lost their chance. If they shot him now, Constantine would get a harpoon through his gut and they'd be, at the very least, unemployed.

As standoffs went, it wasn't very promising, but Hawk wasn't given a chance to worry about it. The flares hadn't even reached their zenith when the blurred *rat-tat-tat* of an automatic weapon echoed through the night. Another of Blackthorne's surprises, Hawk guessed as he saw the guard at the stern fall a moment before Jerry dove for the deck near Constantine's feet. Hawk didn't spare a glance for the other guard aloft, because he knew that if he took his eyes from Constantine, he'd be dead. He moved to the rail without looking where he was going, pointing his gun at Constantine, who looked enraged and, Hawk thought, handled the Steyr as though he weren't familiar with it. That was a bonus, because automatic weapons weren't as easy to use as they looked. On the other side of the coin, though, Constantine himself appeared at the very edge of control. Even so, he didn't shoot, not yet, and that gave Hawk all the leeway he needed.

He made it to the rail and got one leg over the side before he saw the change in Constantine's eyes. He knew then he was going to have to shoot the speargun. He waited until the last second, and not because he had any qualms about killing Constantine. He didn't. Constantine deserved to die, and that hadn't changed.

Hawk still wanted justice, but he'd lost his taste for blood.

In the end, it wasn't his choice. He read in Constantine's eyes what he was going to do a split second before he did it, and that was all the time he needed. The bullets went wide as Hawk jerked to one side, then he fired and the harpoon caught Constantine high in the chest.

Hawk pitched backward into the water and dove deep, keeping one hand on the speargun even though it slowed him. The clock ticking in his brain told him time had nearly run out, but there was nothing for it except to try to get as far away from the *Sea Charmer* as humanly possible.

When he came up for air, he was still much too close, so near that he could hear the shouts of the guards giving each other orders and doing nothing in the way of looking for him. That was good, because he didn't dare dive again. As quietly as he could manage, he turned and began swimming. He wasn't headed toward shore, and that concerned him because he wasn't sure of the tides and if he'd be able to manage them when it was time. It couldn't be helped, though, because the *Sea Charmer* was between him and the shore and he'd be a fool to go near her.

He hadn't gotten far when the muffled thunder of the underwater explosive charges reached his ears. Not sparing even a glance behind because he knew what was coming, he kicked and stroked and fought his way through the waves. He was too late, too close. The explosion reached the diesel tanks and the *Sea Charmer* burst into a million projectiles of fire . . . and death rained down on the sea around him.

From the beach where she crouched barefoot and shivering beneath a blanket someone had thrown around her shoulders, Angela watched in mute shock as the *Sea Charmer* was engulfed in a ball of flame that dimmed the stars and spewed fire and debris across the waves. Throwing off the blanket, she got up and ran across the sand toward the water—*Hawk was still out there!*—but someone caught her before she got her feet wet again and passed her back to the man who was in charge of all the others.

He held on to her and shouted orders at the same time, then took her by the shoulders and made her look toward the water where three men in frog suits were hustling through the waves. They disappeared beneath the water as she watched.

"There's a dinghy out there too," the man said, and she remembered he'd told her to call him Peter. She also remembered he'd said he worked for Micah Blackthrone—which didn't explain anything but was at least reassuring. Blackthrone was the man Hawk had intended to send her to. It followed that his men could be trusted.

Peter continued: "If he's out there, they'll find him."

"Couldn't you see?" Peter had, after all, been using field glasses.

"The flares we used were quick burning, for surprise only. We didn't want Constantine's men to have time to look for our dinghy or, if Hawk got away, to spot him in the water. Unfortunately, there was still too much light for night lenses and too little for regular ones. So no, Angela, I didn't see."

She felt his hands fall away from her shoulders, but she couldn't seem to move or even breathe very well as she stared toward the flames that glowed in pockets between the softly rising waves. "Did Hawk know about the explosion?"

"He planned it."

That confirmed what Angela already thought about Hawk's plan. The blanket materialized around her shoulders again, and she stood beside Peter and waited for news as the sandy beach behind them turned into a parking lot for a half-dozen vehicles.

Angela prayed as she waited, because if Hawk didn't come back to her, she was quite sure she'd never forgive him. Being that angry with Hawk wasn't how she wanted to spend the rest of her life. She had other plans for the two of them, plans that rated ten out of ten and she couldn't wait to share them with him.

If he just came back. If he survived.

At her side, Peter continued giving orders, listened to reports, and looked through first one pair of binoculars, then the other ones that she supposed were for night vision. He was one of several men who had been waiting on the beach when she and her escort of three had surfaced from the deep, slogging in cautious silence through the knee-high surf to the sand.

She'd been told about the men in the dinghy when she had demanded to know what they were doing about Hawk. Peter hadn't had a chance to say anything more, because the flares had gone up then and she'd been too spellbound by the show to press him.

The first burst of gunfire had sent her heartbeat into triple time, but Peter had reassured her without taking his eyes from the field glasses he had trained on the *Sea Charmer* that the shots had been fired from the dinghy, that Hawk was not the target. She'd just begun to breathe again when a second burst made Peter swear and say something she didn't catch into the transmitter at his wrist. He didn't get an answer, and it seemed to Angela that he hadn't expected one. He was waiting for something, though, because for the third time since she'd begun counting, Peter checked his watch.

Moments later, when the explosion rent the night sky and flaming pieces of the *Sea Charmer* fell to the burning sea, she knew it was what he'd been waiting for.

Another dinghy was launched from the shore, this one mounted with a searchlight that swept from side to side across the waves. Peter left her for a moment, and when he came back he pressed a cup of coffee into her hand. She didn't want it, but accepted it anyway because he seemed like the kind of man who didn't take no for an answer.

"The divers should be in the area now," he said. "The men in the first dinghy are searching the perimeter of the wreckage, but they've only got the light of the fire to see by."

"If Hawk was still on the *Sea Charmer*, he's dead." Angela said it because they were searching the wreckage, not the sea around it, and that meant the worst.

"The men in the dinghy saw him go over the side thirty, maybe forty seconds before it blew."

She turned her head very slowly to meet Peter's gaze. "Why didn't you tell me that before?"

"The second burst of gunfire wasn't ours," he said after a moment. "We don't know if he was hit before he went into the water. The men didn't see him again."

She blanched, then gathered her courage and the few shreds of hope she had left and stared back out across the black sea with its diamond-tipped waves. Hawk was out there, and he was alive. It wasn't just that she wanted to believe it. She *had* to believe it.

The Hawk she knew wouldn't swoop into her life, change everything in it, then fly away and leave her wondering what was real and what was a dream. He wouldn't leave her to face it all alone, to sort through the web of deceit and danger he'd unwittingly dragged her into. He was too responsible to desert her now, too honorable.

The Hawk she admired made tough decisions. He'd kissed her and made her want his loving, made her want him, then had denied them both because once would have been too much, too little, too easy. The control that drove her mad was so intrinsic to his character that she knew she'd notice the lack if it were gone—and regret it.

The Hawk she'd come to love had taught her fear, yet what she'd felt for herself was nothing compared with what she felt now, for him. And because she knew that he'd expect it of her, that he'd be proud, she hid her fear behind a mask of hope and dignity.

Disregarding the activity on the beach around her, Angela waited and watched and didn't even notice that the coffee she sipped had long since gone cold. She heard Peter ask if she wanted more, and almost said yes when she realized he wasn't listening, that he was concentrating on the water. Without a word, he switched on his flashlight and played the beam over the shallows, left to right and back again, deeper into the night. Then Peter held the light still, and Angela could have sworn he chuckled, but she didn't ask why because there was movement at the fringes of the light.

She had no sooner focused on the spot than Hawk rose from the sea and surged forward until he was at the center of the beam. Waves lapped at his knees as he stood there and stared unblinking into the light, with water streaming down his face and bare chest and a vicious-looking speargun in his hand.

He was a warrior from the deep, her warrior. If he didn't already know it, he would soon learn . . . and there was no time like the present. Angela handed her blanket and coffee to Peter and asked him to please turn out the light, then she walked into the surf until she was within touching distance of the man she loved.

"So you made it," she said, lifting her gaze to meet his and wishing she'd not asked Peter to turn out the light. She couldn't see more than a vague outline of the features she'd come to know so well.

"You're surprised?" The deep caress of his voice wrapped her in a cocoon of warmth and familiar pleasure.

"Impressed, I think." A cool breeze tugged at hair that had escaped her wet braid and blew it across her face. She ignored it. "What do you do for an encore?"

"Anything you decide, Angel. Anything you decide." He held out the hand that wasn't holding the speargun and waited. He didn't wait long.

A breath later, a step, and her face was buried against his chest as his arm closed on her shoulders. Angela slipped her own arms around his waist and felt a tremor go through him as they stood in the surf and shared the warmth of trust, hope, and love.

FOURTEEN

They made love the first time in the shower.

Hawk hadn't meant for it to happen like that, so hard and fast and without frills, but Angela had taken him at his word. Decisions, he was beginning to discover, were something she was very good at.

He'd gotten his first inkling of her decision-making skills during the hour-long ride from the beach to the hotel. After a private debriefing with Peter while Angela repacked the contents of his sports bag into a borrowed duffel —she was, he mused, overly interested in the task—Hawk had suggested that Angela be flown immediately to Denver on the small jet Peter had left at a private airfield a short distance south. Hawk and the remainder of Blackthorne's men would then drive back to San Rafael and collect the videotape he'd left there.

Without it, Marchand was still a formidable threat.

Angela had not only disagreed, she'd given a handful of reasons why it was a rotten idea—beginning with the fact that Hawk was too exhausted to think, much less think ahead, and ending with the incontrovertible truth that dividing their forces would necessarily weaken them. When

Hawk argued that it was doubtful Marchand would have his apartment in San Rafael under surveillance, Angela pointed out that he'd assumed they hadn't been tracked from Sammy's either, and look where that had gotten them.

Besides, she didn't want to go to Denver, she told him and so long as he'd left the decision making to her . . .

Hawk surrendered, but only after Peter agreed that Angela's reasoning was sound. After a call to Blackthorne, Peter delegated responsibility for liaising with authorities regarding the *Sea Charmer* to his second-in-command, saying his orders were to stick with Angela until such a time as Hawk was no longer distracted by the issues surrounding Marchand.

So it was five trucks that left the beach that dark, cold autumn morning. Hawk's pockmarked Chevy stayed behind with the three men who were still searching for survivors—although no one expected to find any. Hawk and Angela shared the backseat of one truck while Peter sat up front with the driver, so the kind of conversation they both yearned for was impossible. They settled for holding hands beneath the blanket and sharing the occasional tremor of reaction that went through one, then the other, as they remembered how close they'd come to losing it all.

Dawn was shading the black landscape gray when they passed a seaside resort. Angela leaned forward to tell Peter they were going to stop there for a rest.

He looked at her over the seat. "That's a five-star hotel. I don't think we look good enough to pass their entrance exam."

"The only excuse I'll accept is that they haven't any vacancies, and I doubt that because the parking lot wasn't full." She sat back and resettled the blanket. "Trust me, Peter. If they have rooms, we'll get them."

Peter picked up the cellular phone and began calling the others.

Angela was as good as her word. In fact, once she'd had

a private conversation with the manager on duty, it took less time to sort out keys and room assignments than it had to stop the five-strong caravan and turn it around. She even managed to have room service agree to bring early breakfasts all around, although Hawk first had to talk her out of having it served in the restaurant. Wearing a borrowed sweater but still in his damp jeans, he told her he didn't feel up to five-star standards. And despite his personal opinion that Angela looked like a million bucks no matter what she had on, he doubted that she'd agree once she got a look at herself in the mirror. Bedraggled, he thought, was probably the nicest thing she might say about her appearance at the moment.

So they went to their suite to await food, and for the first time in what seemed an eternity, Hawk knew as he closed the door that they were truly safe. Between the man Peter had left stationed at the door and the others whose rooms bracketed Angela and Hawk's, not even Marchand could get at them.

Turning from the door, Hawk saw a trail of blankets and damp clothing leading through the living area and past the huge pedestal bed to what he assumed was the bathroom. The sudden hiss of the shower confirmed it. He reached down to pick up one blanket, then the other one. Draping them over his arm, he took a few more steps and stared down at Angela's damp jeans and sweater.

She'd taken them off while he'd been out in the hallway, not even waiting for the privacy of the bathroom. Blood pooled in his groin as he noticed the wisp of satin and lace peeking out from beneath her sweater, and he realized that as she'd stripped she'd known he would come through the door at any moment.

The noise of the shower filled his ears, and when he took another step he could see that she'd left the bathroom door wide-open. He dropped the blankets and began pulling off his clothes. The jeans were molded tight to his thighs and it didn't help that his erection was hard and swollen, but he finally got everything off and went to take Angela up on her invitation.

The shower was built on the same luxurious scale as the rest of their suite, with glass panels and marble walls defining an enclosure that was bigger than some beds. Twin brass fixtures sprayed water from opposite walls, and Angela stood in the center of it all with her eyes closed as she struggled to free her hair from its braid. Water streamed over her shoulders to spill from the dark mauve tips of her full breasts as other rivulets flowed across her belly to flatten the curls between her legs.

She was completely feminine yet possessed a strength that was, to his mind, her greatest attraction. He wanted all of her for his own, forever. He also wanted her now.

He stepped into the cubicle and watched her eyelids flutter open as he pulled the door shut behind him. "Need some help with that?" he asked, but moved behind her and sank his fingers into the knotted mass before she could reply. She stood passively for a moment, then tried to look at him over her shoulder. He was firm but gentle as he pushed her chin until she resumed her former position.

"Just stand still, Angel. Let me do this for you."

"This wasn't what I had in mind when I left the door open."

"I know." He had half the braid sorted—the bottom part was probably the easy bit, he assumed—but half wasn't good enough, so he kept working, reminding himself that she'd sleep better with her hair free and dry. Besides, he doubted he'd have the energy to work on the mess her braid was in once he'd made love to her.

Then the tip of his shaft brushed her buttocks, sending a shock the size of a tidal wave rolling through him. Before he could recover, Angela spun around and slipped her arms around his neck, pulling him down until their mouths came together in a ravenous kiss that stole his sanity . . . his control. He lost it all in a whirlpool of erotic sensation, in the way her mouth opened greedily to his, the soft crush of her breasts against his chest, the almost painful throbbing of his erection as it pressed into her belly.

Backing her against the cold marble wall, he closed one hand around her thigh and lifted, pulling her upward as he hurriedly tested her readiness with the fingers of his other hand. She was hot and slick, and he needed no more encouragement. Holding tightly to her thigh and without breaking off the hot, unrestrained mating of their mouths, he guided his length to the entrance of her feminine sheath and thrust inside.

Angela cried out, a cry of pleasure so intense that Hawk would have mistaken it for pain and withdrawn had she not raised her other leg and wrapped it around his waist, bringing him closer, deeper. He cupped her buttocks in his hands and, digging his fingers into her soft, muscled flesh, held her firmly against the wall and began to move. Slowly, steadily, he thrust into her, gritting his teeth and sweating and dying a little because it was so good, so unbelievably good to be inside her.

Then, suddenly, almost before he'd begun, she started to convulse around him. He stared into her eyes and was amazed by the passion, the excitement . . . the absolute surprise he discovered in them. It was stunning, the ease with which she'd reached the zenith. His own climax was forgotten in that moment as he became captivated by hers.

She convulsed again, hard and strong, then there was a ripple of smaller contractions. Hawk thrust into her one final time and held his position deep inside as she collapsed quivering and boneless in his embrace.

They stayed like that for a while, water pouring around and between them as he stroked her back and shoulders, their heads bowed and humble. Finally, he slid her up the wall until he was no longer buried in her, then eased her to her feet. He didn't quit his support of her until a long while later when he felt her legs begin to assume her weight.

"I should get back to that braid before we run the entire hotel out of hot water," he said as she looked up at him.

Her eyes were still cloudy with passion, and there was confusion in their depths. "Damn the braid, Hawk, *and* the water. I can't *believe* you just did that to me."

"Did what?" It was hard not to laugh, but he made an effort because anger wasn't one of the emotions he wanted to deal with. "If you're referring to the way we just made love, I'll admit it was a little on the wild side. Next time I'll be more careful with you."

"That's not what I meant!"

"You liked it, then?"

"Of course I liked it!" she fumed. "Couldn't you tell?"

A rosy blush blossomed and spread downward from her cheeks to the upper curves of her breasts. Hawk was entranced. Despite his best resolve, he laughed, then put his hands on her shoulders. Before she could guess what he was about, he spun her around to face the wall. Digging his fingers into her braid, he got back to work, albeit at a somewhat feverish pace.

"I know it wasn't what you meant, Angel. Frankly, though, I can't see what you're upset about . . . unless it's the part of me that's hard against your butt, and I can assure you it won't be like that for long." Without stilling the progress of his hands, he bent to whisper in her ear, telling her graphically what he wanted from her, what he wanted for her . . . and, perhaps most important, what he wanted for the two of them together.

He could tell by the uneven rise and fall of her shoulders that she was excited by his erotic promises. Her sexual fire, her dazzling passion, was unlike anything he'd ever known, and it fed the flames of his own desire. He kept talking as he worked, using the force of the shower to help as he untwisted the knot that seawater had made of her long, luxurious mane.

The instant the last of the braid was sorted, Hawk dropped his hands to her shoulders, then slid them downward to cup the soft weight of her breasts. Her nipples were hard against his palms, and she gave a long, sustained moan as he rolled them in his fingers. Her hands lifted to curl around his wrists, and he pulled her back against him because he could no longer stand the distance, the wanting he felt all the way to his soul.

Nuzzling her hair aside, he explored the soft skin on the side of her throat, found her ear with his tongue, and bit gently on the delicate skin there. Then he slid one hand downward, moving unhesitatingly past the soft, springy curls to explore the wet, hot passage they hid, taking his time to learn the feel of her with his hand, the sensitive pads of his fingers.

She was ready for him again, though he knew her slick welcome was, in part, a result of their recent coupling. She cried out as he pushed a single finger deep inside, and tried to turn in his arms. He tightened his control of her body and slowly removed his finger.

"Spread your legs, Angel," he murmured against her throat. "We're almost there."

He rewarded her compliance by brushing the nub of her passion with his thumb. Her gasp of pleasure nearly broke through the remnants of his control, but he made himself try harder. It was important, these moments of preparation, and not just for her physical comfort. The ecstasy of controlled, lingering foreplay was as much a part of lovemaking as Technicolor fireworks among the stars.

No, he didn't want to rush, but the sensation of her buttocks rubbing against his arousal was almost more than he could stand. Sweat broke out on his forehead and he entered her again, with two fingers this time, and began a rhythmic stroking.

She was ready, had been all along, Hawk knew. Leaving his fingers embedded in her, he toyed with the sensitive, swollen nub a moment longer, then abruptly withdrew his touch and stepped back.

Angela almost fell to her knees at the combined loss of sensation and support. A wildness deep inside her was bursting to get out as she swung around to see Hawk leaning against the marble wall opposite. The gaze that met hers was hot and dark, compelling her without words to go to him.

She hesitated, but not because she was in any way uncertain. Nothing in her life had ever felt so good, so incredibly right. No, she paused because she wanted to remember this forever, this moment, the way Hawk stood proud and strong before her, his chest heaving with deep, uneven breaths, his hard shaft jutting out from its dark thick nest, his hands shaking slightly but enough for her to notice.

It was time. Angela went to the man she loved, the man who was her lover, and put her palms against his chest. The fingers of one hand crept up his shoulder to explore the puckered scar. When she slid her hand around to find the matching wound on his back, it took all her control to keep her expression free of the dismay she felt at what he had suffered. This was a time for pleasure, not pain.

"There's no going back," he said. "I've known almost from the beginning that I'd never let you go, not if we made it this far together."

"I love you," she said simply, and gasped as his heart thudded double time beneath her fingers.

"I've never used those words before." His hands were still shaking as he lifted them to cover hers. "I meant what I said, though. I'll never let you go."

"That's good enough for me." She didn't need the words, not when she could see the love in his eyes. Love, and desire. She focused on the latter. Stepping even closer, she felt the heat surge through her again as the hard, sensitive tips of her breasts brushed the backs of his hands.

"We could do this in a bed, you know," he said. "There's one just a few feet away." He turned his hands to cup her breasts without dropping his gaze from her eyes.

"Later."

He spread his fingers and squeezed her nipples between them. "It would be easier for you, Angel."

She smiled as she slid one hand downward and closed her fingers around his smooth, hard arousal. "We've got the rest of our lives to do things easy."

"Have it your own way, then," he said, and gave her a tender kiss. He lifted his head and shook it almost ruefully as he smiled down at her. "Ready?"

"Together this time?" she asked softly.

"Together." He gripped her hips and pulled her tight against him. "Take a deep breath, darling. Here we go."

Angela did what he said because it didn't occur to her not to, and that was a good thing. It was a very long time before his mouth slid from hers long enough for her to get another breath. Then Hawk covered her mouth again, and as their tongues dueled and mated they sank to the floor and made sweet, hot love beneath the twin sprays of the shower.

If the hot water ran out, they didn't notice.

FIFTEEN

Breakfast was on the cold side by the time Hawk and Angela got to it, but like the temperature of the shower, they didn't really notice. Sharing the omelettes, bacon, and flaky croissants on a table next to a cozy wood-burning fire, they ate everything in sight, then went to bed for several hours of much-deserved rest.

Peter awakened them sometime around noon with coffee and more food, sharing their second breakfast as they discussed the day's schedule. Like Hawk, Angela wore the thick robe provided by the hotel, the one-size-fits-all nearly overwhelming her, while leaving Hawk's forearms and knees exposed. Keeping her gaze from wandering too often to said forearms and knees, she held a coffee cup in one hand, a piece of toast in the other, and ignored them both as she listened to the men. She didn't like what she was hearing.

"If I might interrupt . . . ?" She smiled and waited politely.

"Since when have you asked permission?" Hawk asked, but he smiled back, so she knew he really didn't mean the unsubtle insult.

She put the toast down and wrapped both hands around the coffee mug. "As I understand it, your plan is to get the video back from where you hid it in your neighbor's apartment, make copies, then leave it up to Blackthorne to make sure they get spread around. Am I right?"

"Yes." Hawk poured more coffee for all three, then added, "If you're worried about anything, don't be. There's no reason for Marchand to imagine I'd hide the video where I lived. All he knows is there's a tape and he might be a player in it."

"Which is enough to make him very determined to stop you," Peter said. "The sooner we get that video, the better."

"The thing I can't figure out," Angela said, "is why you haven't used it before. If it implicated Marchand and Constantine, you could have been in the clear months ago."

"I couldn't use it against Constantine because he had his back turned to the camera throughout." Hawk got up and went to lean against the mantel over the fireplace.

"You were bluffing?" Her heart thudded in her chest as she began to understand the chance he'd taken. "But why?"

"It was all I could come up with in the way of a stall. If I was prepared to let you die, Constantine needed to be convinced I had a good reason for coming to the boat."

Angela had to pause and take several deep breaths before the terror of those hours in Constantine's company would subside to manageable proportions. That, combined with the horror of knowing men had died in the explosion, had kept her awake long after Hawk had carried her to bed. At his insistence, they'd talked about everything—witnessed or imagined. She'd finally found comfort in his arms when even logic hadn't been able to erase the brutal images from her mind.

It was easier in the cold light of day to remember that those same men had wanted to kill her and Hawk. Easier, too, when she had something else to think about. Marchand and the problems he posed were ideal for her purpose.

She looked up to find Hawk's gaze on her. "So why didn't you use the video against Marchand?"

"That night when I fled the beach, I'd been wounded and betrayed by a man I trusted. I had no way of knowing how far the rot had spread beyond Marchand, so I just kept running." He studied the back of his right hand and flexed it as though it was giving him pain. "At first I thought I'd only have to keep my head down until I was recovered enough to retrieve the camcorder from the sand dune that collapsed over it. It was two months before I dug it up and saw that the video would be useless against Constantine. I knew then I couldn't let him get away with what he'd done to Jack."

"So you decided to go after him yourself."

"It was the only way." His gaze held a plea for understanding. "If you hadn't come along, I would probably have gone through with it."

Remembering that first night, Angela didn't doubt that for a second. "Constantine doesn't matter anymore, and I refuse to let what might have happened come between us."

"I killed him," Hawk said suddenly. "Constantine didn't die in the explosion. I shot him with the speargun. You need to know that."

"How he died isn't important," she said without hesitation. "Peter told me the explosives were your idea too. Four men died last night because that was the only way you could find to save my life. Those men made their own choices about how they would conduct their lives long before you or I came into the picture. I feel no guilt. Neither should you."

Hawk didn't have a chance to reply because Peter took that opportunity to get the conversation back on track. "Let's concentrate on Marchand, shall we?"

"How can we be sure he won't be waiting at your apartment?" Angela asked.

"We can't," Hawk said, "and that's why I'm not going alone."

"Why can't you just send someone else for it?"

"Because Mrs. Avery would probably call the police if someone she didn't know asked if he could pull up a couple of boards from her living-room floor and take what's under them." Hawk grinned and shook his head. "It's got to be me, Angel."

"Then I've got a suggestion to make." She leaned back in her chair and contemplated Hawk over the rim of her cup. "Why don't you call this Mrs. Avery and make sure the coast is clear before you go barging in?"

Hawk glanced at Peter, and when he looked back at Angela, there was a smudge of chagrin in his expression. "Because," he said, "I never thought of that."

"Simple, but effective," she said, following it with a loud sigh as she got up and went to stand next to Hawk. Sliding her arms around his waist, she smiled at him. "I would feel so much better knowing you're not walking into a trap."

In the mirror over the mantel, she saw Peter nod as the hint of a smile touched his mouth. "The lady's got a point, Hawk. We should have thought of that ourselves."

"All in a day's work," she said, then stepped away from Hawk when a knock sounded at the door. Peter got up to answer it, and she glanced aside to find Hawk watching her. "What?"

"You. You're a natural at this business."

"I'm a planner," she said succinctly. "And unlike some people I know, *my* plans always work."

"And mine don't?"

"You depend entirely too much on luck. If I left as many loose ends as you do, I wouldn't be able to afford vacations in St. Lucia."

"So who's traveling around Northern California with not much more than the shirt on her back and paying a small fortune for a hotel room on an island thousands of miles away?" He hooked a finger in the belt of her robe and drew her close.

"That's the thing about luck," she said, weaving her hands around his neck. "It can foul up the best-laid plans . . . and leave you believing you've won the lottery."

The caravan of four-wheel-drive trucks left the resort after lunch, with Angela at the wheel of the one in the middle and Hawk beside her. Peter had been dissuaded from riding with them, and he'd given in with the proviso that they rearrange themselves before reaching San Rafael. Angela agreed, but didn't tell anyone she had no intention of letting Hawk tuck her somewhere safe while he went on to risk his neck retrieving the video. That refinement to the plan, she decided, could come later. In the meantime it felt good to be dressed in their freshly laundered clothes. Not even the fact that she was back to wearing her high-heeled pumps was enough to dampen her optimistic mood.

"How is it you came to leave something so important back in San Rafael anyway?" she asked, reaching down to fiddle with the buttons on the side of the driver's bucket seat. They were pretty much the same configuration as the ones in her Towncar, and she grinned when she pushed one and the lumbar support filled in the curve of her spine. "It seems to me that a videotape would be right at home in that sports bag of yours."

"Keeping it with me wasn't a good idea, not if I wanted to be sure Marchand didn't get his hands on it."

"So what's wrong with a bank? They're much more anonymous than your neighbor's apartment." She frowned without taking her eyes from the road.

"You have to provide identification to rent a safe-deposit box," he said around a yawn. "Even with a half-dozen fake identities, I couldn't be sure Marchand wouldn't eventually track down all of them. Now that he knows there's something to look for, he's probably already checking out the banks in the area."

She chanced a quick glance sideways. "That's how he found you, through a fake ID?"

"I suspect he's had that information for several weeks. There are a limited number of really good forgers, and the kind of pressure Marchand can exert will eventually wear down even the most tight-lipped of them." He thrust his fingers through his hair, then patted her thigh. "Even so, Marchand wouldn't have known where to start looking if Mrs. Avery hadn't spilled the beans. I'd still be planning revenge and you'd be in St. Lucia, working on your tan."

"Mrs. Avery did this to you?" she exclaimed. "But, Hawk—"

"Don't worry, Angel. It wasn't intentional." He reached over to run his fingers through her hair, which she'd worn loose at his request. "You have to know what kind of person she is to understand what happened."

"So tell me."

"She's—" he began, then a strange look crossed his face and he dug into the breast pocket of his jacket. His expression cleared when he pulled out a cassette and pushed it into the tape player in the dash. "This will tell you a lot more than I can," he said enigmatically, holding his finger on the reverse button until the tape was at the beginning.

"This is WRDY radio out of Pine Forest, North Carolina, and you're listening to 'Fiona's Forum' on Austin in the Evening. *Tonight's subject is men—"*

"What *is* this?" Angela interrupted.

"Hush and listen."

She did, but not because he told her to. She was intrigued by the deejay's outline of the show's format, and even more so when the woman who called herself Fiona began to talk.

"*Don't get too carried away, Austin. I only promise to produce the perfect mate. The end result of any relationship is a matter best left to the people involved.*"

"*You're saying that not even the perfect mate will be a guarantee of happy-ever-after?*" the deejay asked.

"*A lasting relationship takes more than a mere introduction,*" Fiona said. "*Much more.*"

"*My name is Mrs.—*" It was a new voice, and Angela guessed it was a caller.

"Your neighbor?" she asked, beginning to see where at least a part of this was leading.

"Yes."

Angela listened very carefully indeed as Mrs. Avery—Sara—described her next-door neighbor.

"*. . . it's not that he's gorgeous or anything prissy like that. Bob—that's his name—is more the rugged sort, real tall with wonderful broad shoulders and the kind of face that only a very strong woman would think was attractive.*"

"Bob?" Angela said. "Why not John, as in Smith? Real subtle, Hawk."

"Hush. I haven't listened to the whole thing yet."

"*A woman has to be strong to look at Bob?*" Fiona asked.

Angela choked on a laugh, and only just held back another when Sara related how Hawk's smile scared her friend Edna. Angela was thinking Edna needed to get to know Hawk better when Sara started talking about Hawk's—Bob's—injuries. Only then did she begin to see just how much revealing information Mrs. Avery had spread across the radio waves.

Mrs. Avery continued. "*Such a shame, too, that scar on the back of his hand, the right one. He says it happened years ago, but I can tell it still hurts, even now when his other injuries have mostly healed.*"

Hawk responded to Angela's involuntary gasp by patting her shoulder. "That's as far as I've listened. Let's hear it all."

Fiona was speaking. *"A scar on—"*

"It was why he took up needlepoint—for the exercise therapy, you know, to get his fingers working again. Bob does such beautiful work too. He made me a new cover for my footstool last month, a roadrunner it was. Such a thoughtful man. I'm quite worried about him, you see."

"Because he's single?" Fiona asked.

"Of course that's why I'm worried. I wouldn't have called you otherwise. Bob is a lovely man, and I've never once seen him with a woman—or anyone else for that matter."

Fiona asked, *"Does Bob talk to you about this?"*

"If you mean does he bend my ear about how lonely he is, then you've got him all wrong. A body has to work very hard to get any information out of Bob about anything, and then he'll only say as little as he thinks he can get away with. I'd think you would sense that Bob wouldn't talk about himself like that. Are you sure you're a psychic?"

Despite or because of Hawk's pained expression, Angela started laughing and didn't stop until he covered her mouth and told her to watch the road and listen. He wanted to know what woman this Fiona had in mind for him.

"With any luck," he said darkly, "my ideal woman will at least know when to keep her mouth shut."

"Boring," Angela said, then pressed her lips together in an exaggerated way when he glared at her. She listened as Mrs. Avery enumerated Bob's better qualities, and wasn't surprised by any of them. She could even sympathize with her when Fiona gently accused her of being in love with the alleged Bob. Her ears then pricked up at Fiona's prediction.

"Bob is going to meet his perfect mate sometime in the next few days."

"Oh, he is, is he?" Angela didn't like the sound of that.

"Shh! I want to know who to look for," Hawk said.

"It's a good thing I know you're teasing," she said, and was annoyed when he shushed her again.

". . . *medium height, five five or six, with long thick hair hanging down her back. Red, I think—I'm not sure about that, though. It's hard to tell. She's standing somewhere dark, somewhere without windows.*"

Angela felt her mouth go dry, and when she glanced at Hawk, he was staring her with a look of disbelief in his eyes.

"*The woman Bob is destined to fall in love with is holding a gun.*"

Angela's attention was so glued to the incredible thing she was listening to, she almost rear-ended the truck ahead. She corrected herself in time and slowed so she wouldn't have to worry about that again.

"*You see a gun but you can't be certain if her hair is red?*"

"*Sometimes it works like that.*"

"*You're sure it's not one of those fancy corkscrews? I've got a friend—*"

"This is a setup," Angela said, shooting Hawk a dark look.

"Don't look at me," he said, and turned up the volume.

"*I really think it was a gun,*" Fiona said.

"If she says anything about a hidden videotape, I'm turning this truck around."

"*A corkscrew would make more sense,*" Mrs. Avery said. "*Bob sometimes drinks a glass of wine when he sits on the porch in the evening. Is this woman aiming the thing at Bob?*"

"*I hope not.*"

"See, that Fiona doesn't know everything," Hawk said.

"*I'd hate to think this is her way of telling Bob she's not interested in him,*" Mrs. Avery said.

"*Perhaps Bob respects a woman who has strong opinions.*"

There was more, but Angela didn't hear it. She was too busy laughing and trying to keep the truck on the road. The cellular phone rang and she could hear Hawk reassuring Peter that no, there was nothing wrong. Angela was just a little distracted, and maybe they should pull over for a minute or so.

The caravan ground to a halt. After putting the truck into neutral and setting the brake, Angela turned to Hawk, cocked her finger, and aimed it at him. "I wonder what Mrs. Avery would think of her sweet, gentle neighbor if she knew everything you've done to me."

"Mrs. Avery is a smart woman, Angel." Hawk's gaze traveled from her finger to her eyes. "She'd know I'd never hurt you."

"I wasn't talking about the way you go around threatening, drowning, or otherwise torturing innocent women, Hawk." Leading with her finger, she leaned across the console until her fingertip touched his lips. "I was referring to the wild, untamed man who made love to me in the shower. Isn't he a little at odds with the man Mrs. Avery knows as Bob?"

"Mrs. Avery is a smart, not to mention very pragmatic, woman." His tongue darted out to leave a damp trail down her finger, and she shivered in response.

"Which means what exactly?"

"Just that if we get a little loud when I make love to you in my apartment, she won't call the police to report a disturbance." His mouth closed around her finger and he began to suck. Her breasts tingled and arrows of heat and wanting were shooting through her as he added, "If I know Mrs. Avery, she'll probably just turn up the television and pat herself on the back for finding me the ideal mate."

SIXTEEN

It was early evening when the caravan pulled into the parking lot of a grocery store that was about a mile from Hawk's apartment. Peter got out of the vehicle next to them and handed over Mrs. Avery's telephone number, which he'd gotten from directory service. Sitting with the door open so Peter could listen at least to one end of the conversation, Hawk and Angela put their heads together with the phone snug between them.

He had decided to ask Mrs. Avery to look after his apartment for a while, as he'd been called out of town unexpectedly and didn't know when he would return. If anything unusual had happened in his absence, that would give her the opportunity to tell him about it. When he showed up at her doorstep soon after to retrieve the video, he would have to do a better job of explaining things. Pulling up her floorboards wasn't something she'd be likely to miss.

Mrs. Avery was delighted to hear from Bob and said she would, of course, be very pleased to watch over things. His African violet would need watering—if it wasn't already dead, her tone implied—and she'd begun collecting the newspapers for him. As for everything else, well, a lot had happened since he'd been gone.

The postman had screwed in the new lightbulb Mrs. Avery had bought for the front entrance. She'd made a big batch of the apricot nut cookies Bob favored, and had given them to the grocery delivery boy two days after Bob had disappeared. She would, of course, make another batch when he returned. In the meantime Mr. Tompkins had told her he was thinking of looking for another apartment, one on the ground floor. But he'd also brought her flowers and asked her out for a meal. She was pretty certain she knew which apartment he had in mind.

When Mrs. Avery ran out of news, Hawk thanked her, gave her the number of the cellular phone in case she needed to reach him, then disconnected.

"Mr. Tompkins's days as a bachelor are numbered," Angela said.

"Remind me not to vacate my apartment right away." Hawk grinned and put the phone on the dash. "Heaven only knows what would happen if Mr. Tompkins had to choose betwen marriage and a ground-floor apartment."

"One favor deserves another?" she asked, laughing.

"Something like that." Hawk turned to Peter. "If anyone is watching the building, they're keeping their distance."

Peter nodded in agreement. "Even so, we need to proceed with caution. I'll have the men check the area before you go in."

"Mrs. Avery will probably spot them."

"Since you'll be on their heels, it won't matter." Peter turned away and gave the men their final instructions. They'd spent the afternoon studying the map Hawk had drawn of the local area, so they were already familiar with the neighborhood. Three got behind the wheels of trucks and left to scout the vicinity while six others set off on foot. Not counting Peter, Hawk, and Angela, that left two trucks and three men—all with nothing to do except wait. Hawk and Angela sat in the truck, holding hands but not speaking because they'd already said it all.

When Hawk's cellular phone rang a few minutes later, Angela assumed it was one of the men reporting in. She picked it up and was passing it to Peter when Hawk stopped her.

"Give it to me, Angel."

It rang again as she handed it over, but it took Peter's worried frown for her to realize something wasn't right. "What's wrong?"

"The men wouldn't use this number." Hawk let it ring once more, hoping against hope that it was something simple like Mrs. Avery not being able to find her key to his apartment. His gut told him otherwise. Turning so he didn't have to see the worry and apprehension on Angela's face, he flipped the phone open and held it to his ear. "Yes."

"Hello, Bob," said a voice from his past, one he'd not heard since that night eight months ago. "I stopped by to see if you'd left anything interesting lying around, and your neighbor told me she'd just spoken with you. I have to admit I was rather surprised."

Hawk mouthed "Marchand" to Peter, who immediately ran over to the other truck and began sending out warnings via phone to the men in the field.

"I want to speak with Mrs. Avery," Hawk said, checking his watch. The men on foot wouldn't have had time to get to his street yet. Mrs. Avery was on her own.

"Not right now," Marchand answered. "I'm more interested in what happened to my friend Constantine. I heard rumors that something went wrong. Hard to get any real information, though. The Coast Guard isn't giving anything away."

"Probably because they don't know anything. The *Sea Charmer* resembled a pile of jigsaw-puzzle pieces when I last saw it." Hawk put his thumb over the mouthpiece as Peter leaned inside and whispered that one of their trucks had done a drive-by. Unless Marchand had someone inside with him, he'd come alone. The streets appeared clear of any backup, and his men were taking close positions.

"Mrs. Avery and I would like for you to join us here," Marchand said. "I'm assuming, of course, that you're very close. I don't think you would have called just to ask her to watch your apartment, which leaves me to believe you wanted to make sure I wasn't hanging around."

Hawk thought about denying it, but knew that would place his neighbor in even greater danger. Marchand would have no compunction about knocking her out or otherwise hurting her so that he'd be free to search Hawk's apartment. Angela chose that moment to put her head next to his so she could listen in. He couldn't bring himself to push her away, so he made a motion for her to keep her mouth shut and angled the phone between them.

"I can be there in five minutes," he said. "If you hurt Mrs. Avery—"

"Yes, yes," Marchand interrupted. "I'm familiar with your protective instincts. Speaking of which, why don't you bring the woman with you? Angela, I believe her name is."

Hawk squeezed the phone so tightly, he wouldn't have been surprised if it shattered in his hand. "She's not—"

Marchand cut in again, and he was a lot more impatient this time. "Constantine had her on the *Sea Charmer*. He had you as well. If you survived, I have to believe she did too. I know you too well, Hawk. Bring her—no, *send* her along first. Give us a couple minutes to get to know each other."

"She won't come."

"She will, or the old lady will pay for it."

"How do I know you'll let any of us go once you have what you want?" Hawk asked. He didn't expect a guarantee, but not asking would raise Marchand's suspicions.

"I've decided to get out before things blow up in my face. With all the money Constantine funneled my direction, there's enough for me to retire and live very well indeed. Unfortunately, the country I've chosen for that purpose will overlook almost anything—except drugs. They're rather straitlaced about that particular vice. If the video were to surface, things would get very ugly indeed."

"So you'll let all of us go?"

"After a suitable delay. I wouldn't want you fouling my getaway. Ten minutes, Hawk. The woman first." Marchand disconnected.

Hawk turned his head to find Angela looking at him, dismay pooling in her eyes.

"It's my fault," she said. "If I hadn't suggested that you call first—"

"If you hadn't done that, I would have walked right into him. This way I've been warned." He cupped the side of her face. "You aren't coming with me, Angel."

"But I have to," she protested, pushing her hair back over her shoulder with an impatient hand. "He said—"

"Marchand won't hurt her, not if he wants to get his hands on that video."

"Maybe, maybe not." Angela grabbed his wrist and dug her fingers into it, not hurting him but definitely getting his attention. "I'm not going to take that chance. At least if I go, it will be two against one."

"It's already two to one," he said. "Mrs. Avery is no slouch."

"I'm not joking."

"Neither am I." Gently, he pried her fingers from his wrist and transferred her grip to the steering wheel in front of her. "If I let you go anywhere near Marchand, I'd be too worried about you to do what I have to." He looked across her to Peter, who stood just outside the driver's window. "We go now, before he has time to get nervous. Leave two men here with Angela.

"I'll be back," he said to Angela, then kissed her hard and got out of the truck. There was no way he was taking her, and that was that. He slammed the door and had taken a couple steps away from the truck when he started thinking about how easily he'd gotten his way with her. Too easily, he mused as a wave of uneasiness coursed through him.

The dull thunk of door locks falling into place put him on alert, but it wasn't until he heard the truck's engine start that he turned around. By then it was too late; Angela was reversing out of the parking slot. Short of throwing himself onto the front hood—a dramatic but essentially ineffective maneuver—there wasn't anything they could do in the crowded parking lot except take the other truck and try to get there before her.

So Hawk and the rest jumped into the truck and gave chase. They would have succeeded in at least keeping up had it not been for the woman who came out of nowhere with a cartful of groceries and cut right in front of them. Rubber burned the parking lot as the driver jammed on the brakes and swerved. The woman swerved, too, but the cart's suspension wasn't up to it. Groceries spewed across the road as the cart went flying one way and the woman the other. Holding manfully on to his patience, Peter told one of the men to get out and help. He was out and gone before Peter finished speaking, but by the time they'd reversed the truck and gotten to the road, it was already too late.

Angela was long gone.

Hawk nodded in agreement as Peter advised the men in the field to watch out for her, but not to interfere. Their presence was the only leverage they had left, and showing their hand before Hawk got inside was a risk they couldn't afford.

A minute or so later Peter's men reported Angela's arrival at Hawk's apartment. She went up the walk just as the truck Hawk was riding in pulled to a stop a block away.

Hawk handed Peter his gun because he knew Marchand would take it away, then got out of the truck and started walking.

As he went past the houses, duplexes, and cut-up Victorians that lined the street, he promised himself that when he got Angela out of this one last mess, he'd lock her in a room and refuse to let her out until she agreed to stop taking such huge risks.

Failing that, he'd take her to a deserted island and make love to her until she was too weak to spell the word *risk*, much less take one.

Angela's hands were trembling as she walked toward the house. Her defiance of Hawk was as much to blame for her shaken nerves as the coming encounter with Marchand, and she had to force herself not to look over her shoulder for the men she knew were somewhere near. Her affinity for detail had enabled her to determine the best route to Hawk's apartment, though she'd debated the entire way the consequences of her actions.

In the end, it came down to facts. Hawk didn't want her at the apartment because he didn't want her hurt. Marchand, on the other hand, wouldn't hesitate to harm Mrs. Avery if Angela didn't show. There was, Angela concluded, no other course of action. If she could convince Marchand to let the elderly woman go, so much the better.

That didn't make it any easier to climb the front steps, enter the building, and knock on the door on the right. An elderly woman with pink-hued hair and eyes as round as saucers opened it, then stood back for Angela to enter. It didn't take a genius to know Marchand was behind the door and probably pointing a gun at Mrs. Avery, so Angela went straight in without giving him cause for alarm.

She had gotten as far as the burgundy velvet sofa with antimacassars draped across the arms and back when the door slammed shut behind her. Turning, she saw a tall, gray-haired man wearing a short-sleeved pink shirt tucked into cream-colored chinos. He had a vaguely preppy look about him that reminded her of a popular Miami-based cop show, but she imagined it was the gun he was holding as much as his outfit that raised that particular image.

"I was certain Hawk wouldn't let you come," he said. He carelessly pushed Mrs. Avery into a nearby chair and came to stand so close to Angela, she could smell the bitter fragrance of aftershave gone sour. "He must be slipping."

"Don't push her around like that," Angela said sharply, ignoring his reference to Hawk. It was better, she thought, if he didn't know Hawk had been caught off guard. "She's old. You'll hurt her."

Taking Marchand by surprise, Angela ducked around the other side of a low marble-topped coffee table and knelt beside the older woman. "Mrs. Avery, are you all right?"

Angela got worried when Mrs. Avery just stared at her with her mouth open and the fingers of one hand covering it. Angela repeated her question. "Mrs. Avery, has this man hurt you?"

"You're her," Mrs. Avery finally said. "The redhead Fiona told me about."

"I prefer to think of it as auburn, not red." She pushed a wave of the stuff over her shoulder, then winked at the woman. If she could just convince Marchand that Mrs. Avery was helpless, it would be a point in their favor. "You look pale. Are you sure you're all right? Is there anything I can do?" She winked again, and saw the moment Mrs. Avery got the message.

"My heart *is* a little fluttery, dear. This is all so distressing."

"How about some tea? You look like a cup would do you good."

"I didn't ask you here to make tea," Marchand said from behind her.

Angela got up and stood between the elderly woman and Marchand. "Mrs. Avery can make it. It will keep her from worrying."

"I don't want her out of sight."

"What do you think she's going to do? Hightail it down the back steps or come after you with a butcher knife?" Angela shook her head disparagingly. "Get real, Marchand. She's an old lady. Harmless. Just look at her." She stood aside and gestured dramatically at Mrs. Avery, who had somehow managed to age twenty years in the last twenty seconds. Shoulders that had been squared were now hunched, her blue-veined hands shook visibly, and she kept her eyes cast downward as though she were afraid to make eye contact.

"See what I mean?" Angela said. "Harmless."

A knock sounded at the door, but Marchand didn't let the distraction affect the direction in which his gun was pointing. "Go make tea, Mrs. Avery," he said. "Perhaps it would be better if I spoke with Hawk and Angela in private. Don't do anything stupid. I'll be listening, and I've got a gun pointed at this young lady."

Mrs. Avery got up and scurried out of the room before he could change his mind. Marchand made Angela open the front door, standing behind her with his hand fisted in her hair to hold her still and the barrel of his gun dug into her side.

Hawk stood with his hands at his sides and looked straight past her to Marchand. Angela had expected him to show at least a little anger, but he didn't and she realized he was probably saving it for later. The prospect of *later* was reassuring, and she turned her attention to the present difficulty.

Hawk opened his jacket to show Marchand he was unarmed, then followed them into the apartment as Marchand drew Angela backward. He shut the door and leaned against it, his gaze searching the small living room before darting back to Marchand.

"Where's Mrs. Avery?"

"I sent her out to make tea," Angela said, then winced as Marchand tightened his grip in her hair. The clatter of china and silver reached them from the adjoining kitchen, and Angela realized Mrs. Avery was doing exactly as she'd been told. So long as she stayed out of the way, Angela thought Hawk would have a better chance at reversing the situation. It was why she'd sent her to the kitchen in the first place.

"Where's the tape, Hawk?" Marchand asked. "As much as I enjoy cuddling your lover, I don't want to waste any more time here than necessary. You know the story—things to do, places to go, people to see."

"About this unnamed country you're retiring to," Hawk said conversationally. "I assume they don't have an extradition treaty with the U.S." He crossed his arms on his chest and stared at the man holding Angela. The gun was now leveled on her shoulder and pointed at him, and he wished Angela knew enough to use that to their advantage. Unfortunately, she was untrained in close combat.

"It's one of the reasons I chose it," Marchand said. "That, excellent weather, and reasonable access to neighboring islands with accommodating banks." He brushed the barrel of his gun across Angela's cheek. "Don't worry, Hawk. Once I'm gone, I won't be back. You can come up with any story you want to explain your absence for the past eight months, and I won't care."

"Without the video, I won't have much of a job to go back to." He watched Angela cringe as the metal touched her cheek, and had to force back words of encouragement to her. It was bad enough that Marchand assumed Hawk and Angela were lovers. What Marchand would do if he discovered that Hawk had fallen head over heels in love with Angela didn't bear thinking about.

Marchand wasn't a nice man, and until Hawk was in a position to object, anything Marchand did to Angela would go unavenged.

Marchand sneered at him. "Your job is your problem, Hawk. I'm reassured by your concern, though. Obviously, you don't have any copies lying around to support any wild accusations you might make."

"Copies were dangerous," Hawk admitted. "It's hard enough to hide one object of value when people are hunting you. Anything more is taking a stupid chance." He knew that if Marchand believed there *was* only one tape—the truth, as it happened—he would be less likely to kill them all before trying to leave. Unfortunately, killing them was probably what Marchand planned to do in any case. Even though he was leaving the country, it wouldn't do to leave witnesses of any sort behind. If Marchand was going to the island Hawk thought he was, even rumors of drug dealing would raise uncomfortable suspicions—and that would be enough to put an end to his tropical idyll, not to mention his life.

For now, Hawk's job was to keep Marchand calm and talking. The longer he could manage that, the better chance they all had of getting out alive. The men in Peter's assault team had to get close and tight in order to succeed.

"Let the women go, Marchand. They've nothing to do with this."

"All in good time. First, the tape."

Mrs. Avery appeared in the kitchen doorway just behind Marchand's right shoulder. He must have seen her out of the corner of his eye because he dragged Angela tighter to him without pulling his aim from Hawk. "Come sit down, Mrs. Avery. Hawk is going to get the tape and I don't want either of you ladies out of my sight."

"But the cups," she said, holding up the china teapot, one hand on the spout, the other on the handle. Hawk noticed there was no lid on the pot. "They're still in the kit—"

"*Sit down!*" Marchand thundered. Angela winced at both the loud voice in her ear and the arm tightening around her. She frowned as Hawk appeared to ease away from the door, then Marchand suddenly tensed against her. His shrill scream filled the air, and Hawk dove straight for them.

Angela caught the full power of Hawk's charge in the stomach as Marchand's gun went off. The double assault left her deafened and winded, and she wasn't much of a help to Hawk as he somehow jerked her hair free and shoved her out of the way. She let him at it, knowing that without the gun, Marchand was helpless. Mrs. Avery obviously thought so, too, because she seemed quite content to stand in the corner and watch as Hawk gave Marchand a good pounding.

Scrambling on all fours, Angela headed for the wall and hadn't even caught a decent breath when Marchand's gun came skittering across the rug to bounce against her feet. Because it seemed a good idea, she picked it up—then swung it around to point at the men who came rushing through the front door.

Their reflexes were superb. Freezing into respectful statues, they waited until Peter pushed past them to hunker down next to Angela. He smiled and took the gun. "Hawk warned me you've picked up some bad habits over the past few days. I take it this is one of them?"

She looked over his shoulder where Hawk was allowing some of the others to pick up whatever pieces he'd left of Marchand. In very short order, they removed him from Mrs. Avery's living room and shut the door behind them.

"Considering how often I find a gun in my hand," Angela said, "I should probably get one of my own. It will save having to pick them up all the time."

"Not necessary." Hawk put his back to the wall and slid

down it to join Angela and Peter. "If I get my way, the closest you'll ever come to a gun again will be the water cannons our kids are going to use to persecute each other." He took her hand in his slightly bruised one and kissed the back of it.

"Fiona was wrong and I'm going to call and tell her," Mrs. Avery said as she put the china pot down on the coffee table and looked at Angela. "You didn't point that gun at Hawk, not even once. She obviously got her wires crossed."

"Who's Fiona?" Peter asked.

"Don't ask," Hawk said, grinning at Mrs. Avery. "You were brilliant."

The pink-haired woman blushed and smoothed her pleated skirt. "It was Angela's idea, really. If she hadn't suggested the tea, I would never have thought of it."

"Thought of what?" Peter asked, looking more confused by the minute.

"She poured boiling hot water down Marchand's back," Hawk said.

"You did?" Angela said, blinking rapidly as she reassessed the woman.

"I was a little worried I might get some on the roadrunner," Mrs. Avery said. "It was just behind that horrible man."

"What roadrunner?" Peter asked.

"The one Bob—excuse me, *Hawk* sewed for me." She bent down to swipe a surprisingly steady hand across the needlepoint-covered footstool. "I don't think Fiona believed me when I told her about this."

"Who's—" Peter began, but shut his mouth and just shook his head.

Hawk pushed himself to his feet and pulled Angela up behind him. "Peter, I trust you won't need me for a while."

"I think I can handle things, thank you," he said, rising also. "But the video—"

"It's under the floorboards next to the bookshelf,"

Hawk said, pointing, then he turned to Mrs. Avery. "I know I owe you an explanation for all this, but do you think it could wait—"

"You take your lady and go home, Hawk," she said, obviously delighting in his new identity. "With all this activity, Mr. Tompkins is surely busting a gut to know what's been going on. I think I'll get out the sherry and tell him all about it. We might even give Fiona a call."

Hours later, perhaps days—Angela didn't know; time was irrelevant when everything you wanted in life was breathing down your neck and holding you tight—Hawk rolled over until he was on top looking down and she was caught between the hard mattress and his equally hard body. She loved it.

"What?" she asked when he didn't say anything.

"What I said about kids," he began. "We haven't talked about it—"

Squirreling a hand up between their bodies, she covered his mouth to keep him from going on. "We haven't said anything because we both agree," she said simply. "If you didn't want children, you wouldn't have made love to me without taking precautions. Ditto for me. End of debate."

He grinned. "I didn't know you'd noticed."

"I did. I also didn't leave the bathroom door open without understanding the consequences." She smoothed her fingers over his brow. "Changing the subject a bit, do you think you'll get your job back now?"

"It doesn't matter. If you don't have any objections, I thought I'd go private. Give Blackthorne a little competition." Shifting his hips until she took the hint and opened her legs wider, he added, "On the other hand, I could always work for you. What do you think, Angel? Would it work? Don't you think I'd be a great meeting planner?"

A mild panic assaulted Angela at the thought of spend-

ing every working minute of every working day with a man
whose planning skills could be engraved on the head of a
pin. Fortunately, Hawk's growing arousal and her response
distracted them both enough that when she finally said no,
he couldn't work with her, he didn't seem to mind.

Much later, as they lay with limbs entwined and her
head snuggled into his shoulder, Hawk reached over to
snap on the bedside light and gathered the strength he
needed for one last question before they slept.

"Angel?"

"Hmm?" She answered without opening her eyes or
her mouth.

"This hotel in St. Lucia."

She opened one eye and looked at him. "What about
it?"

"Well, since the room is already paid for and you've got
over a week left . . ." He yawned and shut his eyes against
the questions in hers.

"What about it?" When he just yawned again, she
thumped him on his chest with her fist. "Come on, Hawk.
Get to the point."

He looked at her through narrowly slitted eyes. "This
might sound just the slightest bit tacky—I know the groom
usually takes care of the honeymoon arrangements—but I
was thinking that if we flew through Reno, we could get
married and the hotel room in St. Lucia wouldn't go to
waste."

"Let me get this straight, Hawk." Angela propped her
elbows on his chest and stared at him. "Is it the honeymoon
or the quicky marriage in Reno you're wanting an answer
for?"

"Both." Cupping her chin in his hand, he smiled into
her eyes. "I thought that with your passion for detail, you'd
like to help me settle these tiny ones."

She looked at him for a long moment, then smiled so

brightly that the gold bits in her eyes sparkled. "You're learning, Hawk."

"Learning what?"

"Not to leave anything to luck."

"That's right," he said, sliding his fingers into her hair and drawing her close. "I'm leaving it all to love."

Sitting alone on the screened porch of her North Carolina home, Fiona drank herbal tea and watched contentedly as lightning ripped across the night sky. Suddenly the back of her right hand began to throb and she had to put down the cup so the tea wouldn't slosh out. Before she could do anything to soothe the pain, though, she was struck by the startlingly vivid image of a hawk soaring high and strong. It turned in the wind, and Fiona gasped with pleasure as she saw the angel beneath its wings.

Then they were gone, a union of power and light that took the pain from her hand and left Fiona content with her glimpse of the end.

THE EDITORS' CORNER

The four new LOVESWEPTs headed your way next month boast the sexiest season's greetings you'll ever read. While the chestnuts are roasting, be sure to treat yourself with romances guaranteed to put the sizzle in your holidays.

Marcia Evanick charms our socks off again with **MY TRUE LOVE GAVE TO ME,** LOVE-SWEPT #770. When she awakens Christmas morning, Megan Lemaine gazes, astonished, at the pear tree—with a partridge—in her backyard! Then Tate Brady comes courting, seducing her senses with fiery kisses while a dozen days of enchantment fill her with wonder. With this funny, touching, and utterly irresistible tale of love as magical as a Christmas miracle, Marcia Evanick creates a romance to cherish for always!

BORN TO BE WILD, LOVESWEPT #771, is

the next smoldering novel in Donna Kauffman's <u>The Three Musketeers</u> trilogy. Zach Brogan is sexier than sin, a globe-trotting wild man whose bad boy smile beckons Dana Colburne to taste thrills only he can deliver! He'd always sensed the secret wildness that burned inside his childhood pal, had tempted her into trouble more than once, but now he wants the woman she's become to feel his fire. Untamable, outrageous, explosively sexy, Donna Kauffman's heroes like dancing on the edge and women who don't make it easy—but no one sizzles hotter than guys who act bad to the bone but are oh-so-good!

Romantic Times award winner Laura Taylor explores the darkest shadows in the human heart with **SEDUCED,** LOVESWEPT #772. He'd loved Maggie Holden for as long as he could remember, had ached as she wed another, but now Noah Sutton wants to make the hauntingly beautiful widow his at last! Tainted by a tragic betrayal, her innocence destroyed, Maggie has retreated from the world. Noah stuns her with passion, igniting a soul-deep longing to be cherished—and to be believed. Rich with poignant emotion, thrilling in their intensity, Laura Taylor's novels celebrate the healing power of hope.

Bonnie Pega sets pulses pounding in **THE REBEL AND HIS BRIDE,** LOVESWEPT #773. Annabelle Pace was Gregory Talbot's true love, until she left him with no explanation. Now the beautiful seductress is back in town, and he is determined to get answers, if he can keep his hands off her delectable body long enough. Annabelle refuses to play second fiddle to the minister's causes, but with one kiss, he unleashes all her pent-up desires and recaptures her soul. Brimming with desire, Bonnie Pega offers a novel of passion too fierce to be denied.

Happy reading!

With warmest wishes,

Beth de Guzman

Shauna Summers

Beth de Guzman   Shauna Summers

Senior Editor   Associate Editor

P.S. Watch for these Bantam women's fiction titles coming in January: From Jane Feather—the incomparable author of the national bestsellers VIOLET and VALENTINE—comes **VANITY,** her newest unforgettable romance. **BREAKFAST IN BED,** a classic romance by *New York Times* bestselling author Sandra Brown, will be available in hardcover. In **DEATH ELIGIBLE** Judith Henry Wall sets out to discover how far one family will go to protect itself—when one of them is guilty of murder. Tamara Leigh, author of PAGAN BRIDE, presents **SAXON BRIDE,** the story of a fiercely handsome warrior and the breathtakingly lovely woman who leaves him torn between his duty and an agonizing truth. And finally, **NIGHT SINS,** the acclaimed national bestseller from Tami Hoag, will be out in paperback. Be sure to see next month's LOVESWEPTs for a preview of these remarkable novels. And immediately following this page, preview the Bantam women's fiction titles on sale *now*!

Don't miss these extraordinary books
by your favorite Bantam authors

On sale in November:

AMANDA
by Kay Hooper

HEAVEN'S PRICE
by Sandra Brown

MASTER
OF PARADISE
by Katherine O'Neal

TEXAS OUTLAW
by Adrienne deWolfe

July, 1975

Thunder rolled and boomed, echoing the way it did
when a storm came over the mountains on a hot
night, and the wind-driven rain lashed the trees and
furiously pelted the windowpanes of the big house.
The nine-year-old girl shivered, her cotton nightgown soaked and clinging to her, and her slight body
was stiff as she stood in the center of the dark bedroom.

"Mama—"

"Shhhh! Don't, baby, don't make any noise. Just
stand there, very still, and wait for me."

They called her baby often, her mother, her father, because she'd been so difficult to conceive and
was so cherished once they had her. So beloved. That
was why they had named her Amanda, her father had

explained, lifting her up to ride upon his broad shoulders, because she was so perfect and so worthy of their love.

She didn't feel perfect now. She felt cold and emptied out and dreadfully afraid. And the sound of her mother's voice, so thin and desperate, frightened Amanda even more. The bottom had fallen out of her world so suddenly that she was still numbly bewildered and broken, and her big gray eyes followed her mother with the piteous dread of one who had lost everything except a last fragile, unspeakably precious tie to what had been.

Whispering between rumbles of thunder, she asked, "Mama, where will we go?"

"Away, far away, baby." The only illumination in the bedroom was provided by angry nature as lightning split the stormy sky outside, and Christine Daulton used the flashes to guide her in stuffing clothes into an old canvas duffel bag. She dared not turn on any lights, and the need to hurry was so fierce it nearly strangled her.

She hadn't room for them, but she pushed her journals into the bag as well because she had to have *something* of this place to take with her, and something of her life with Brian. *Oh, dear God, Brian* . . . She raked a handful of jewelry from the box on the dresser, tasting blood because she was biting her bottom lip to keep herself from screaming. There was no time, no time, she had to get Amanda away from here.

"Wait here," she told her daughter.

"No! Mama, please—"

"Shhhh! All right, Amanda, come with me—but you have to be quiet." Moments later, down the hall in her daughter's room, Christine fumbled for more clothing and thrust it into the bulging bag. She helped the silent, trembling girl into dry clothing, faded jeans and a tee shirt. "Shoes?"

Amanda found a pair of dirty sneakers and shoved her feet into them. Her mother grasped her hand and led her from the room, both of them consciously tiptoeing. Then, at the head of the stairs, Amanda suddenly let out a moan of anguish and tried to pull her hand free. "Oh, I *can't*—"

"Shhhh," Christine warned urgently. "Amanda—"

Even whispering, Amanda's voice held a desperate intensity. "Mama, please, Mama, I have to get something—I can't leave it here, please, Mama—it'll only take a second—"

She had no idea what could be so precious to her daughter, but Christine wasn't about to drag her down the stairs in this state of wild agitation. The child was already in shock, a breath away from absolute hysteria. "All right, but hurry. And *be quiet*."

As swift and silent as a shadow, Amanda darted back down the hallway and vanished into her bedroom. She reappeared less than a minute later, shoving something into the front pocket of her jeans. Christine didn't pause to find out what was so important that Amanda couldn't bear to leave it behind; she simply grabbed her daughter's free hand and continued down the stairs.

The grandfather clock on the landing whirred and bonged a moment before they reached it, announcing in sonorous tones that it was two A.M. The sound was too familiar to startle either of them, and they hurried on without pause. The front door was still open, as they'd left it, and Christine didn't bother to pull it shut behind them as they went through to the wide porch.

· The wind had blown rain halfway over the porch to the door, and Amanda dimly heard her shoes squeak on the wet stone. Then she ducked her head against the rain and stuck close to her mother as they raced for the car parked several yards away. By the time she was sitting in the front seat watching her mother fumble with the keys, Amanda was soaked again and shivering, despite a temperature in the seventies.

The car's engine coughed to life, and its headlights stabbed through the darkness and sheeting rain to illuminate the graveled driveway. Amanda turned her head to the side as the car jolted toward the paved road, and she caught her breath when she saw a light bobbing far away between the house and the stables, as if someone was running with a flashlight. Running toward the car that, even then, turned onto the paved road and picked up speed as it left the house behind.

Quickly, Amanda turned her gaze forward again, rubbing her cold hands together, swallowing hard as sickness rose in her aching throat. "Mama? We can't come back, can we? We can't ever come back?"

The tears running down her ashen cheeks almost but not quite blinding her, Christine Daulton replied, "No, Amanda. We can't ever come back."

HEAVEN'S PRICE

by Sandra Brown

AVAILABLE
IN PAPERBACK

"One of romance fiction's brightest stars."
—*Dallas Morning News*

With one huge bestseller after another, Sandra Brown has earned a place among America's most popular romance writers. Now the New York Times bestselling author of TEMPERATURES RISING brings us this classic, sensuous novel filled with her trademark blend of humor and passion, about a woman who thought she knew her destiny until she learns that fate—and her heart—have something else in store.

From the award-winning author of PRINCESS OF
THIEVES

MASTER OF PARADISE

by Katherine O'Neal

*As the privateer bore down on her ship, Gabrielle Ashton-
Cross recognized all too well the magnificent, leonine figure
at its prow. Once she had resisted his arrogant passion, had
survived his betrayal to become the toast of London. And
even now she might escape him, for her sword was like
lightning. Yet the moment their gazes locked across the
rolling deck, she knew that Rodrigo Soro had every intention of taming her to his will at last. Gabrielle hadn't
journeyed so far from home to fulfill a lifelong dream only
to surrender to a pirate king. But this time when he took
her in his arms, would she have the strength to fight the
only man who could ever promise her paradise?*

"Ella â minga," Rodrigo had told his men. *She's mine.*

He was so confident, so secure. Yet there were
some things even his carefully placed spies couldn't
know. Things that had long ago closed the door on
any future with Rodrigo—even if he hadn't thrown
his life away to become the bloodiest pirate of the
seven seas.

Gabrielle thought of that night, eight long years
ago, when they'd said their farewells. She'd seen the
proof back then of his dark passions, of the menacing

sensuality of the inner self he'd hidden from an un-suspecting world. Of the cold, ruthless way he could pursue his goals. Hadn't she learned that night to pursue her own aims just as coldly, just as ruthlessly? But she'd never seen this anger, this impression of raw, unrestricted violence that sparked the air between them. It scared her suddenly, as she realized for the first time where she was—alone in a locked room with the one man who was truly dangerous to her designs. With her ripped skirts up about her hips. With him pressing his all-too-persuasive body into the softly yielding flesh of her own. With an erection fueled by years of frustrated desires.

As if reading her thoughts, he softened his tone. Still holding her head in his hands, he said, "But that's over. We're together now. I've come here to rescue you."

She put her hands to his shoulders and pushed him away. "Just what is it you're rescuing me *from*?"

"From the clutches of England, of course."

She couldn't believe what she was hearing. "I rescued *myself* from England, thank you very much! Did you imagine I'd wait all this time, like some damsel in distress, for you to fashion a miracle and rescue me? When I had no indication that you ever thought about me at all?"

His hand stilled in the act of reaching for her breast. "I thought about you always. I never stopped longing for you."

"You never sent me word. Was I supposed to read your mind? Wait for a man who walked out of my life without so much as a backward glance? Without regrets of any kind?"

"You're wrong, Gabé. I regretted very much having to leave you behind."

"You *regret*? You knew what you were going to do and you didn't tell me. I can't believe the arrogance of you thinking you could waltz back into my life and dictate my future after all you did to me."

His hand made the arrested journey and slid over her breast. "Is a future with me so formidable a prospect?" he asked in a husky tone.

She shoved him away and fought to sit up. "Future? What kind of life would I have with you? A pirate's wench? Hunted by the law? Hung by the neck till I'm dead? You don't seem to understand, Rodrigo. You stand in the way of all I hold dear. You once told me I didn't fit into your plans. Well, now you don't fit into mine."

"You have no feelings for me at all, I suppose?"

She lifted her head defiantly and said, "None!"

He took her wrists and wrenched her up from the bed so she came crashing against his chest. The blow was like colliding with a brick wall. "I *know* you. I know the passions of your soul. It matters not what you say. You're mine now. This time I surrender you to no man. I made a mistake with you once before. But that," he added bitterly, "is a blunder I won't make again."

You're mine now. Staking his claim. Taking possession of her like a bauble he fancied. As if she had no feelings. Permitting her no say at all.

"I shan't let you do this," she vowed. "Your men already tried to take me against my will. Do you think I'd fight them off, only to let another pirate succeed where they failed?"

He was insulted, as she'd intended. She could see it in the tightening of his jaw, in the ferocious flare of his lion's eyes. She pulled away, but he followed, pushing her back to his bunk as he stepped toward her with stormy eyes. As she backed away across the expanse of red silk, she came up sharply against the wall—the one with the collection of weapons within handy reach.

He caught the flash of the blade as she snatched it from the wall. Incensed, he grabbed her arm and yanked her to her feet. But he didn't know what an expert swordswoman she'd become. Determined to fight him, she swung the sword around and put the cutting edge to his throat.

TEXAS OUTLAW

by Adrienne deWolfe

For a lady train robber, seduction was a game—until a handsome lawman changed the rules. . . .

In this sneak peek, Fancy Holleday has only a few minutes to dispose of Marshal Rawlins before her band of outlaws boards the train. And desperation drives her to a reckless act.

"Marshal!" Fancy's bellow rattled the windows and caused at least one passenger to douse his lap with turtle soup. "Arrest this man!"

"You want the preacher cuffed, eh?"

"Yes, sir, I most certainly do!"

"What in blazes for?"

Fancy hiked her chin. Obviously, Mama Rawlins had neglected to teach her son the finer points of etiquette.

"Because that . . . that *beast* of a man dared to . . ." She paused dramatically. "To grope me!"

Rawlins chuckled, a rich, warm sound in the breathless silence of the car. "Whoa, darlin'. No one was over there groping anything that you didn't give away a good long time ago."

She bristled. He had seen through her ruse! Despite her stylish emerald traveling suit and the demure black ringlets that framed her face, Cord

Rawlins had pegged her for a trollop. She wasn't sure she could ever forgive him for that.

"If you're not man enough to defend my honor," she said coolly, "then I shall be happy to speak to the railroad detective whom I saw dining here earlier."

Every eye in the car shifted eagerly back to Rawlins. He appeared undaunted. Hooking his thumbs over his gunbelt, he strolled to her side. She was surprised when she realized he was only about three inches taller than she. Standing in the doorway, he had appeared much larger. Nevertheless, the lawman exuded an aura of command.

"Well, preacher?" Rawlins tipped his Stetson back with a forefinger. A curl so dark brown that it verged on black tumbled across the untanned peak of his forehead. "Speak your piece."

The cleric continued to gape. "Well, I, um . . ."

"Spit it out, man. Did you or did you not grope this . . ." Rawlins paused, arching a brow at the straining buttons of Fancy's bodice. ". . . this, er, lady."

She glared into his dancing eyes, then let her gaze travel down his face. The man had dimples. Bottomless dimples. They looked like two sickle moons attached to the dazzling white of his grin. She thought there should be a law somewhere against virile Texicans with heart-stopping smiles. Cord Rawlins had probably left dozens of calf-eyed sweethearts sighing for him back home on the range.

"I'm sure there must be some reasonable explanation," the preacher meanwhile babbled. His scarecrow body trembled as he towered over Rawlins. "I'm sure the young lady just made a mistake—"

"The only mistake I made," Fancy interrupted, "was thinking that this lawman might come to the defense of a lady. No doubt Marshal Rawlins finds such courtesies an imposition on his authority."

"Begging your pardon, ma'am." He indulged her this time with a roguish wink. "I thought you did a mighty fine job of defending yourself."

Oh, did you now? She seethed. *Then just wait 'til you get a load of my .32!* If only that blessed moment would come. Where in hell was Diego?

"Show's over, folks." Rawlins waved his audience back to their meals. "Your pigeons are getting cold."

"That's it?" She gaped. "That's all you're going to do to help me?"

" 'Fraid so, ma'am. You aren't any the worse for wear, as far as I can see. And I reckon Parson Brown isn't any worse off, either."

"Why, you—!" Fancy remembered just in time that ladies didn't curse. "You can't just walk away," she insisted, grabbing Rawlins's sleeve and hoping he would mistake her panic for indignation.

"Says who?"

A nerve-rending screech suddenly pierced the expectancy in the car. Fancy had a heartbeat to identify the braking of iron wheels; in the next instant, the floorboards heaved, throwing her against Rawlins's chest. Silver, crystal, and a diner's toupee flew; she cringed to hear the other passengers scream as she clung to her savior's neck. Rawlins's curse ended in an "umph." Fancy was grateful when he sacrificed his own spine rather than let hers smash from the table to the carpet. For a moment, Rawlins's tobacco, leather, and muscled body imprinted themselves on her senses. Then her mind whirred back into action. She had to get his Colt.

Having made a career of outsmarting men, Fancy found it no great feat to shriek, thrash, and wail in a parody of feminine terror. She wriggled across Rawlins's hips and succeeded in hooking her heel behind his knee. She knew she could pin him for only a moment, but a moment was all she needed to slip her Smith & Wesson from her boot—and jam its muzzle into his groin.

"Whoa, darling," she taunted above the distant sounds of gunfire.

His face turned scarlet, and she knew he had assessed his situation. He couldn't reach his holster without first dumping her to the floor. And that would be risky, she gloated silently. Most risky indeed.

"Have you lost your goddamned mind?"

"My dear marshal, you really must learn to be more respectful of ladies," she retorted above the other passengers' groans. "Now real slowly, I want you to raise your hands and put them behind your head."

On sale in December:

BREAKFAST IN BED
by Sandra Brown

NIGHT SINS
by Tami Hoag
available in paperback

VANITY
by Jane Feather

DEATH ELIGIBLE
by Judith Henry Wall

SAXON BRIDE
by Tamara Leigh

To enter the sweepstakes outlined below, you must respond by the date specified and follow all entry instructions published elsewhere in this offer.

DREAM COME TRUE SWEEPSTAKES

Sweepstakes begins 9/1/94, ends 1/15/96. To qualify for the Early Bird Prize, entry must be received by the date specified elsewhere in this offer. Winners will be selected in random drawings on 2/29/96 by an independent judging organization whose decisions are final. Early Bird winner will be selected in a separate drawing from among all qualifying entries.

Odds of winning determined by total number of entries received. Distribution not to exceed 300 million.

Estimated maximum retail value of prizes: Grand (1) $25,000 (cash alternative $20,000); First (1) $2,000; Second (1) $750; Third (50) $75; Fourth (1,000) $50; Early Bird (1) $5,000. Total prize value: $86,500.

Automobile and travel trailer must be picked up at a local dealer; all other merchandise prizes will be shipped to winners. Awarding of any prize to a minor will require written permission of parent/guardian. If a trip prize is won by a minor, s/he must be accompanied by parent/legal guardian. Trip prizes subject to availability and must be completed within 12 months of date awarded. Blackout dates may apply. Early Bird trip is on a space available basis and does not include port charges, gratuities, optional shore excursions and onboard personal purchases. Prizes are not transferable or redeemable for cash except as specified. No substitution for prizes except as necessary due to unavailability. Travel trailer and/or automobile license and registration fees are winners' responsibility as are any other incidental expenses not specified herein.

Early Bird Prize may not be offered in some presentations of this sweepstakes. Grand through third prize winners will have the option of selecting any prize offered at level won. All prizes will be awarded. Drawing will be held at 204 Center Square Road, Bridgeport, NJ 08014. Winners need not be present. For winners list (available in June, 1996), send a self-addressed, stamped envelope by 1/15/96 to: Dream Come True Winners, P.O. Box 572, Gibbstown, NJ 08027.

THE FOLLOWING APPLIES TO THE SWEEPSTAKES ABOVE:

No purchase necessary. No photocopied or mechanically reproduced entries will be accepted. Not responsible for lost, late, misdirected, damaged, incomplete, illegible, or postage-die mail. Entries become the property of sponsors and will not be returned.

Winner(s) will be notified by mail. Winner(s) may be required to sign and return an affidavit of eligibility/release within 14 days of date on notification or an alternate may be selected. Except where prohibited by law entry constitutes permission to use of winners' names, hometowns, and likenesses for publicity without additional compensation. Void where prohibited or restricted. All federal, state, provincial, and local laws and regulations apply.

All prize values are in U.S. currency. Presentation of prizes may vary; values at a given prize level will be approximately the same. All taxes are winners' responsibility.

Canadian residents, in order to win, must first correctly answer a time-limited skill testing question administered by mail. Any litigation regarding the conduct and awarding of a prize in this publicity contest by a resident of the province of Quebec may be submitted to the Regie des loteries et courses du Quebec.

Sweepstakes is open to legal residents of the U.S., Canada, and Europe (in those areas where made available) who have received this offer.

Sweepstakes in sponsored by Ventura Associates, 1211 Avenue of the Americas, New York, NY 10036 and presented by independent businesses. Employees of these, their advertising agencies and promotional companies involved in this promotion, and their immediate families, agents, successors, and assignees shall be ineligible to participate in the promotion and shall not be eligible for any prizes covered herein. SWP 3/95

DON'T MISS THESE FABULOUS
BANTAM WOMEN'S FICTION TITLES